Karl Stieler, Hans Wachenhusen, Friedrich W. Hackländer

The Rhine

from its source to the sea - Vol. 1

Karl Stieler, Hans Wachenhusen, Friedrich W. Hackländer

The Rhine
from its source to the sea - Vol. 1
ISBN/EAN: 9783337368807

Printed in Europe, USA, Canada, Australia, Japan

Cover: Foto ©Andreas Hilbeck / pixelio.de

More available books at **www.hansebooks.com**

THE RHINE

FROM ITS SOURCE TO THE SEA

TRANSLATED BY

G. C. T. BARTLEY

FROM THE GERMAN OF
KARL STIELER, H. WACHENHUSEN
AND F. W. HACKLANDER

NEW EDITION, REVISED AND CORRECTED

VOL. I.

ILLUSTRATED

PHILADELPHIA
HENRY T. COATES & CO.
1899

CONTENTS.

(v)

LIST OF ILLUSTRATIONS.

VOLUME I.

(vii)

THE RHINE.

INTRODUCTORY.

THE great rivers of the world must have added a charm to Nature even in the first era of Creation. The summits of mountains are dumb, and icy repose ever dwells in their heights; but in the flowing tide there is endless change, and the dashing water suggests strength and eternity.

It was a sublime moment in the world's history when man for the first time subdued the stormy wave, and compelled the current to carry far and wide his power and his thoughts. The rivers were the original boundaries of nations, and their beds were sacred; within their depths dwelt gods, and the destinies of mankind were determined on their banks. Thus have rivers become, as it were, the fundamental lines of the world's history, and the guides of every great hero. The poet, however, looks deeper, and makes the river the symbol of life. He watches it as it struggles forth, the rivulet of youth, emerging gradually into the broad energy of manhood, and finally losing its individuality in the ocean of the community. He sees in it the image of turbulent passion, and of the thousand obstacles which bar the road of life between the beginning and the end.

> "A life lived loveless to its end
> Is like a stream in sandy ground,
> Spent and dried up before it found
> The sea, that goal to which streams tend."

Foremost among rivers is the Rhine, which, even two thousand years ago, was a watchword among nations. Its banks were impressed with the foot-prints of Cæsar's legions and Attila's cavalry; and centuries later, accompanied by a rejoicing people, King Conrad descended the Rhine to Mainz for his coronation.

Legend also has grown as luxuriantly as History on the banks of the Rhine. As the ivy clings to the old castle walls, so do traditions fasten themselves to actual events. On the Rhine stood the Castle of the Niebelungen, and on the Rhine the Lorelei sang. What country can compare in richness to that through which the Rhine flows, from the snow-clad Alps down to the very sea in which it is lost?

Here lay the cities of the old empire and the great seats of ecclesiastical pomp, which lavished as reck-lessly as they grasped all that came within their power. Both wished to proclaim afar their magnifi-cence; and to do so minsters and cathedrals were built, so that when the traveller towards evening dragged on his weary way, he would see from afar the slender tower, and cry with joy to his companion,

" Yonder is Strasburg !" Out of the morning mist, also, the mariner, who had come down the Rhine overnight, would see the dark mass of the Cathedral of Cologne rise before him like a ship, but built with stone flanks and stone masts.

Indeed, who does not feel the wealth that lies in the words " The Rhine," the wealth of Nature and of Art, of History and of Legend, of old and new life ?

THE RHINE SONG.

"THE Rhine!   That little word will be
For aye a spell of power to me,
And conjure up, in care's despite,
A thousand visions of delight:
The Rhine!   Oh! where beneath the sun
Doth our fair river's rival run?
Where dawns the day upon a stream
   Can in such changeful beauty shine,
Outstripping Fancy's wildest dream,
   Like our green glancing, glorious Rhine?

"Born where blooms the Alpine rose,
   Cradled in the Bodensee,
Forth the infant river flows,
   Leaping on in childish glee.
Coming to a riper age,
   He crowns his rocky cup with wine,
And makes a gallant pilgrimage
   To many a ruined tower and shrine.
Strong, and swift, and wild, and brave,
On he speeds with crested wave;
And spurning aught like check or stay,
Fights and foams along his way
O'er crag and shoal until his flood
Boils like manhood's hasty blood."

                         —PLANCHÉ.

CHAPTER I.

THE SOURCE OF THE RHINE.

HARK! what is that trickling amidst the icy waste that surrounds us? We have ascended, through the valley, past the last house and the last tree. Higher and higher we mount, clinging close to the narrow path; but now the goal is reached, and the Rhein-wald Glacier lies before us in regal majesty.

We gaze breathless—so vast is this gigantic white wall on which our eyes rest; the clouds which pass slowly over the peaks give a dignity and a depth of coloring to the huge masses; but in the midst, in the wall of the glacier, is a small fissure, and from it a slender thread of water breaks forth, white and foaming, and leaps joyously to the earth. This is the Rhine. Now that it has seen the warm light which never penetrates to the depths of the glacier; now that it has once touched the blessed soil of Mother Earth, it will stay and wander for hundreds of miles, until from the recesses of the mountains it returns to the bosom of the sea.

The Rhine, as is well known, is formed of two principal arms, the Upper and the Lower Rhine, which unite at Reichnau. A third and smaller arm, which rises at Lukmanier and empties itself at Dissentis, is described as the Middle Rhine. But this branch is unimportant, so far as historic and artistic interest is concerned.

We will begin with the Lower Rhine. It has its source close by where we stand. What an heroic future has its birth here; what an amount of life hangs on this silver thread! This rivulet, the future Rhine, has torn itself free from its lonely home. It will glide farther and farther, while, in mute silence, the giant mountain gazes after it as it flows away. The cleft in the glacier-side gapes like a wound in its breast through which its life is ebbing.

The enigma of birth, of the pain of parting, and the rapture of freedom, are embodied here on this solitary plain.

The course of the Lower Rhine is altogether as wonderful as its origin; its path is, perhaps, the wildest that ever led from the mountains to the valley. Who does not know the sombre name of the *Via Mala?*

In Holland, where this same river flows broad and majestic, it is the custom to ask a young man who is a candidate for an office, or an aspirant for a maiden's hand, whether he has " sown his wild oats ;" and when this question is answered in the affirmative, it is taken as the security for an earnest, active life. And thus it is with the Rhine: a wild, stormy youth precedes the wonderful, active work which it accomplishes for the culture of mankind—its course through the ravine of the Grisons is not a journey, but a torrent, a cataract—it is "sowing its wild oats."

At the very beginning of its course, scarcely half a mile distant from its source, the battle of the young stream with the old boulders may be seen in very earnest; the river is hurled precipitously into an abyss of yawning depth; the rocks cover it, it has vanished, it is buried—choked. It looks almost as if the rocks would imprison it anew just when it has escaped. The thunder of its roar echoes above as it wrestles for life and for freedom. But it cuts its way victoriously through; and, as the infant Hercules strangled the two snakes, so has the Rhine in its cradle conquered the two great powers that endangered its existence, namely, Ice and Rock.

Its childhood is an augur of its giant future. Even the names which accompany its origin have a mystic grandeur, for the mountain plain which lies opposite the source of the Lower Rhine is called " Paradise," and the abyss into which it falls is called " Hell."

The first elevated plain through which the Rhine flows is called the Rheinwald Valley, and the first village we meet with bears the name of the young stream. In spite of the lofty and rugged situation, we are surrounded by the most beautiful woods of fir and larch. The inhabitants claim to be descended from the time of Barbarossa, who colonized the valley

with Germans in order to guard the old military road
over the Alps.   But much more remote traces of
human life are found, for in places where the earth
has been washed and worn away by the elements,
primitive household utensils have been discovered;
and in one spot, which is more fully exposed, a Roman
temple must have stood.   In fact, it is believed that
the glacier in the Rheinwald Valley has considerably
increased in the course of centuries, and that the climate was formerly much milder than it is now.   There
have been found nests of birds which have not built
there within the memory of man.   Swallows and jays
have migrated forever; only the sparrow-hawk, gray
as the rock on which it builds its eyrie, circles in fitful
flight high over our heads; only the rock-falcon pecks
and flits and skims shyly away when it becomes aware
of the presence of man.

Out of this solitude we step on to the next lower
plateau into the Schamser Valley, through which the
celebrated Splügen Pass leads from Chur to Chia-
venna.   It was opened in 1822.   The most remarkable point in it is the ravine, which reaches from
Andeer to Rongella.   Here the ominous words *Via
Mala* become a reality.

The powers of Nature which were active enough
here centuries ago to tear a yawning cleft in the close
wall of rock, inspire us, even at the present day, with
thoughts of terror.   The stone walls rise precipitously
for two thousand feet, and sink perpendicularly an

The course which the Lower Rhine travels from its source to its junction with the Upper Rhine at Reichnau does not amount to more than fifteen miles, but the height through which it falls within that distance, over the three huge valley steps, shut in by the ravine, is nearly four thousand feet. A comparison of these figures will give the best idea how turbulent the youth of the great stream is, and what mighty powers are at work here.

The origin and course of the Upper Rhine, which we will now notice, are less solemn, but still of exquisite loveliness. Once more deep solitude surrounds us, gray boulders are scattered about, and the grass sprouts sparsely between the mighty masses. No human footfall, no sound of life, no ray of sunlight greets us, and only by straining the eye forward and upward can the deep blue of the distant sky be distinguished.

And yet there springs out of this deep, dead solitude a life which none other equals in greatness—we hear it gently murmuring—that murmur is the cradle-song of the Rhine. Here, again, we stand beside its source. The country in which we find ourselves is the Grisons, the wildest canton of Switzerland, where, even at the present time, the eagle soars and the bear crawls through the clefts. We are in the midst of that rocky mountain-chain over which the St. Gothard towers. The glaciers are ranged around, covered with eternal snow—Crispalt and Badus, and, in the distance, Furka. It is the original watershed between the stormy, dark North Sea and the smiling Mediterranean. It is one of those wonderful places where Nature hides her mightiest work in solitude.

Three streamlets form the source of the Upper Rhine. One comes straight down from the crag, the second flows timidly along the earth, the third forces its way through the impenetrable rocks. The small basin where they first unite is called Lake Toma. Its length is scarcely more than three hundred paces, and its breadth scarcely two hundred; its depth also is inconsiderable; but the dark mirror stands out in wondrous beauty of color, and from the clefts an Alpine flower peeps, here and there, among the snow.

Here the waters gather quietly, and prepare, as it were, for a rush down over the stony mountains to Chiamunt and Selva, until the Middle Rhine flows into them at Dissentis. The village itself lies deep in the valley; the sound of the vesper bell comes down from the chapel which stands up among the green meadows.

The peasant of whom we ask our way looks wonderingly at us. The language in which he gives us information is a *patois*, and only fragments of it are intelligible. The countenance of this solitary man is of a harsh, rough character, but still not wanting in truthfulness. When we are seated in the little circle of the village inn, we hear for the first time all that has happened here in the olden times.

Dissentis was not always so lonely as it is at the present day. For a whole century after Attila, the Great Scourge of God, had been carried to his grave, dispersed bands of his nomadic army hung about the neighborhood, until the Rhætians conspired against them and exterminated them to the last man. On the hills which surround the village the disciples of St. Benedict built themselves a dwelling-place, which they inhabited for more than a thousand years, hidden among the peaceful mountains, far away from the stream of time and history. Then time came to them in the shape of the wild soldiers of the Republic, with their flapping tricolors, who burnt down their village and destroyed their cloisters.

Although the Rhine does not always run beside us on the path which now leads us from Dissentis to Ilanz, it is still our guide, for, even where we cannot see it because of the fir woods and rocks which hide it from our view, we, nevertheless, hear close beside us the roar with which it beats out its foamy path. On the road we meet with little villages, often composed of only a few weather-beaten cottages—at one a mountain stream rushes down from the hills, and at another the beat of a forge-hammer rings through the silent depths of the wood. We may mention that trout-fishing is very fine here, fish weighing as much as twenty pounds being caught at times.

Just before we enter the village street of Trüns there stands the trunk of a renowned old tree; it was once a maple with rustling boughs, under which, more than four hundred years ago, assembled the founders of the "Gray Covenant," who gave their name to this part of the country (the Grisons). The little chapel which stands just above is consecrated to its memory. Whatever relics of that time remain in the way of records and treaties are preserved in the old court-house at Ilanz, the first town on the bank of the Rhine.

The road has already lost much of its former rough-ness; it leads over broad, green meadows studded with thick alder-trees, and even the hamlets that lie away from the road have a sweet charm that induces us to loiter. The little village that stands near the so-called "Forest Houses," where the road takes a wide sweep to the left, is called Flims; on every side are murmuring streams running to the Rhine. Before us lies the Flimser Lake, with its pale green water— a sunny idyl, where the herdsman lies dreaming in the rich grass, with his charges pasturing lazily beside him. But the river lies away to the right; we can hear the sound of its ripple coming over the summit of the wood, whilst now and then an island covered with trees rises out of the stream, or the ruins of a fallen castle look down on us from the heights.

Here also we meet more than once with witnesses of a cruel period of oppression. Prominent among them is Hohen Trüns, the history of which reaches back to the time of the Merovingians. The village

The Via Mala, Switzerland.

enigmatical names, a church that has stood for more than a thousand years, narrow streets over whose stony pavements the heavy mail rumbles, and, towering over all, is the lofty Kalanda. Foreign sounds greet our ears on every side, for this is the centre where all the roads of the Grisons meet: here is the gathering-point of all that immense traffic which goes over the Splügen and St. Bernard to the south.

The history of the town is as gloomy as its walls, which in the time of the Romans bore the name of *Curia Rhætorum*. The Emperor Constantine set up his winter-quarters here, which first led to the enlarging of the city; and here, as early as 451, Christianity was established. The Bishop's Palace stands high, and, together with the Cathedral and the buildings belonging to it, has almost the appearance of a bold fortress. In the quarter of the town which surrounds this priestly stronghold the Catholics still preponderate.

In the lower town—which is rich in original architecture, in pointed gables and dark archways—active, arduous life abounds, and the houses reach far into the valley, out of which the river Plessur rushes to the Rhine. The population, which two hundred years ago was exclusively Roman, the town being called not Chur, but Quera, is now considerably changed, and a large industrial trade is carried on, though sometimes it may be thought that the stubbornness of the soil is reflected, as it were, in the character of its people. This may readily be accounted for, for a national character which springs out of free unmolested action forms itself differently from one which is the outburst of oppression.

Beyond Chur we meet, as before, with witnesses of the period of national tyranny; lonely castles, whose very names announce the hardness and insolence which dwelt in them—Krottenstein, Haldenstein, Leichtenstein—frown on us as we quietly follow our path along the valley, thinking here of a song, there of a beautiful maiden who once looked down from those balconies.

Passing on, however, we soon find ourselves in quite a different scene; we are in the midst of the "vortex of fashion," the high life of the present day and its busy hum. We are at the baths of Ragatz, which in the summer season of the year are the fashion, and they have within the last thirty years attained a European reputation.

The warm spring which rises at Pfaffers, and whose water is conveyed in iron pipes for nearly half a mile to Ragatz, was discovered by a huntsman about the middle of the thirteenth century. It belonged to the renowned order of Benedictines, who were enthroned high up on the mountain in one of the strongest and oldest abbeys in the kingdom.

For a long time the spring was enclosed in a little frail hut, similar to those depicted as bath-houses of the middle ages, and the sick crowded to it from all

quarters to be healed. About a hundred and fifty years ago the abbot raised a new building in the expansive style peculiar to the time, and especially popular with the cloister. Now, however, that the whole institution is the property of the State, gigantic palaces stand in the usual splendor of the modern Spa, and fifty thousand visitors come here annually to be healed.

But there is, beside this outward comfort. a beauty of Nature, which also silently exerts its healing power. The Flascherberg, covered here and there with dark woods amidst cloven rock, looks down into the valley through which the Rhine rushes hastily; and above the rock the snowy summit of the Falknis shines with silver brightness. That deep cutting over which the road leads to Bregenz, fortified with a strong bulwark, opposite the imperial frontier, is the St. Luciensticg; the two castles whose ruins peep down from among the bushes are Freudenberg and Nidberg. The latter is particularly rich in legends, one among them being especially known by its gloomy fascination and the passion which it reveals.

The Knight of Nidberg was dreaded far and wide; his towers seemed to be inaccessible, and his strength invincible, whenever an enemy attempted to besiege him. But that which valor had not been able to achieve was accomplished by the treachery of a woman, driven to revenge by outraged love. She well knew his chamber and his deep slumbers; and she led the foe by a secret path up the steep castle hill till they stood opposite the battlements.

There they could see into the open chamber, where the invincible knight lay sleeping; the gentle breeze played in at the window, and the full moonlight fell on the closed lids and heaving breast. It was scarcely five paces across, but neither bridge nor hand stretched over the yawning abyss which parted the sleeper and his foe; but the arrow has wings, and will find neither the abyss too deep nor the way too long. "Fix your arrow, and aim true," whispered the enraged woman in the foeman's ear. For a moment he stood half-terrified on the edge of the rock, so powerful was the form of the sleeper; but then the whirring bolt sped through the window; it struck its aim, and the knight passed from life to death.

If Ragatz, with all its splendor, makes a delightful impression on us, the grandeur which we meet with in its wildest form as soon as we have passed Pfaffers does so still more. Here the Tamina, which falls into the Rhine at Ragatz, has worn itself a path through an awful ravine; and *here*—not outside, in the smiling landscape—lies the secret of the old healing spring.

Dark walls of rock which rise precipitously six hundred feet on either side confine the rushing torrent, and have an inexpressibly gloomy appearance, even at summer noon. The narrow overhanging path, washed by the restless flood, clings painfully to the left. In about three-quarters of an hour we reach the bath-house which the monks erected here in 1704, a long dark building in whose passages the rays of the sun fall but sparely. There is accommodation here for many guests, for it was the only asylum for strangers before Ragatz had developed into a bathing-place.

But we have not yet seen the most impressive part of the ravine, for heaven still casts its blue gaze down on us, and though confined, we are yet in open Nature. Behind the bath-house, however, where the path continues for about five hundred steps, we pass right into the interior, into the very bowels of the rock. Here the ravine becomes a chasm; and even if the July sun be shining outside, it is damp and dark within. On every side we are surrounded by rocks, which appear to threaten us with approaching destruction.

We proceed timidly along the path, till suddenly a steaming vapor rushes towards us, and it seems as though it must stifle and kill if we step within the forbidden circle. Not destruction, however, but blessing, rises out of these obscure depths; for here lies the beneficent spring to which thousands owe their restoration to health and life.

Truly, it is marvellous! The deepest creative powers of Nature have not their origin on the bright sunny soil, but, as it were, in the darkness, and drag themselves through to the light with supernatural struggle. Who does not think involuntarily of the great minds of the human race? One of them stands especially near to our memory in this place, and his name shall be gratefully spoken before we leave the spot—it is Schelling, the philosopher, who lies buried at Ragatz. His monument in the churchyard there was erected by King Max II., of Bavaria, who called himself a scholar of this noble master.

It is said that the devil once took up his abode in this narrow ravine above Ragatz, where the hot springs rise, and lying in wait for a victim he saw Anna Vögtli pass.

He knew that she was a witch, and spent her nights on the mountains, when the moon was full, gathering herbs and weaving baneful spells. So he promised her great success in finding what she needed for her black art if she would only go down into the little church and throw away the holy wafer that was on the altar.

The girl, who had long since given up going to mass, and had already sold her soul to the devil, did not consider this a hard task, and started immediately to obey Satan.

She stole into the church, but no sooner had she laid her hand upon the sacred Host than the ground shook, the thunder rolled, and the lightning gleamed, until the mountains began to waken to the sounds.

Terrified, Anna Vögtli rushed out of the sacred place, throwing away the holy wafer as she ran. It fell on a thorn-bush, which immediately put out a silvery rose, whose petals, closing round the wafer, protected it from harm.

A flock of sheep, passing, reverently bent the knee, and a wolf, springing out of a thicket to fall upon the sheep, lay down like a lamb beside them.

The peasants, attracted by these miracles, plucked the silvery rose, and laid it upon the altar of the Church of Ettes Wyl, where it has performed many miracles.

If we continue to go northwards we soon reach— at Sargans—the place where, in prehistoric times, there lay a diverging point of the Rhine. For, as many geologists maintain, the course of the river did not originally lead it to Lake Constance, but turned left to Wallenstadt and Zurich, where fewer obstacles lay in its path. This opinion is founded from observations of numerous marks in the rocks, by which the old river-bed may still be identified; and the watershed between Lake Constance and the Lake of Zurich is, at the present time, so low that it is not difficult to believe this supposition. In the fearful inundation of 1618, the chronicles tell us the water-level of the Rhine had already risen so high that it was feared that the river would break away a second time to Lake Wallenstadt.

The whole valley which we now pass through, as far as the huge basin of Lake Constance, is called, *par excellence*, the Rhine Valley. The proud castle of Werdenberg reminds us of the lords who governed it. The tower hangs, like an eyrie, high up on the rock; and here lived the old counts, as quarrelsome and as fond of plundering as the Montforts, from whom they sprang. Now, indeed, they have slept for many long years in their stone coffins, but formerly their banners floated proudly on the battlements. The one over Werdenberg was black, that over Sargans was white, and those of Vorarlberg and Swabia were red. How strange that the colors of the mightiest race that ever ruled on the banks of the young Rhine should compose the banner which, hundreds of years later, set free the stream, and now waves from every steamer that plies from the Rhine to the sea!

But, we are reminded as our feet tread its soil, the great kingdom has forgotten one little spot, and that is the little land of Leichtenstein. For half a century it was the Benjamin of the holy German Confederation, and now, though that good body is dead, no one has adopted the blooming orphan. The five-and-fifty soldiers stand at peace, the faithful subjects live without a state under the Castle of Vaduz, with few cares and few taxes, whilst the father of the country tarries in his Austrian possessions. *Vallis dulcis*—that is the fragrant root from which the name of Vaduz springs.

As we approach Lake Constance the valley grows broader; the mountains recede noticeably, and in the place of wild beauty striving against cultivation, we have lavish fertility. It is not improbable that, as Strabo relates, in his time the whole Rhine Valley was covered with marshes, between which the stream ran in its deep bed. The land owes its fertility to the deposit of mud which was left behind on hill and valley.

Vines were planted in the Rhine Valley as early as 918, and the market towns scattered at distances in the valley were soon among the most charming places of South Germany. It is true that fire and drought, endless war and discord, intruded amongst these plenteous blessings; but they could only destroy what was created, and not the creative power which is here specially peculiar to Nature. She gave her gifts willingly, with a full, indeed prodigal, hand; the fields in the valley were covered with heavy crops, and over the hills the vine clambered, until, indeed, it became almost unvalued from its very abundance.

The time of the vintage was appointed by the common council, and also the price of the wine, which even at the beginning of our own century was restricted to seven kreutzers the measure. The supply was indeed almost inexhaustible, and the proximity of the Rhine made it impossible to dig cellars which would remain free from water. A great portion of the harvest therefore had to be disposed of abroad, especially in the frontier land of Appenzell, which gave in exchange the produce of its cattle.

Boats plied to and fro over the stream, and in quite early times the markets which were held by imperial privilege in the Rhine Valley obtained a fine trade. No ship floated more proudly over the blue surface of Lake Constance than the great market-ship from Rheineck, no other booty was more eagerly watched for by the hunting or pirate-ship which cruised about the lake filled with marauding troops.

It was natural that so much wealth and prosperity should strengthen the courage and the self-consciousness of the citizens—and indeed they needed all their courage; for at one time they had to defend themselves against a governor who cruelly oppressed the people, and at another against insolent neighbors who broke over their frontier in company with a foreign power.

Then came the Reformation, whose mighty influence was felt even in the most distant valleys. In the middle of the winter of 1528 the people of the Rhine Valley were called upon to say which religion each man would adopt; the alarm-bells were rung, and the new teaching made a triumphal entry to their sound.

In the meantime the conflict became more fierce, and the strife of minds became the strife of arms, when the Thirty Years' War broke out in full blaze even in the provinces of the Rhine Valley. The Evangelicals attacked not only the Imperialists, but also their own countrymen; the corpses which the

Rhine washed ashore lay unburied all around, food for the famished and maddened dogs. The prices will show to what a pitch famine, and consequently usury and extortion, had risen : the ducat at that time was worth seven florins, and a quarter of corn cost five and a half florins.

In the wars of the eighteenth century also the Rhine Valley suffered severely, and it was long before those quiet, blessed days returned of which the river Rhine is now the witness.

The last great stronghold, which stood commandingly at the exit of the valley, was Rheineck—a fortress the possession of which was contested even in the time of Stauffen by the Bishop of Constance and the Abbot of St. Galle. Now, of the two castles, the one is levelled to the ground, and the vine grows luxuriantly on the hill where it once stood; of the other, nothing but the ruins look down into the valley. But below, on the Rhine—which at this place first becomes navigable for large vessels— the little town lies strong and well built. It has a fine hall of commerce for its brisk trade, especially in timber, which is floated down from Chur in rafts.

The proximity of the mouth of the river is announced by the depression of the banks, which are covered with thick sedge; barely a mile more, and the noblest of rivers vanishes from our sight, and the blue shimmering surface of Lake Constance lies before us. The stormy history of the upheaval of this lovely lake is thousands of years old, but its smiling mirror ever greets us with the sparkle of eternal youth.

CHAPTER III.

LAKE CONSTANCE.

Standing on the banks of Lake Constance we feel that we have before us the most beautiful lake which Germany possesses. The snow-capt mountains of Switzerland tower around; on one side is the mighty Säntis, on the other is the Kurfirsten chain, with its cloven summits. Cheerful towns stand on the shore, and the breeze carries the sound of morning bells over the blue surface.

What wealth of color gratifies our eyes, what a delicious, refreshing air fans us as we gaze over the strand where yonder boat is tossing! The water glistens like an emerald with the sun shining through it. Farther off it is deeper, and the strong north wind raises the waves, so that the sail flaps and the foam washes the sides. Hark how it rustles!—a firm hand must guide that rudder, for beneath the keel the lake is of an unfathomable depth.

Of all the German lakes no other offers so great a variety of sounds: on its shores at times we hear the tender song of the wavelets, and at another the roaring howl of the hurricane; and the painter will find from rosy twilight to stormy midnight as great a variety of colors and tints here as he can possibly desire. In these waters marvellous beauty is joined to a frightful power such as Nature only, and not man, can combine, and herein lies the unknown fascination which Lake Constance, in common with all great lakes, exercises over us.

Lakes are the secret working-places of Nature. Here, where no human eye can penetrate, inestimable blessing and utter desolation seem to flow in a way which we can neither understand nor control—at times the lake rises in a glassy flood nearly a foot over the banks, and then hastily recedes; often a great volume of water is pressed into the small northern arm, till the moist south wind breaks over the mountains and throws it back into the broad open basin. Then the flood is stirred to its very depths, no boat is safe upon it, and even the strongest steamer scarcely dares leave the harbor! In this way it is swayed by the warm wind which blows over the mountains in the spring and autumn, and when winter comes the frost lays the waves with its icy breath till they remain quiet and motionless, as if they had been wrapt in sleep. The effect on a wild December night, when the imprisoned flood knocks at its dungeon door and forces it, so that the ice bursts from one bank to the other with a deafening roar, when once heard is never to be forgotten.

The lower lake freezes annually, but the whole surface is so rarely covered that the years when such an event has happened are historical. An example of this phenomenon occurred in 1695, when a great shooting festival was held on the ice, and passed off merrily.

Gustave Schwab has depicted the terrible side of the picture in his well-known ballad. Who does not remember the horseman who hunted for hours over the snow-covered plain—the plain which was Lake Constance! But figures only can give a correct idea of its size and the scope which it offers to the elements. It is two hundred and seven miles in area, forty miles long, seven and a half miles wide, and, in some places, eight hundred and twenty-five feet deep.

Through the midst of this mass of water the Rhine flows invisibly. Nature has taken it once more into her quiet, hidden sanctuary, as a mother takes her wayward boy into her silent chamber, from which he emerges grave and moved, with his whole character changed. Such an hour of quiet lies here. The lake is the secret chamber where the change in its inmost being is completed, and when the stream has once more left the lake the Rhine has started on a noble, active, dignified life, the wildness and danger of youth being for ever left behind.

It is lost to sight, but though we do not see it, we still feel its tide, and we are conscious of the Rhine current running through the water of the lake. The color of the shore is a yellow green, such as the old legends describe the banks of the Rhine, and yonder, in the waveless tide, we feel a slight heaving motion, which is the heart-throb of the great stream running through the depths below.

The charm which this spot possesses attracted men in very early times, and they penetrated the wilderness, sword in hand, to build their towns on the shore —the strong constantly giving place to the stronger. Even now, as if in remembrance of the many alternations of conquerors, the lake is the boundary of many countries—Austria, Bavaria, Wurtemburg, Baden, and Switzerland, all have a share and touch the water of this inland sea. It is a gem too costly for the possession of a single kingdom, and five countries with dark wood and golden grain form the setting for this glittering jewel.

The old Romans were the first who came to contest the dominion of the Rhætians, and the first town that adorned the shore was Bregenz. Both Strabo and Pliny knew it under the name of Brigantium, by which name the lake also was distinguished; its present designation is of much more recent date.

A Roman writer of the fourth century gives a description of Lake Constance which is very striking in its powerful simplicity. At that time gigantic forests reached down to the water's edge, and heavy mists hung over the lake, so that it was with difficulty that the axe hewed the first road to the shore. But through the "lazy repose of the lake" (says the narrator) there flows a river with strong current and "foaming eddy," which carries its waters to the outlet, unmixed with those of the lake. In the finest bay in the lake stood the old castle of Brigantium, all wild and desolate, but strong and well protected, and a prosperous town grew up under its shelter.

But its prosperity did not last long; fresh races came and were in their turn superseded by others, until at last the first missionaries came over from Ireland and introduced gentler manners. They were St. Gallus and Columba; they also first set foot in the south-eastern part of the country, where the towns of Bregenz and Lindau now stand; here lay the key for the civilization of the whole district.

We too, then, will begin our description at Lindau, whose youthful image presents itself to us in these later days in its beautiful name. At the present time, when commerce has constructed iron roads everywhere, and made firm land even where nature thought fit to place water, we scarcely remark that Lindau stands in the middle of an island, for the railway carries us into the very heart of the town. But at the time when our ancestors gave the place its name the green island was washed all round by the blue waters, and no bridge led over from the mainland to the sunny meadows (Au), where the wind played among the old lindens.

The first buildings raised by German hands were the church and the cloister, which were erected in the time of the Carlovingians, and numerous dwellings were soon erected near them. Long before Rudolf of Hapsburg mounted the throne the town had be come a free city, and its situation being accessible, commerce and traffic increased unusually fast. It had close relations with the most powerful cities of the kingdom, and its political influence was known even with the German house in Venice. Its activity manifested itself intellectually and in no small degree when the first note of the great Reformation sounded.

The Thirty Years' War was the first turning-point in the fate of the town. In order to keep off war, it was fortified and surrounded by strong outworks, but these precautions only invited the attacks of the enemy. The wrathful General Wrangel threw thousands of shot into the beleaguered town, which was defended by the Imperialists; and, though he retreated, followed by the jeers of the citizens, without having accomplished his aim, their welfare was impaired for centuries.

That time had gone forever when (as Achilles Gasser proudly relates) more than fourteen hundred vehicles, and people from thirty towns, appeared at the weekly market of Lindau. The population dwindled as the wealth disappeared, and want greatly helped on the downfall, when the town fell into the hands of the Bavarians in 1806.

After these disasters every possible effort was made to raise its fortunes again; streets and gardens were laid out, and the varied forms of modern progress were quickly fitted into the frame of the antique picturesque bastions, part of which is still preserved. The most important points of the modern town are naturally the railway, which runs from the mainland to the island over a massive viaduct, and the harbor, which is now the finest on the lake.

On approaching the town by water, two prominent objects are seen towering above it—the handsome light-house, with its indented top, and the old lion of Wittelsbacher, which keeps its lordly watch on a lofty pedestal. Not far from it stands the bronze monument of the noble Max II., who died in 1864, the prince to whom Lindau specially owes its prosperity.

But the greatest increase of prosperity has been in the lake traffic, for there are now many steamers used in the service. Amongst them there is a ferry-boat which carries trains bodily over to the Swiss side. The first steamboat was built by Church, an American, in the year 1824. It bore the name of King William of Wurtemburg, who had it built, and it remained in use till 1847.

Previous to this there were vessels on Lake Constance which were adapted for the transport of huge burdens, and frequently carried one hundred to one hundred and fifty tons at a time. They were fitted with a gigantic sail composed of some six hundred yards of canvas, which bore them slowly over to Constance.

Lindau was for many centuries the centre for the fishing as well as of the shipping trade; the inhabitants of the town, indeed, had a monopoly of the former; and on the "fish days," which were appointed annually, it was agreed how and where the productive right should be used. The lake abounds in trout and in a small fish called Felchen (which we do not know); and even at the present day thousands of the so-called "Gang fish" are caught in the spring, and sent in large quantities throughout Germany.

Lindau has long since lost all these privileges, but it has exchanged them for advantages which are infinitely more valuable; the fishery is almost free at the present time, and the permission to enjoy the sport is granted with praiseworthy liberality to the visitors to the lake. No one complains, and the fishes, who alone might offer an objection, are dumb.

Thus everywhere we feel the action of progress, but many traces remain of those old primitive days when the canoes of the Alemanni crossed over from the mainland. The so-called "Heathen Wall" is supposed to be a fragment of the gigantic watchtower which Tiberius erected here; the church of St. Peter, which is used at the present time as a granary, is a memorial of the Carlovingian period; and the Town Hall illustrates the beautiful style of the old imperial town. The arms of Lindau are still a linden on a white field, and the most beautiful point in the neighborhood, the Lindenhof, preserves the idea of the verdant origin of its title.

Bregenz is the neighboring town to Lindau, and, although the boundary of two great empires parts them, they are united by nature, whose divisions are not those of man. If Lindau is an island town, Bregenz is, in the fullest sense of the word, a gulf town; and while the one has been sometimes compared to Venice, the other has been called the German Genoa or Naples.

We, however, will have nothing to do with comparisons, but give ourselves up without reserve to the pleasure which this beautiful piece of country awakens in every sensitive soul—we will not dwell upon imaginary pictures, for before us lies the loveliest picture of reality.

The soft blue bank of the lake bends crescent-wise, and the town rises towards the mountains in light terraces, overshadowed by the lofty Pfänders and the Gebhardsberg, with its little glistening church. Old forests of beech and fir lie around, though many a gap has been made by the axe. Mountain town and coast town are here united.

The oldest part is that which lies upon a hill sloping gently on three sides. It is generally agreed that the Roman castle stood here, and the extent of the former town has been determined by many researches and discoveries. Burial-grounds and beautiful mosaic pavements, statues and metal-work have been discovered, and everywhere rusty coins, bearing the images of the Cæsars, have been brought to light after the feet of the Huns, for thousands of years, had trodden them into the earth.

Here, as on the Riviera, the oldest part of the town retires as much as possible into the land, and is huddled together on the slope of the mountain, while the new parts stretch towards the shore for the sake of trade. The modern busy Bregenz stands below, on the harbor and on the railroad. This is a striking proof how social development follows historical development. Formerly the existence of the town depended on protection; now it depends on traffic. At its first building that point had to be selected which was the safest; the present growth seeks that situation which seems to be the most accessible.

It is true that beauty is sometimes lost sight of, and in the erection of barracks and huge storehouses architecture sinks from the domain of Art to an arithmetical calculation. So many square feet, and so many rooms, must be provided at so much rent. These considerations are rarely compatible with the architectural genius of the present day.

Even on the coast of Bregenz, therefore, we are not altogether safe from such defects, though the objects which disturb us are exceptions. Taken altogether, it is not easy to find a little town which strikes us so pleasantly; for, let builders do what they may, the great architect who designed the ground-plan was

Nature, and human hands can hardly help following her lines. The population of the town is small, and has a somewhat official air, from the fact that every possible dignitary is to be found here, Bregenz being the capital of Vorarlberg. But other dignitaries have also established themselves in the town, whose distinctions do not depend upon imperial decrees, for Lake Constance has always possessed a special attraction for poets.

Gustave Schwab has sung its praises, and the great poet of gloom, Hermann Ling, has often delighted in his visits to its shores. Victor Scheffel, the fortunate master of Ekkehart, lived in Rudolfszell, and in Bregenz Alfred Meissner wrote his well-known romances. How the charm of a country increases, and the delight of a journey through it is enhanced, when we can rest beside the hospitable hearths of remarkable men! Adelaide Procter, the English poetess, has sung of the Maid of Bregenz—how, three hundred years ago, she was forced to leave her native town to serve in the Swiss valleys. As the years went by she became attached to her new home, and her childhood in the Tyrol seemed to fade from her mind; but one day she overheard her neighbors talking of a plot against Bregenz, and boasting that the town would be surprised and captured before the dawn of another day.

Then the maid's love of country asserted itself, and she stole silently away to the stable, saddled a fleet horse, mounted, and turned his head towards Bregenz, to warn the inhabitants. On they fly through the night, horse and rider. She hears the bells ring eleven while she is still far from her journey's end; she urges her horse, and on they go, faster; and just as midnight strikes they reach the city gate:

"And out come serf and soldier
  To meet the news she brings.

"Bregenz is saved ! ere daylight
    Her battlements are manned ;
Defiance greets the army
    That marches on the land.
And if to deeds heroic
    Should endless fame be paid,
Bregenz does well to honor
    The noble Tyrol maid.

"Three hundred years are vanished,
    And yet upon the hill
An old stone gateway rises,
    To do her honor still.
And there, when Bregenz women
    Sit spinning in the shade,
They see in quaint old carving
    The Charger and the Maid.

"And when, to guard old Bregenz,
    By gateway, street, and tower,
The warder paces all night long
    And calls each passing hour ;
'Nine,' 'ten,' 'eleven,' he cries aloud,
    And then (O crown of Fame !)
When midnight pauses in the skies
    He calls the maiden's name !"

Bregenz is at the extreme point of the long blue upper lake. It is only when the air is exceptionally clear that we can see the minster tower of Constance looming in the far distance. That is the goal to which the steamer is now bearing us, but on either side, on the German bank as well as on the Swiss, we see many agreeable halting-places and many pleasant, snug retreats.

Over yonder on the left bank, Rorschach and Romanshorn have become the centre of traffic, and between them the little town of Arbon lies on a narrow peninsula. It was one of the most select points on the lake, and was fortified by the Romans, the leader of the cohorts dwelling there in a strong castle. The harbor was built far out into the lake, and some of its huge foundation-stones are still visible on the bottom when the sun shines through the quiet water.

The old name, the sound of which is still partially preserved in the modern one, was Arbor Felix. When the Romans were exterminated or driven away, the representatives of the German prince came into the town, and brought in their train the young Conrad, who tarried with them before taking the fatal road to Italy. What a tragically beautiful form it is that rises before our imagination, blue-eyed and golden-haired, on the cross-road between happy youth and earnest manhood! How often the music of love-songs must have sounded over the lake from the lips of him in whose veins the warm blood of the Staufens flowed!

His golden head fell beneath the axe, and the name of Conrad, at the present day, stands unabsolved in history.

The little village with the church which we see yonder, nearly opposite Arbon, is called Wasserburg. The church stands prominently on the shore, and the parsonage is further inland, for the waves wash over the building when the lake is exceptionally stormy. On sunny days, however, the reverend inmate has the advantage, for lofty green trees spread their shady canopy over his garden, and though, close at hand, the country people are engaged in bustling occupations, he strolls quietly up and down, feeling as secure and proud on his land as ever did his neighbors the Counts of Montfort. That name has an old world-renowned sound, for the owners of it for many centuries possessed the proud castle which rises abruptly from the lake at Langenargen.

It was at first on an island which was afterwards united to the mainland by a dyke. No race in the district of the Rhine Valley and Lake Constance was mightier than they. No castle was more stately—it asserted its ancient majesty even in its ruins. Now, however, it has all disappeared, in order to make way for a modern artistic edifice which the rulers of Swabia have erected for themselves. The new Montfort has cost many thousands, but the old wave-washed walls will not bear the modern burden which has been laid upon them, for it is stated that from time to time the pillars show unmistakable signs of giving way in many places.

But the real summer retreat of the Court of Wurtemburg is Friedrichshafen, lying a few miles distant, with its fine landing-place, its lofty light-house, and its broad quay, where the bustling, chattering Swabian life goes on.

What confusion of men and goods! The engine of the train whistles, the bell of the boat rings. Stop! another passenger before the bridge is drawn away. Now he is on board, safe but breathless, the vessel is pushed off, and in a few minutes the open blue water bears us on again. And now we first see clearly the beautiful elevation of the castle, with its long rows of windows and its broad terraces. Lofty lime-trees shade the entrance, and the garden with its fragrant flower-beds spreads round it on all sides, whilst the flag on the summit of the building flaunts in the breeze.

This charming town did not always bear the name which it now possesses. Friedrichshafen came into existence in the present century, after the old monastic settlement of Hofen was broken up and united to the town of Buchhorn.

At Buchhorn dwelt the good knight, Sir Ulrich, beloved by all his people. Then a summons came and he rode off to the wars, and nothing more was heard of him for many a day. At last a messenger rode up to the castle, bringing the news to his sorrowing wife that Sir Ulrich had fallen in battle, fighting bravely until the last.

From that time the Lady Gertrude gave herself up to working for the poor, and on the fourth anniversary of her lord's death she gathered together all her people, and all those dependent upon her bounty, and begged that they would pray for the soul of Sir Ulrich.

Among those assembled was a pilgrim, in rags, who begged that the noble lady would give him a robe to replace his tatters. The Lady Gertrude handed him the robe, and asked for his prayers, also, for the soul of her dear lord, when, instead of thanking her humbly, the pilgrim took her in his arms and kissed her! Throwing back his cowl he disclosed the features of Sir Ulrich, who had been kept a prisoner all these years, and had finally escaped and made his way home to his dear wife.

At Buchhorn, as far back as the time of the Carlovingians, a council was held, called by the old German term a Thingstätte. Trade also, and barter, were carried on to a very large extent. The rulers who dwelt there were called Counts of Linzgau.

The light from the windows of the castle, which we are now approaching, is so clearly and brightly reflected on to the lake below, that even more than a century ago the people of the neighborhood were accustomed to say, "That glitters like Meersburg." At its foot lies the little town of the same name,

which was founded in the reign of King Dagobert.
It was here that the princely ecclesiastics from Constance dreamed away the golden summer in times of
peace, and entrenched themselves and their treasures
in times of war.

The steep position and antique coloring of Meersburg give it the appearance of a strongly-fortified
little town, and this impression is naturally greatly
increased by the appearance of the two castles which
overtop the whole. Between them is an open ravine
which Bishop Nicholas caused to be made by blasting, in order to defend his castle more surely. Luxuriant vines grow all over the hills, and in the distance the snowy peaks of the Bernese Alps are
visible.

Guelphs and Staufens were lords of the castle, and
the manuscript of a message still preserved in Meersburg tells us that once the Bavarian and the Swede
knocked at their doors and threatened to level their
walls to the ground. This message is contained in a
yellow, time-stained letter burnt at the four corners,
and written by the colonel of Horn's regiment. It
states that it shall fare no better with the town than
with the letter; that it also shall be set fire to, at the
four corners, if it does not surrender. Meersburg,
however, did not surrender.

At the beginning of the present century the district looked very waste and desolate: the walls of the
old castle stood dreary and dismantled; the bishopric

was abolished, its property secularized, and the town itself passed to the government of Baden. This was a period when many existing conditions were broken up—justly indeed, but harshly.

Destruction would have overtaken the old castle had not one of the noblest men of his country chosen it for his home. The Baron von Lassberg became the owner of the castle, and in the gallery where the bishop's library formerly stood he arranged his intellectual treasures, comprising manuscripts of all ages. In the balcony, where his great arm-chair was placed, he sat and basked in the sunshine.

The Rhine Gate, Constance.

CHAPTER IV.

CONSTANCE.

WE have seen that the history of Meersburg is closely connected with that of Constance, and the road also is near at hand which brings us within reach of the proud old episcopal town; Constance forms in one sense the keystone of the upper lake, for here the great basin is divided into two slender arms, one of which is named after the town of Ueberlingen, and the other is called the Lower Lake, or the Zellersee.

In these arms are the two beautiful islands of Mainau and Reichenau, on which we will land as soon as we have finished our walk through Constance. The history of this town has been similar to that of Lindau and many other places of the old empire; its population and its importance to the world at large rapidly retrograded, and instead of fulfilling a great historical mission, it was called upon simply to form the centre of a narrow, modest circle.

Its nature and its merits must be measured accordingly, though it will be acknowledged that for this class of town Constance stands in the foremost rank. Its inhabitants, which now number about sixteen thousand, have retrieved in intellectual freedom the position which its forty thousand residents formerly held, for this last was its population when that renowned council was held which crowned its deeds with the death of the great Huss, instead of with the purifying of the church.

The origin of the town reaches as far back as the wars of the Emperor Constantine with the Alemanni, and the colossal substructure of the Castle was discovered during the Thirty Years' War, when the Swedes were digging their trenches. Its prosperity, and consequently its importance for the great empire began early, for nearly all the German princes down to the time of the Staufens passed through its gates and rewarded its hospitality with rich honors.

When Charlemagne went to Rome in order to receive his imperial crown, he rested in Constance with Hildegard, and the German kings very often spent Christmas or Easter here. Brilliant regal assemblies were held when the nobles of the kingdom gathered round their chief. It was in Constance also that the ambassadors from Milan appeared before Barbarossa when he received the golden key which the Italian states sent him as a token of their submission.

All the splendor, however, of this last event vanishes before the spectacle of sensual and sinful ostentation which is known by the name of the Holy Council of Constance. This was held in the year 1414, at a period when the wild, devastating spirit of arrogance, of indolence and immorality, had penetrated the great structure of the Romish Church. Love songs resounded through the cloister, and quarrels of the reverend inmates with their neighbors were even at times fought out in the open streets. At the head of these wild practices were three rival Popes— namely, John XXIII., Benedict XIII., and Gregory XII., who in turn made war upon each other. No one knew any longer who was the real head of the Church, but those who suffered most were the men whose beliefs were honest.

The Council of Constance was summoned in order to amend this state of things, and to reform the Church throughout its entire constitution. In this way the little town became for four years the central point of European history. Ulric von Reichenthal, a contemporary writer, describes with charming *naïveté* the pageant of princes and prelates, and how " one after another heralds and fifers came, with all sorts of servants, in order to secure lodgings for their masters. They bespoke food and straw, and fixed their masters' badges on the houses and doors."

The Cardinal of Ostia came in the middle of August, being entrusted with the preparations, as Lord High Chancellor of the Holy Church; more than eighty horsemen followed in his train. The Archbishop of Mayence rode into the town clothed in armor from head to foot. The Margrave, Frederick von Meissen, came accompanied by a crowd of nobles, and followed by twenty-one heavily-laden wagons and above five hundred horsemen.

The citizens looked on in alarm, for the town continued to fill. The delegates came even from the East and from the distant North, and no one could foresee what would be the end of all this splendor. Late in the autumn, when the snow had already begun to fall among the Alps, the Pope himself appeared. The sledge which brought him over the Arlberg upset and was almost buried in the snow before he reached Thurgau. Duke Frederick of Austria received him there with great honor, and accompanied him and his party to Constance, where he was to make a triumphal entry. He rode, clothed in the white papal robes, under a canopy, and before him there walked a horse with a bell on its neck, and the Holy Sacrament on its back; four councillors bore the canopy, and the shouting mob streamed by in thousands. The Emperor Sigismund alone was absent, though he too made his appearance on Christmas Day, accompanied by the empress and a countless train of followers.

The influx of strangers constantly increased, their number being roughly estimated at eighty thousand, and at the time of the greatest pressure it must have amounted to one hundred thousand men, who had at their disposal thirty thousand horses. All the curiosity, and a good deal of the vice of Europe flowed together here, for more than a thousand women ministered to the pleasure of the worthy prelates.

To turn from these considerations of outward splendor, how did it fare with the great duties which this assembly had been summoned to fulfil, and with those reforms which Christendom so sorely needed? What did the Council of Constance do for the development of history and for the salvation of the human race? Nothing, and less than nothing! For when this question is asked, the splendor that was paraded there sinks at once into foul ignominy, and we are confronted, not with a deed of glory, but with a ghastly crime. It is true that after much trouble the three rival popes were prevailed on to relinquish their dignity in order to give place to a fourth.

Very soon after, however, Pope John broke his sacred oath, fled from the Council, and having reached Italy, attempted to strengthen his dominion afresh. But the inquiries made in the meantime by the Council as to his mode of life resulted in such an exposure of vice that he was solemnly deposed, and Cardinal Colonna was chosen in his stead.

This gloomy incident was soon followed by a second, which is almost unequalled in horror. It was, naturally, much easier to condemn heretics than to endanger the safety of the existing Church; the Council found, therefore, their most pressing duty to be that of vengeance. The support which the doctrines of John Huss had met with in Bohemia had for a long time roused the hatred of the Romanists, so the renowned teacher was summoned from Prague to Constance, in order to defend himself before the Assembly. Sigismund took the precaution of giving him a guarantee of safe conduct, and had promised to protect his life. The emperor, however, broke his word, as the pope had done before, for he was easily persuaded that no man was bound to keep faith with a "heretic." The execution of this great, steadfast man, who mounted the scaffold with stoical calmness, is a stirring picture, and cannot be related without a feeling of angry shame.

First of all his clerical clothes were torn off him with horrible curses, then his long hair was cut off, then a rusty chain was put round his neck, and lastly a crown on which demons were painted was placed, in mockery, on his head. Huss did not resist, nor did he beg for mercy, but all along the road to the stake he prayed aloud that God would forgive his enemies; and while the flames played round him he praised God and sang till the smoke stifled his voice, and hid his mutilated form. Thus died "the heretic," and the Church whose edifice rests on love to one's neighbor had burdened itself with a fresh and a horrible crime.

As to the important question which had been placed before the Council at Constance—namely, that of purifying the Church—nothing was done. It was at last openly determined that the performance of this duty should be deferred to a "later" Assembly, and the Council dispersed with a feeling of hopelessness. Even worse than this, their departure was covered with shame of the meanest description, for the Emperor Sigismund was so deeply in debt that the citizens would not allow him to depart without leaving the whole of his baggage in pledge. It remained for years in the custody of the State, and when every hope of it being redeemed had vanished, and the chests were opened, it was found to contain—not silver vessels, as was supposed, but stones.

Such was the course and such was the end of the celebrated "Holy Council of Constance." An emperor and a pope both proved themselves traitors to their word, the town was inundated with a profligate crowd, an irrecoverable debt was incurred, and, above all, the scaffold of John Huss had been erected as an endless blot on the fair city of Constance. Truly, the smoke from the martyr's pile still pervades these memories.

When we turn from the past to the present time we still find in the outward appearance of the town many things that remind us of the middle ages. The Town Hall, erected in 1388, in which the conclave was held, is especially remarkable. It is an extensive building, and stands close to the water's edge. The lower portion is of stone, the upper of dark, weather-beaten wood, so that it has almost the appearance of a huge shed, though at each of the four corners of the roof there is a little overhanging projection, which gives an air of originality to what is in itself a somewhat clumsy structure.

On the first story is the " Council Chamber," as it is called. It is a large but low room, entirely lined with polished wood, the roof being supported by pillars. The frescoes which adorn the walls represent the most important events in the history of Constance. They were done in 1875–85 by Philip Schwörer and Frederick Pecht, of Munich.

The Cathedral, which was begun in the middle of the eleventh century, stands out, both historically and architecturally, above the other churches of the city. The style of the architecture was originally Roman, but the many additions which have been made from time to time are of the Gothic order. A dreadful fire once occurred within the walls, which melted the entire peal of bells and caused great destruction. In spite of these disasters, however, the minster is still the finest church on the lake.

Constance having become the seat of a bishopric as early as 781, the city grew rich in consequence, and a succession of remarkable men who labored there added much to its renown. The greater proportion of the inhabitants are Catholic. The impression left from the days of the great Assembly sunk so deep that the citizens at that time rushed with open arms to meet the Reformation, and the bishop left the city. The Lutheran opinions became daily more open and decided, and when the town immediately repudiated the "Interim" which Charles V. laid upon it, open strife broke out.

One of those wars followed in which the self-respect of the citizens sets itself with the courage of despair in opposition to the superior strength of their rulers. The soldiers of the city encountered the Spanish infantry, which the emperor sent against them, on the Rhine bridge; but after a bloody fray the imperial troops obtained the upper hand. It was indeed a Pyrrhus-like victory, for the emperor repaid with care the heroism of his enemies, and made the city, which had formerly been a free town, part of Austria. All Protestants were obliged to flee, and their property was confiscated.

Constance had again to suffer the calamities of war when the Swedes encamped before its gates. On this occasion Field-Marshal Horn stormed the walls three times, but the resolute defence of the inhabitants forced him to retire. After this, quieter times came. Commerce and industry began slowly to flourish once more, and Nature unconcernedly brought forth her golden treasures. A permanent change, however, had been wrought, for the great free city has become a quiet, homely, provincial town, and only one thing still reminds us of the past: this is a disposition to freedom which the town proves in every way, and which it especially attests in its ecclesiastical government. Many noble hands were held out to the people, with offers of assistance, in their time of effort; notably those of Joseph II. and the great Wessenberg, who, when Bishop of Constance, raised for himself an imperishable monument by his humanity and his cultivation of art and learning.

We have still to mention the two large islands, which, like Lindau, were in early times distinguished as meadows or pastures. One was named, from its wealth, Reichenau; the other, from its beautiful May breeze, Mainau. For a long time both belonged to the same owners.

Mainau was for many generations a subordinate property of the great abbey on the Lower Lake, till the abbot himself gave it away. It then came at second-hand to the German order, who possessed it till 1806. The wide, princely house of this order— a mixture of castle and cloister—stood with its great wings on the high plateau of the island. In the long galleries and handsome rooms were hung the banners of the commanders, and in the chapel the consecrated bell sounded, sending its peaceful music far over the lake; while above glistened Säntis, and in the hazy distance the towers of Old Bregenz could be distinguished.

Strangers in those days who visited the island found hospitable entertainment at the farm and the inn attached to it. In later years, when the commandery had long fallen away, the glory of the order and its noble lords left its own peculiar impression on the island. The old good-natured host would sit for hours and narrate to his guests how the armed knights Von Hiltpolt and Werner Hundbiss defended the island against the Swedish ships, just as though he had himself been present. Now, since the reigning family of Baden have fixed their summer residence here, these pictures of the past have faded before the brilliancy of the present.

In the villages at the end of the Ueberlingen Lake there are some dark caverns which are called "Heathen Holes." They are narrow chambers hewn in the rock, and are thought by many people to have been a kind of catacomb, and to have served the early Christians as hiding-places. Others take them to be Roman graves, dating back as far as the times of the wars with the Alemanni.

The neighboring island of Reichenau, in the Lower Lake, presents an entirely different picture; its circumference is considerably greater, and its history is much older. No spot of land round about surpasses it in richness of soil or in political and historic renown. Amongst all the monasteries that arose in the middle ages, Reichenau was specially favored by fortune—four archdukes and about twenty counts were its lieges; and as Charles V. boasted that the sun never set upon his dominions, so did the abbot of Reichenau boast that he slept every night on his own territory when he travelled to Rome to see the Pope. He was a prince of the Holy Roman Empire. Emperors and princes sat at his table, and the noblest knights from the neighboring districts served him as high steward and cup-bearer when he entertained his guests.

In Reichenau, however, they attended not only to the full enjoyment of the senses, but also to the enjoyment of intellectual cultivation, and the monks prided themselves that no town in the southern part of the empire could compare with them in culture. The nobles sent their sons from all parts of the country to be educated here, and more than eighty bishoprics were filled by scholars of the abbey.

But Fortune had been too prodigal to be lasting; the turning-point came under the Hohenstaufens, and ruin rushed in with overwhelming force. Instead of giving themselves up to meditation at Shrovetide, the monks went to Ulm for the Carnival, and danced and played with the townswomen, so that, in order to exclude them from the town, the abbot sold all the property which he possessed there.

One hide of land after another went to cover debts, and soon the income of the monastery had sunk from fifty thousand florins to three silver marks. The disorganization increased, and at last an hour arrived when it was indescribable, and the abbot, with his own hands, tore out the eyes of five inoffensive fishermen because they were subjects of the city of Constance, with which he was at war.

In this state of affairs the bishops of the neighboring city, who had long conceived a plan of annexing Reichenau to their own possessions, saw that the moment had arrived when the ripe fruit might, of itself, fall into their lap. Without much trouble the abbot was persuaded, in consideration of a small sum, to betray his trust; and he himself, in 1540, delivered the monastery over to Constance.

Such are the thoughts and memories which accompany us as we walk through this beautiful island. The effect is strange; the old church, consecrated in 806, still stands. We step through the carved porch among the gray pillars; we pass the tombs, the coverings of which are adorned with crozier and mitre, but the broken light which environs us is oppressively gloomy. The place seems haunted by a spirit of powerlessness, which, perhaps, proceeds from the imperial grave of Charles the Fat, great-grandson of Charlemagne, who died here, unthroned and unhonored. The sacristy, with its rattling iron bolts, contains the treasures and relics of the abbey. Here are to be found the Gospels on fine parchment, chalices, costly vestments, and ivory carvings. Here is also a huge emerald, which indeed, to our eyes, looks no better than green glass.

We unconsciously draw a deep breath of relief when we step out of these dim, gloomy rooms into the open country, which well deserves the name of the "Rich Pasture." Fruit-laden trees and sunny vineyards surround us, and the three villages of Ober-

zell, Mittelzell and Unterzell peep out among the
meadows, adding much to the beauty of the scene
over which the summer breeze plays so pleasantly.

On the shore are seen the ruins of the old Scopula-
Burg, destroyed in 1384, where the monks entrenched
themselves in times of danger. All along the edge
of the lake little white-looking towns and villages rise
before us, Iznang and Horn, Steckhorn to the south
and St. Rudolf's Cell to the north.

But presently the neighborhood changes; a peculiar contest between land and water begins, and the
bottom of the lake presses up close to the shallow
surface. It is preparing an outlet for the Rhine, for
between the mainland and Reichenau it is so shallow
that in the height of summer it is almost possible to
walk across dryshod.

We are now in Switzerland; the great castle which
we see yonder, where the Rhine flows from the Upper
to the Lower Lake, is called Gottlieben. The poet
has rightly imagined that those square towers, which
look so gray and sad, were built by Melancholy, and
that they have received only sad guests. The Bishop
of Constance retired here, in anger, before the hatred
of the Emperor Frederick II.; here Jerome of Prague
was a captive; here John Huss lay imprisoned before
he was led to the stake; and here the profligate Pope
John was kept in custody when he was captured at a
wrestling-match, disguised as a messenger.

Even the last hand which attempted to revive and

adorn the old castle was without a blessing; it was the hand of the third Buonaparte—Louis Napoleon—who wished to restore the building in the Gothic style. He was living, as is well known, near at hand, in Arenenberg, which Queen Hortense inherited from a patrician family, and had enriched with delightful pleasure-grounds.

It was from this place that he went to Paris as President of the Republic, and the Second of December soon followed. He exchanged the quiet, retired country-seat for the Tuileries, and for nearly two decades all Europe hung anxiously on his mysterious words, during which Arenenberg lay desolate and forgotten.

The place where all constraint is completely thrown off, and where the great stream reigns once more free and independent, is called Stein on the Rhine, a little town which claims a Merovingian origin. Formerly it had walls and trenches, and it had need to be ever watchful of its freedom, for not only did the stronghold of the Lords of Klingen tower above it, but many a quarrelsome neighbor lay ready outside its ramparts.

Once, indeed, the burgomaster himself conspired with the Lord of the Castle of Höhgau to give the town into his hands. A night attack was made, but the citizens kept off the enemy with unexpected vigor, and having seized the traitor they tied him in a sack and hurled him into the Rhine.

Höhgau, which we have just named, may without doubt be considered the most important tract in the whole Lake Constance district. Its name, which signifies "hill district," appears as early as the time of Charles Martel, and it well describes the nature of the country, with its numerous rocks and boulder blocks, which overrun plain and forest. What a gigantic and mysterious power has hurled them up from the depths of the earth or down from immeasurable heights!

Formerly more than twenty castles stood in Höhgau, and the oldest families of the Empire dwelt there. The most beautiful picture of the past, in which rugged power is strangely mixed with gentle sentiment, is framed within this lovely landscape. Ekkehart's turret chamber was here! Hadwig, the learned Duchess of Swabia, dwelt at Hohentwiel, which looks over the open blue Lake of Constance. The beautiful ruins stand out on the rock like a high watchtower stationed there to command river and lake. Close behind, and steeper still, are the ruins of Hohenkrähen. What memories this rock covers! It is a monument of the history of the land and of its people.

The little town of Singen lies nearly at the foot of Hohentwiel, and the numerous Roman antiquities which have been found there lead to the inference that the legions of Tiberius had found out this beautiful spot. A guide meets visitors at the farm which lies on the ascent to the castle, and conducts them

The Concilium Saal (Town Hall), Constance

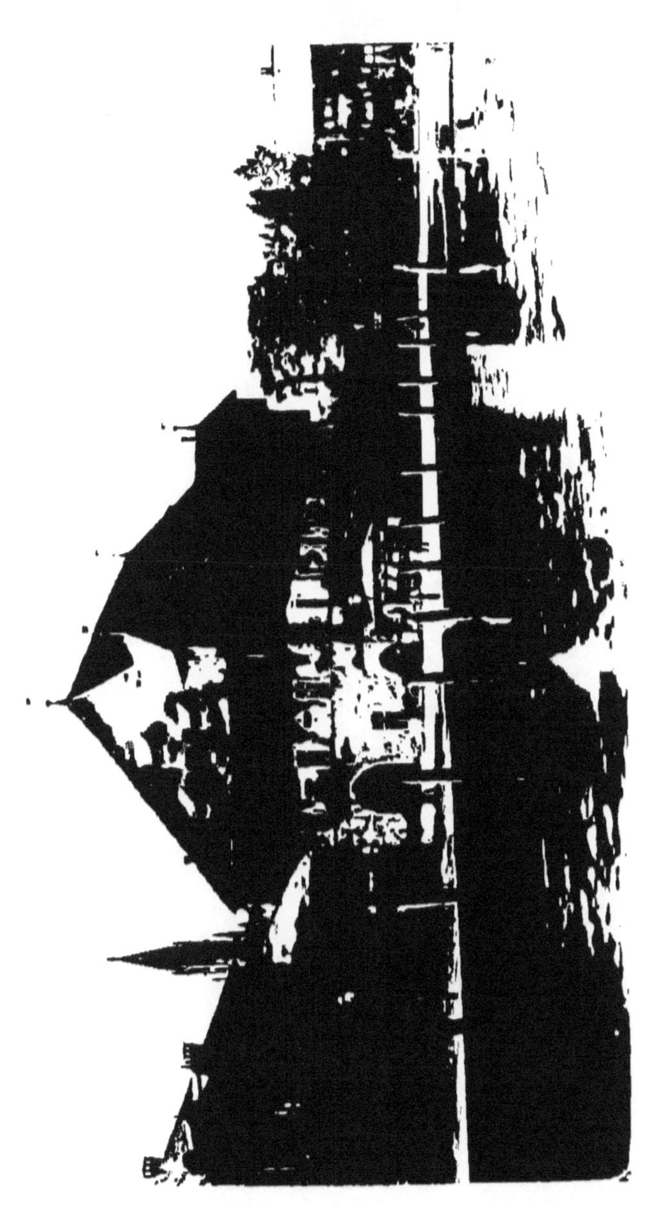

silently past the old lindens and the steep rock wall, the stones of which are here and there streaked with red.

In about a quarter of an hour the real fortress is reached, and we are surrounded by ruined bastions, ditches and walls. Though everything is broken and fallen, there is still an appearance of strength which neither time nor foe has been able to destroy. This castle has, indeed, been associated with suffering to many; for, among the purposes which it has been made to serve in the course of ages, is one which is terrible enough. It has been a prison, and within its walls men, such as the noble Moser, have languished. Many who had entered it with golden locks have left it, if they have ever again passed its portal, with hair white as snow.

Hohentwiel became a part of Wurtemberg, to which it belongs at the present time, in the middle of the fifteenth century; though it was then, as now, a detached or outlying territory, surrounded on all sides by Baden. The waves of the Thirty Years' War beat against its walls, but the brave Wiederhold, into whose hands the defence of the place was given, remained firm, and yielded neither to the gold nor to the sword of the enemy. He deserved the inscription which was formerly carved over the shattered door of the stronghold:

"Der Feind hat's fünfmal zwar geschreckt,
Doch hat der Herr zum Schutz erweckt

> Den Wiederhold, der fünfzehen Jahr'
> Dasselb' beschützt in Feindts Gefahr."*

But there was not always a Wiederhold to command at Hohentwiel, and impregnable though the fortress seemed its hour at last came. Its star sank at the opening of this century, at a time when empires and dynasties were engulfed. Who destroyed it? The same power which at that time carried destruction throughout Europe—namely, the army of Buonaparte, which invaded Höhgau to the number of twenty thousand men. The officers of the garrison capitulated unanimously, with the exception of one lieutenant; but the conditions on which the surrender was made were broken, and the demolition and blasting of the stronghold was the result. This work lasted for nearly a year; mines were laid, not only in the building but in the rock itself, and nothing more than ruins were left of the proud home of the beautiful Hadwig. Five hundred inhabitants of the neighboring villages were compelled to assist in this disgraceful work.

That is the last sad remembrance that surrounds the "Rock," but it shall not be the impression with which we take our leave of it. Ruthless hands might raze the walls to the ground and destroy the master-

---

* "Five times the din of dreadful war
In vain did on those ramparts roar,
For Wiederhold, God's trusted knight,
Fifteen long years maintained the fight."

pieces which adorned its stone halls; but one picture was imperishable; it could as little be touched by the hands of the destroyer as its beauty can be expressed by rapturous description.

Let us look out into the golden distance and into the blue depths, for the lovely picture lies before us in the clear morning air. Here we see a mountain-chain that reaches from Mont Blanc to the Ortler, a country which can scarce contain the fulness of its blessings; and that pearl, the sparkling jewel which meets our gaze in this open treasure-house of nature, the blue shining lake over the long surface of which our eye lingers. In primeval times, further back than the existence or the thought of man, Höhgau also was a part of the lake. Teeth an inch long are occasionally dug out of the gravelly ground, and are supposed to have belonged to huge fish, which moved under the vast waters. In the lapse of ages the water slowly retired, wrestling with the earth inch by inch, till it found its limits in the huge basin which to-day lies smiling before us.

What a vast horizon, what warmth of color, what harmony of sounds, when the evening bells ring over the waters! The fiery ball of the setting sun sinks lower and lower; it glows over the water like the re-flection of a great conflagration; the gray cloud draws its veil over the edge of the disc, gradually covering it little by little. The gold changes into purple, the purple becomes violet, and now the last faint ray disappears, and the evening breeze rustles among the trees. How gratefully the great sail, which still floats on the lake, will catch the breeze; but soon the sail too has vanished, and is lost to us in the thick curtain of the twilight.

CHAPTER V.

SCHAFFHAUSEN.

THE Rhine has left Lake Constance, and has emerged once more on its course. It has still the vivid, impetuous character of youth, but may be said to resemble a youth earnestly striving towards a great future. Such is the character of its course from Stein to Basle.

Only once, not far from its outlet, there comes a critical moment, an outbreak of its old passion. This occurs at the Rhinefall at Schaffhausen, where a gigantic bank of rock, over three hundred feet wide, stretches itself right across the stream; it is nearly eighty-five feet high, and was formerly still higher, as may be seen from the columns which rise out of the whirlpool.

Nature has thrown up this fortification to obstruct the path of the lordly stream, and here must the Rhine descend. It is a leap for life, but with a shout of joy it extricates itself from the seething depths into which it falls, and the liberated waters flow on again gleefully through forest and mead.

The Rhinefall is seen to the greatest advantage on approaching it from Neuhausen, for then the picture of the splendid cataract confronts us set in a framework of green woods. On the right bank, the Schweitzerhof stands like a palace, with its showy façade; the fashionable world crowds the wide terraces, and the high windows glitter in the sun. There is a short way to the shore by a steep flight of steps, but the more convenient approach to it is by a gravelled path which winds through the park. The opposite bank is steep; the rocks rise full of crevices moistened with spray, and overgrown with green bushes which cling to every cranny.

On the hill the Castle of Lauffen stands, with its indented gables and battlements, reminding us, with its straggling out-buildings, of an old fortress. It has recently been converted into an inn. The magnificent spectacle of the waterfall presents itself before us in sublime beauty; mountains of foam are heaved and tossed and torn until they are shattered into myriad drops of spray.

It is, indeed, a battle; and the last of those rocky columns, which are the remains of a stony phalanx, stand in the vortex, like heroes who have survived the battle unshaken. Day and night, summer and winter, for years and for centuries, the unruly tide has stormed against them; the foundation is already undermined, and many of their companions have sunk into the foaming depths.

Through how many more generations will those which remain continue as they are now? But though it is a battle, and a gigantic one, it is quite devoid of any element of gloom; it presents no picture of destruction, but one of victory. The sparkling stream casts itself down with such a shout of joy that it can be heard for some leagues on a clear night; and in the morning the sun streams through the silver spray till it is reflected in all the colors of the rainbow.

If we visit the place at the height of the fashionable season we see entirely different pictures—we find visitors from every part of the globe, and in their midst we realize the aphorism that it is but a step from the sublime to the ridiculous.

A Frenchman complains that the beauty of the cataract has considerably decreased since 1870, and that he misses that "parfum de l'électricité," which Delrieu remarks in his Rhine book. He speaks in a loud voice, "pour dominer le bruit du cataracte;" he talks enough for two, and so it is no wonder if his neighbor, the pale Anglo-Saxon, is inexorably silent. "Le touriste est une créature machinale," says the Frenchman, again quoting his Delrieu, "il a besoin d'un dada." He was right, and nowhere does this cockneyism of travel work more painfully than when we stand before a truly noble object of nature.

We would involuntarily see enthusiasm or rapture reflected in the face of every person with whom we share the delight of such a sight. Instead of this, how often do we find a melancholy want of appreciation, and we feel alone in the midst of a chattering crowd—one complains that the Rhinefall is too daz-

zling, another that it is too noisy, a third unconcernedly reads up the chapter in his guide-book and ticks
off the name as if to erase a burdensome debt.   He
has "done" the Rhinefall.

The Rhinefall and Schaffhausen are generally described as one geographical object, but this is not at
all the case, for they lie nearly a league apart.   When
we have sufficiently admired the Fall we turn our
gaze back to the tidy antique little town, whose
gabled roofs and arched doorways promise hospitable
entertainment.

Schaffhausen itself is but small, and lies straggling
along the bank of the Rhine, but the style of the
buildings, as well as the whole character of the town,
show the substantial independence of the citizens to
have reached a high stage of development.

The old citadel of Munoth frowns down from the
heights with its impenetrable walls, and the towers
of the cathedral, erected 1052–1101, have become
gray with age.   Its bells, as is well known, bear the
inscription which Schiller prefixed to his incomparable poem: "*Vivos voco, mortuos plango, fulgura
frango.*"   The manufactures of Schaffhausen enjoy
a considerable reputation, and its trade is doubly
profitable on account of the great water-power it
possesses, and from the stoppage of all vessels caused
by the Rhinefall.   In this way the venerable town
has added the modern power of wealth to that which
it possessed in bygone ages, as the "Key of Swabia,"

and the same public spirit which formerly animated it still survives. The noblest institutions which the town possesses for public use have proceeded from the liberality of individual citizens, and fresh instances of such liberality are constantly being given.

Legend tells us that in the earliest times only a few boatmen's huts stood on the spot where Schaffhausen now is, and the name itself may easily be traced back to such an origin; as early as the twelfth century, however, the unpretending place received the privileges and honors of a town. Many a siege also was sustained by the fortifications with which the citizens surrounded their home; nor were the inhabitants, indeed, exempt from other visitations of various kinds.

In one year more than four thousand were carried off by the plague. Fire and water vied with each other to devastate the beautiful town, and the war which brought all the arms of Europe together in Switzerland, at the opening of this century, at length robbed the town of one of its most remarkable ornaments. This was the old bridge over the Rhine, which is here more than three hundred feet wide. It stretched from one bank to the other without a single support, for the one pier which stood in the middle of the stream belonged to an earlier structure, and in no way assisted in carrying this bridge. The celebrated wit, Madame Roland, expressed the greatest admiration for this remarkable viaduct in her letters from Switzerland; but the men who set fire to the bridge and burnt it to the ground, in the spring of 1799, were the compatriots of Madame Roland.

Leaving Schaffhausen, in a short time we enter the district of the so-called "Forest Towns," which for centuries belonged to the house of Hapsburg. The first of them is called Waldshut, a name having precisely the same signification as that of *Custodia Silvæ*, which it bore a thousand years ago. In those days what is now a town consisted only of a solitary forest-house standing in the pine-covered wilderness.

Near this place the Aar runs into the Rhine. It is a wild mountain-stream which descends nearly seven thousand feet from the Grimsel, and in its rapid course collects all the watery treasures of the Bernese highlands in order to offer them in homage to the Rhine.

The landscape through which we now pass corresponds to the name which the four towns bear. It is covered with forest, high beeches stand on either side, and the lovely stream glides almost hidden under the branches. The waters are as blue as the sky above, and so clear that the sun pierces to the gravel on the bed beneath. Only a smoking kiln or a floating raft reminds us of the hand of man. Gradually the banks widen, the beech wood becomes less dense, green fields border the strand, and in the distance there stand the reapers, merrily bringing in the harvest.

Yonder is Lauffenburg. The change in the landscape is startling, a sharp turn of the stream, which brings out the full force of the current, lies suddenly before our eyes—the broken rocks draw together, narrow and rugged, and between them the river wearily beats out its way. The water eddies and splashes round the deeply-embedded boulders, the white foam crests the points, and many of them are already so washed away that it seems as though every hour they must crash together.

This is a last relic of the river's stormy youth, it is a weak echo of that great feat which the Rhine performed at Schaffhausen; and we recognize it in its present name, for these rapids are called "the Lauffen." At one time, if it was required for ships to go farther, they were let down by ropes; but it is rarely that any one attempts this perilous journey now. It was attempted, however, by young Lord Montague, who was drowned in the river on the same day that his ancestral home in England was destroyed by fire.

Even apart from this melancholy fact, which still remains indelibly fixed in the minds of the inhabitants, Lauffenburg has a dull, almost gloomy, character. The weather-beaten houses which stand high up on the narrow bank look as though they had grown up out of the splintered rocks. The front is turned away from the stream, and the gray wall at the back is enlivened with but few windows.

The town stands somewhat peculiarly. Below it

is the roaring whirlpool, the gray houses are perched on the rocks, and above them stretches a dark-green wooded hill, on the summit of which stands the walls of a castle. This castle has long been ruined and tenantless, only the old tower still stands in its ancient majesty; no banner waves from its walls, but a fir-tree which planted itself hundreds of years ago among the battlements now stands like a symbol of the glory which has past.

A narrow bridge, half composed of wood, joins the towns of Great and Little Lauffenburg, and unites Switzerland to the German Empire. Down on the smooth-washed shingle below all kinds of fishing-tackle are spread out, together with fine nets stretched on pegs; for this is one of the most important places for salmon. In one part, where the water is shallow and sunny, the number of young fish is sometimes so great as to darken the surface. The fishery is the most important trade in the whole of this district, though, near at hand, we hear the iron hammer of the quarry ring out from the woods, and the piled-up logs on the bank show that the timber-trade also flourishes.

Soon we reach the last two of the four "forest towns," Sackingen and Rheinfelden. The former, which is considered to be the oldest town of the neighborhood, had a religious origin, having been founded by one of the missionaries who came over from Ireland at the beginning of the sixth century.

The Rhinefall at Schaffhausen.

The Rhinefall at Schaffhausen.

"Jusqu'à ce temps, Satan avait exclusivement regné sur le grand-duché de Bade," says one of the French chroniclers whom we have already quoted; the holy Fridolin, in order to put an end to the heathen customs and disarm the arts of the devil, erected a monastery to oppose the great enemy.

This monastery, which was also a citadel, soon gained worldly power as well as spiritual dominion, and is said by many writers to be the oldest monastery standing on German ground. The princely splendor which it once possessed has long since passed away, for Fridolin has lain for more than a thousand years enshrined among his own relics, and probably but few of the inhabitants of the empire would have known anything of Sackingen had not the celebrated "Trumpeter" spread its fame throughout the world. The impression that the present town makes on us is that it much resembles the little municipal towns of Baden.

Rheinfelden, the last of the four forest towns, lies on Swiss territory. It has old weather-worn walls, gates, and towers, and was formerly one of the outposts of the Holy Roman Empire. In the stream is that whirling eddy called "Höllenhacken," and near by are the famous salt works on the Rhine.

For those who have time to remain, there are several things to be learned even in Rheinfelden. A dreaded stronghold once stood on the rocks which lie in the middle of the stream. The name of the castle was Stein, and many a wild conflict raged around its walls before they were finally destroyed, and many an anxious conference has been held by the citizens in the old town hall, when the Imperialists, Swedes, Swiss, or the hordes of Louis XIV., demanded admission through its gates.

CHAPTER VI.

BASLE.

BUT we must press on to Basle, the place which for many miles around is the centre for all traffic. Thither the river hastens, and thither all our present interests centre, for it is the first really important town on the Rhine.

We soon land beneath its walls; in the distance we see shining the dark tips of the Black Forest range, as well as those of the Jura and the Vosges, and in the broad valley which they enclose lies the level land rich with golden grain and green vineyards. It is here that the Rhine takes its last decided turn to the north, towards Germany, to which henceforth all its splendor and all its renown belong.

The very first effect of Basle, as it lies on both sides of the river, is striking and varied. Nature and history, and not simply accident and population, have formed it into a town. It could not help becoming what it has. There is every development of natural power, and the charm of this impression is increased by the antique historical character on which its present condition is based. The prosperity of Basle has been handed down for centuries. Of late handsome villas have been built in the suburbs; but the older parts of the town remain as they have been for hundreds of years, and the old-fashioned burgher character runs through the nature of the people, and holds them fast to their liberties. Fischart has deservedly sung aloud the praises of the " charming town " of the Rhine.

The Rhine was the great storehouse from which the town drew its wealth, and became what it was. It was the Rhine which carried thousands of foreign guests and foreign treasures to Basle. A regular water traffic was established between Basle and Strasburg as early as the sixteenth century, when long caravans of merchants were still wearily dragging along the high-road. The paving of the streets began in 1417, and the wells were so numerous that Æneas Sylvius observed that whoever would count them must count the houses as well. The old Rhine town was always proud of its name, and the bold struggles it made would vie with those of many a city in which princes raised their thrones.

The Rhine is here spanned by three bridges. The wooden bridge, Alte Brücke, partly supported by stone piers, was originally built in 1225. In its centre rises a chapel of the sixteenth century, also a column, containing a barometer and a weathercock. Above this wooden bridge the river is crossed by a modern iron structure; at each entrance of this bridge stand two basilisks—the well-known standards of the town; they are as much feared and honored as many a princely lion, or imperial eagle. The third bridge, also modern, crosses the river still further down.

The Romans recognized the strategical value of Basle for the rulers of the Upper Rhine, when they settled their colony at Augst (Augusta Rauracorum), the parent of the present town. It was from here that the Emperors Constantine and Julian endeavored to keep down the rising power of the Alemanni, when it became but too apparent that the nations of Europe were slowly gathering into a flood wherewith to overwhelm the Roman countries, and to sweep the worn-out races of antiquity from the earth.

Every opposition to such a force was powerless, and Basilēa fell like other towns into that vast inheritance which the barbarians wrested from the hands of the dying Romans. Golden-haired Alemanni ruled here and far around in Alsace until the Franks came, and the struggle for power began afresh. Burgundy and Germany, bishop and burgesses (among whom various families had distinguished themselves even in Barbarossa's time) constantly contended for the mastery; and whenever the storm swept over Europe, the great town at the bend of the Rhine bore its part in it.

The zealous monk, Bernhard, of Clairvaux, preached the Crusade in the cathedral at Basle. Alexander III. hurled a thunderbolt of excommunication into the town because it remained true to the Emperor; but the citizens of Basle seized the Papal legate who proclaimed the interdict, and threw him into the Rhine. Civil and party contentions of all kinds have, at various times, inflamed the citizens; but their character for energy always led them triumphantly out of their dangers and difficulties, and the town, which now has a population of 90,000, remains in its flourishing condition at the present day. In 1356 a fearful earthquake occurred, and in 1348 a still more fearful plague raged among the people.

It is unfortunate that we cannot here enter into a more detailed history of Basle, for in its firm independent exclusiveness, in the wealth of its intellectual and political tendencies, it presents one of the most attractive subjects of study.

Varnhagen von Ense, who has treated one of the historical episodes of Basle in the form of a novel, well draws out the peculiarities of the inhabitants in powerful language. In the background of the picture the mighty forms of imperialism are always standing out in strong relief. In the distant past we find Saxon and Frankish Emperors; later on, those of the Hohenstaufen line; and, in still more recent times, the Counts of Hapsburg are presented to us. Some are girt with the sword of war, whilst others are conspicuous only in the bright garments of festivity.

Here, as in many of the imperial cities, the bishopric originally formed the nucleus from which the town spread, and the free men who settled here from other places put themselves under the protection of the Church. The ecclesiastical possessions constantly increased, and so it may well be inferred that in the infancy of the town the bishops were its popular rulers.

Their power was increased by the fact that they were often members of noble families, and generally stood by the Emperor. Haito was the devoted friend and confidant of Charlemagne; Adalbero was the same to Henry II.; Burchard von Hasenburg stood, with unswerving fidelity and all the power of that warlike time, by Henry IV., who went to Canossa to do penance to the Pope. Bishop Ortlieb rode to the Holy Land with Conrad III., and Bishop Henry fought beside Rudolph of Hapsburg, at Ganserfeld, against the powerful Ottokar. Rudolph was for a long time the bitter enemy of the town, and had striven to force its gates with fire and sword; but his election to the monarchy, which put an end to the fearful "rulerless period," at once brought peace to Basle. The feelings of all parties changed; the gates of the city, which had been resolutely closed to the count, opened voluntarily to the king, and the two contending parties in the town came to an arrangement—Rudolph atoning for past injuries by lavishly bestowing a double amount of favor on the citizens.

The burgesses did not extricate themselves from the toils of this spiritual supremacy without a hard struggle, and then only by the exercise of all their strength. At length, however, their hour of victory came. If it might be said, during the first epoch, that Basle belonged to the bishop, it might truly be said, in the second, that Basle belonged to the citizens. The city had to preserve and adapt this independence through serious trials of all kinds both at home and in the field; but its historical importance increased in proportion to those trials.

Its banner waved at the battle of St. Jacob, which has been called the Swiss Thermopylæ, and the Council which sat within its walls in 1431–1448, during which time Pope Felix V. returned from the Conclave, drew the eyes of Europe to Basle. That was the time when it was a Free City, and it was undeniably the period of its greatest prosperity. All its powers, moral and physical, were in the highest state of development, and were brought out by the difficulties it had to encounter.

Out of the broad framework of political relations which Basle possessed as a Free City of the Great Empire, there arose gradually a closer and firmer combination by its becoming related to and influenced by its proximity to the Swiss Confederation. The formal and solemn completion of this step of confederation followed later, in the July of 1501; but, although the boys in the streets sang "*Hie Schweitzerboden,*" the city itself remained true to its German forms, and the feeling of the intellectual commonalty found a new lever in the growth of learning.

Thus the Swiss town rose out of the Free Town, which in its turn had taken the place of the bishop's town, and Basle entered upon a third and a new epoch in that form which brings us down to modern times. It is from this view, in spite of all the glory of its wars and history, that the present importance of the town is based.

The first road which we take through Basle leads straight up to the Cathedral, which lies high up on one of the two hills where the earliest settlement was established. It is built of red sandstone, and, with its two slender towers, is a conspicuous feature. Nothing remains of the original building; of the second (which is often attributed to St. Henry, while at other times it is said to belong to the twelfth century) there is still to be seen the choir and the centre of the nave; all the rest was destroyed by that terrible earthquake that ruined castles and churches for miles round. But the Minster was soon opened again for worship, by the active influence of Bishop Senno of Münsingen, though the building was not completed until the sixteenth century, when it exhibited that ingenious combination of various styles which assuredly has a charm of its own.

The Cathedral thus restored became an edifice which, even in its present form, has a great effect on every unprejudiced observer. The sculptures on the façade represent the Virgin and Child. Near the principal doorway are the figures of St. George and St. Martin on prancing horses, and next them the Emperor Henry, with a model of the Church, and the Empress Kunigunde. On the northern side is the St. Gallus porch, which is rich in symbolical figures. It was built in the thirteenth century, and is adorned with statues of the Evangelists and John the Baptist. A relief of the Wise and Foolish Virgins is over the door. In six niches on the sides are the Works of Charity; and at the top sits Christ on the Judgment seat, at the Last Day, surrounded by the angels.

The effect of the interior is more striking than is suggested by the outside. The building is light and lofty, and the eye travels unobstructedly down the long space which is terminated by a magnificent rood-loft, built in 1381, which supports a fine organ. That and the chancel, which rises gracefully, are the remarkable points of the Cathedral. The side-aisles are rich in monuments of various periods, many of them being memorials of entire epochs.

A review of the whole pomp of the Imperial power in Germany, and of the prosperity of the Free Town, passes before our eyes as we gaze upon the tomb where Rudolph of Hapsburg laid his wife to rest. And who does not think of the brilliant rise of learning when he reads upon the stone: " Erasmus of Rotterdam!" In his time Basle reached its highest

Basle, Switzerland.

intellectual point. All branches of learning found distinguished representatives in the young colleges of the town, and near at hand the art of printing had its birth—an art by which in a few generations the world was to be almost transformed. No feeling of jealousy checked the common efforts; in those days of intellectual power "you might have supposed," wrote Erasmus to his friend, " that all possessed but one heart and one soul."

Hans Holbein, who lived in Basle from 1515 to 1526, did for Art what Erasmus did for Learning. A great number of his finest pictures are collected in the Museum of the town, which, next to the Cathedral, is indeed its most important treasure. It was established only as far back as 1849, on the site of the former Monastery of St. Augustine, for the purpose of collecting everything serviceable to the study of the Arts and Sciences.

We should go far beyond the limits of our space were we to attempt the enumeration of the treasures which are collected here, or the description of their artistic and historical value; this work has been already done by abler hands. We will content ourselves with saying, that every one who wishes to study Hans Holbein cannot omit Basle.

Holbein was born at Augsburg in 1494; but when he was quite a boy he followed his father, who was a painter of some note, to Basle. There he contracted an intimacy with Erasmus, whose portrait he painted;

and it was Erasmus who was responsible for his leaving the fatherland and going to England, for Erasmus gave him a letter to Sir Thomas More, who introduced him at Court.

Henry VIII., recognizing the genius of the obscure German artist, made him Court painter, and gave him a liberal pension. But Holbein did not forget Basle, for in painting his famous picture of the Virgin as the Queen of Heaven, now in the Dresden Gallery, he made Jacob Meyer, of Basle, with his family, appear prominently in the picture.

In the Library at Basle is a fine series of panels by Holbein, called the "Passion of Christ." Hans Holbein died in London during the plague, in 1553.

Traces of the great master are to be found not only within the walls of the Museum, but also in the open streets. The Well with the Peasant's Dance, designed by Holbein, still flows merrily; and, although the colors may be effaced by wind and weather, the houses are still pointed out which have been adorned with frescoes from Hans Holbein's pencil. Had he not gone to England, in 1526, Basle might perhaps have maintained a school of painting of European reputation.

Some fragments of his celebrated fresco painting, "The Dance of Death," are still to be seen. These peculiar figures inspired Goethe to write the following poem.

"The warder looks down at the mid hour of night
    On the tombs that lie scattered below ;
The moon fills the place with her silvery light,
    And the church-yard like day seems to glow.
When see ! first one grave, then another opes wide,
And women and men stepping forth are descried,
    In cerements snow-white and trailing.

"In haste for the sport soon their ankles they twitch,
    And whirl round in dances so gay ;
The young and the old, and the poor, and the rich,
    But the cerements stand in their way ;
And as modesty cannot avail them aught here
They shake themselves all, and the shrouds soon appear,
    Scattered over the tombs in confusion.

"Now waggles the leg and wiggles the thigh,
    As the troops with strange gestures advance,
And a rattle and clatter anon rises high,
    As of one beating time to the dance.
The sight of the warder seems monstrously queer,
When the villainous tempter speaks thus in his ear :
    'Seize one of the shrouds that lie yonder !'

"Quick as thought it was done ! and for safety he fled
    Behind the church door with all speed ;
The moon still continues her dear light to shed
    On the dance that they fearfully lead.
But the dancers at length disappear one by one,
And their shrouds, ere they vanish, they carefully don,
    And under the turf all is quiet.

"But one of them stumbles and shuffles there still,
    And gropes at the graves in despair,
Yet 'tis by no comrade he's treated so ill ;—
    The shroud he soon scents in the air.
So he rattles the door—for the warder 'tis well
That 'tis blessed, and so able the foe to repel,
    All covered with crosses in metal.

"The shroud he must have, and no rest will allow,
  There remains for reflection no time ;
On the ornaments Gothic the wight seizes now,
  And from point on to point hastes to climb.
Alas for the warder ! his doom is decreed.
Like a long-legged spider, with ne'er changing speed,
  Advances the dreaded pursuer.

"The warder he quakes, and the warder turns pale,
  The shroud to restore fain had sought ;
When the end—now can nothing to save him avail ?—
  In a tomb formed of iron is caught.
With vanishing lustre the moon's race is run
When the bell thunders loudly a powerful one,
  And the skeleton falls, crushed to atoms."

At the end of the sixteenth century a man was born in Basle who, in another department of Art, may be said to have gained European renown. We refer to Matthew Merian, the illustrator, engraver, and publisher, who, in a set of works which are still much valued, set before the cultivated readers of his time a description of countries and towns, much in the same way that we are endeavoring to do in these pages. Many other names might be given of men who have distinguished themselves, but we should need volumes instead of pages to describe them.

Among the specimens of architecture of past ages, the Town Hall, erected 1508–1521, deserves to be mentioned, with its statue of Munatius Plancus. The various city gates also should be examined. These old gates are often met with, and some of them are very fine. The reason of this may easily be seen, for in the idea of a city gate there is something more than that of a spacious barrier—it involves the principle of a dividing-point between the burgess who rules and the peasant who serves. The whole feeling of the political power of the town is embodied, as it were, visibly in its gates, and this feeling has reflected itself on the artistic power; the architect would naturally, therefore, feel that such a work had a deep ideal meaning, as well as a practical one, and would enrich the rough stone with many fanciful adornments over and above what was requisite for the material end for which the gate was to serve.

The Spahlenthor, erected in 1400, is, without doubt, the most beautiful of the gates of Basle. A pointed top with colored bricks covers the middle tower, which is adorned with three figures of saints, objects which were for a long time venerated in all Sundgau. The two side towers are round, and firmly enclose the indented gateway which affords the only exit. The traffic is naturally the greatest in that quarter of the town lying near the Rhine, and it becomes more busy as we approach the long bridge which unites the two parts of the town, Great and Little Basle.

Thus we have sought to give a sketch of Basle in a few lines, but the changes which the town has experienced within the last few years are truly astonishing. Its whole aspect has been varied; everywhere we see the effort to give unbounded dominion to the ideas of the present day, and on every side we feel that Basle also has entered into the great competition of the period.

It resisted modern innovations as long as possible, and even the most obvious improvements were adopted very slowly. While Hanover was lighted with gas as early as 1829, not a single lamp appeared here. Forty years ago it seemed an impossibility that Basle should ever possess a so-called " Quay," like other towns situated on rivers. Now, however, each year millions are spent in public works.

Art galleries, music halls and theatres have been built, as well as two palatial schools, each of which cost half a million of francs. The change as regards the question of education is most important, for in it lies the great problem of the present and the key to the future. With astonishment we relate that there are teachers in Basle who are millionaires. " You mean, of course, individual professors, who work in your colleges," we said to the learned friend who gave us this information. " Not at all; I mean ordinary teachers; for it is not everyone who can be a professor ! The position itself, whatever school he may belong to, is so distinguished with us that no one thinks himself too rich or too noble for it." Under these circumstances, the old opposition which existed between intellectual and material possessions has been beneficially reduced—the understanding which exists between the rich merchants, the patricians and the scholars is so cordial and unconstrained that we can only wish it existed elsewhere.

Thus the character of the citizens has on all sides changed for the better. It is true that wealth is still an important and ruling element in Basle, but the consciousness of its possession has long been associated with the knowledge that true worth must be weighed, not counted. Many of the leading young merchants go through a thorough academic course, and more pride is felt in performing public benefits than in indulging in personal ostentation.

The domestic life of these people is generally distinguished by a rigorous simplicity—and it is only on the occasion of a public festival or some other important event that any brilliant parade is exhibited. It happened that during the time we spent in the hospitable Rhenish town a great race took place on the shooting-ground, and all classes, from the beggar to the millionaire, streamed out of the town to the race-course. It was the right time to see the people in a body, and to study their manners and customs.

It was on a Sunday afternoon, and the sky was cloudless. As early as one o'clock the motley bustle began; carriage after carriage flew along the road which leads through the Spahlenthor into the broad meadows where the soldiers formerly were drilled; the harness of the horses was adorned with colored ribbons which waved in the wind; then came a wagon drawn by four great horses decorated with fir-branches and filled with soldiers in dark uniforms —a dozen comrades who had joined together to enjoy themselves. At last came the music playing merrily. All the footpaths were covered with cheerful pedestrians in light clothing, for the air was of summer warmth, and the pretty women smiled as gaily as though it were their own special gala day.

We drove noiselessly over the smooth turf on to the course, followed by itinerant vendors of programmes. Next to the steeplechase, which was brilliantly carried out, the greatest interest was shown in a military race in which the cavalry appeared mounted on their chargers. They were mostly the sons of old burgher families, who flew past on their fine horses— though in coarse uniform, for only the soldiers and subalterns were admitted. Nearly every competitor was, naturally, known to all Basle, and each one was at this critical moment looked upon as the son of the whole town. The shout of delight with which the townspeople greeted the smallest advantage which anyone of their own men gained over a native of Zurich or Schaffhausen, and the popularity of the competitors, infected even strangers with a feeling of sympathy—it was that local patriotism which may be recognized still in the free cities—a burgher pride giving itself unrestrained expression. Still more interesting, however, than the entertainment itself were the observers, the *élite* of whom were in the inner circle of the race-course. Here the most beautiful

The Spahlenthor, Basle.

equipages were stationed carriage after carriage; the old gentleman with the white beard and delicate profile talks earnestly with his business friend, while his beautiful daughters stand on the dark-blue cushions and look eagerly at the course through their opera-glasses. Oh, how they laugh and smile when a handsome rider flies past!

At length the last bugle has sounded from the judges' stand, and preparations are made for the return home, which forms no unimportant feature in the amusement of the day. The whole way back is thronged with a lively crowd, and every variety of visitor is to be met with. First of all comes at a dignified pace, and with powdered footmen, the gala carriage of a rich Spaniard who lives in Basle—which even reckoned a Swedish king among its citizens. This is followed by a dashing four-in-hand with dapple-gray horses—then comes the successful gentleman rider, in his jockey costume, driving an elegant phaeton, and he is followed by a steady old gentleman in more sober apparel. The whole form as lively a cavalcade as one would wish to see, as one after another comes up at a brisk trot, and dashes past with some hasty greeting.

At about six o'clock in the evening the great table at the Three Kings is laid for dinner. This hotel is named in remembrance of the time when the Emperor Conrad II. and his son Henry met Rudolph of Burgundy. The three princes possibly took up their abode at this place, though it must have undergone great changes since that time. Now, by the light of numerous wax candles, visitors from all the countries of Europe assemble in the stately dining-room. All sorts of curiosities and antiquities adorn the walls, and a lofty drawing-room, hung with damask curtains and mirrors, receives the guests when dinner is over. Outside there is a broad terrace, where groups of friends assemble under the starlit sky and talk of the old days of the town, while the flowing river at their feet catches their words and bears them away on its ripples.

CHAPTER VII.

BREISGAU.

AFTER passing Basle, the Rhine goes silently and majestically for some distance northwards without presenting any object which specially attracts our attention. The fortress of Hüningen, that bold sally-port which Vauban built for his king, has long been razed to the ground, so that our eyes can follow the whole panorama without obstruction.

About three miles from here is the extensive establishment which, since 1852, has been replenishing the neighboring waters with fish. Thousands of trout and salmon are placed every year in the Rhine and Moselle, and large quantities of smaller fish are sent to the streams of Upper Alsace.

The landscape is more peaceful than beautiful, and for some distance may almost be called monotonous. On all sides we see partially-deserted river-beds, which are deep and green; moist pasture and high sedge cover the banks; and on both sides of the broad plain rise blue hills. We are midway between the Black Forest range and the Vosges.

The former extends far down to the south, and its heights reach for twenty miles, from Säckingen to

Pforzheim. Its breadth also is considerable, deep valleys opening out from its fir-covered solitudes into the broad valley of the Rhine. Neat villages and homesteads are dotted here and there on the dark mountains, where the carved brown wooden clocks tick in the snug little dwelling-room, while the axe outside rings in the forest and lays low the primeval trunks, which are then carried down to Holland by the Rhine.

How poetic are all the surroundings of the district! The mere name of the Black Forest possesses a peculiar charm which no other mountain-range can rival. Elves and water-sprites still sport among its streams. Who does not remember the beautiful, though melancholy song, in which the home-sick wanderer regrets his departure from his beloved Black Forest? How we have shuddered as children while reading the fairy tale of the tall ghostly man who sold his peace of mind for gold! In the night he broke off the most gigantic trunks as easily as if they had been dry rushes, and every ship that carried even one plank of his wood went hopelessly to the bottom. He was called Dutch Michael, but the name of the story is "The Cold Heart," and the story comes, with many others like it, from the Black Forest.

The blue mountain-chain which stretches along the other side of the Rhine is the Vosges, the old Was-gauwald, which reaches from Saverne down to Mülhausen. It is covered with tall beeches and firs, and on the rocks weatherworn castles stand like eyries. Their ruins still speak to us of the glory of the races that dwelt here; for, as the Black Forest was the country of the peasants, so the Wasgau was the country of the nobles. We hear in its retired valley not only the woodman's axe, but also the smith's iron hammer fashioning the metals that are found in the neighboring mines, and we see the blue smoke of furnaces rise languidly towards the deserted castles. Those extensive plateaus which are so numerous among the mountains of the Black Forest are met with much more rarely in the Vosges; and although it must be admitted that usually mountains have a greater effect from their massiveness than from the fine arrangement of their forms, yet here the variety and the grouping strikes us as being much more impressive than that in the Black Forest; the summits rise one above another threefold and fourfold, like giant forms leaning one upon the shoulder of another.

Passing on, we come to Breisach. This was once regarded as the most secure portion of the Holy Roman Empire, for Breisach was considered the key of Germany, and seemed to be so strongly fortified as to be safe from every enemy. It stands two hundred and forty feet above the Rhine, and, as late as the tenth century, the river is said to have flowed around the town. But, like so many things connected with the Holy Roman Empire, it only seemed secure. No war occurred between the two countries from which the town did not emerge with gaping wounds. Its worst time was in 1793, when the ragged soldiery, to the cry of the "Marseillaise," satiated with crime, overran the weary empire, which shook to its very centre; even to this day the town has not quite recovered from the destruction which it then suffered. Nor was this its last trial, for in 1870, on a cold November night, the hissing shells flew hither across the Rhine, and for six days the enemy's fire continued to pour into the town until the French fortress, New Breisach, surrendered.

The landscape in which the two towns are situated, as we have already stated, is not striking, and may, indeed, be said to be somewhat melancholy and mournful. The two chains of mountains, the Vosges and the Black Forest, lie far apart; the low-lying land between them appears as a large level plain; the sky overhead is dull, and is reflected in the river, with gray rain-swollen clouds. As we pass, herons rise from the stagnant waters, which are parted from the river by strong embankments, and even the broad handsome street that leads across into Alsace looks quite deserted. Thus there seems to be a curious sense of loneliness about this place which is increased by a damp mist, which often fills the air, and forms a suitable background for the brown weatherworn town.

The rock on which old Breisach is perched falls precipitously towards the bank of the Rhine. The turrets of the Minster tower above the dark gabled roofs, walls, and fortifications, its commanding and characteristic appearance influencing the form of the whole town. The church is dedicated to St. Stephen, one of the great martyrs, who courageously faced his persecutors even while dying under their stone missiles. The proud temple is indeed worthy of its noble patron, for, as the watch-tower of the German Empire, it may also be said to have often suffered martyrdom. It still stands, however, in spite of the cannon of the enemy, and is now being restored.

We cannot leave the neighborhood of Breisach without making an excursion inland, for at only a short distance is situated Freiburg in Breisgau, one of the loveliest of South German towns.

After a short drive from Breisach we reach the mountain-chain of the Black Forest, which descends in long soft lines into the valley; it is the place where the Dreisam emerges from the mountains into the plain, and there the old Zähringers built their castle. The town extends at its feet along the hill-side. The antiquated gray houses are almost out-numbered by the handsome villas lying among their gardens; but high above them all, seeming as we ap-proach it to overlook even the outlines of the moun-tains, we see the huge Cathedral buildings. The graceful perforated spire stands out against the background, not clear and sharp, as elsewhere, but almost as if shaded with sombre gray.

As we approach, the grandeur of its form increases, until we stand actually before it. As the Cathedral was the first object which met our eyes in the distance, it shall be the first visited when we have reached the place; for, indeed, it is one of those wonderful works the beauties of which increase rather than diminish on a closer inspection. The Cathedral of Freiburg, founded by Conrad, brother of Berthold III., in 1123, is of inestimable value to the history of Art, from the fact of its being the only German church which the middle ages have handed down to us completed, though it is true that later times have made many superfluous additions.

Viewed from the outside the nave of the church appears much lower and shorter than it really is on account of the height and position of the spire, which is placed immediately over the principal doorway. This false impression, however, vanishes as soon as we are inside. Suddenly everything grows to majestic proportions, the gray pillars rise high on every side, and the eye can scarcely take in the whole width from the door to the choir in one glance. The great transepts on each side of the Gothic high-altar are adorned with paintings by the hand of an old German master, and on either side are the richly-carved stalls of the church dignitaries. Here, as in all great cathedrals, the aisles which run parallel with the nave are more or less the domain of the dead.

Along the walls are the tombs and sculptured figures of knights who have assisted to establish the prosperity of the town, either by enriching it with their goods or defending it with their swords. The Minster of Freiburg has had its friends and its rich donors, of whom it was proud. Their renown is handed down to posterity in graceful monuments; all the little chapels which adorn the outer circumference of the choir are crowded with such memorials. One belongs to the university, and contains the tombs of the great scholars who have become celebrated there. The altar-piece of the university chapel is by Hans Holbein, painted in 1520, and represents the Wise Men from the East humbly adoring at the manger of the Holy Child.

In another chapel we find costly wood carvings, and the light breaks with wonderful effect through a stained-glass window. The Byzantine crucifix of heavy embossed silver was brought here from the Holy Land by a Crusader, and dedicated to the service of the sacred place; for these walls were standing even at the time of the Crusades, when Bernhard of Clairvaux preached in the unfinished building, and with burning zeal called all Christendom to arms.

Seven centuries have passed since that time, and the battle-call has often sounded for far different aims;

yet still, as we stroll at twilight within these massive walls, when the last rays of the setting sun fall through the pointed windows, it seems as though the stony figures move again, and a breath of the glowing spirit of that inspired monk still lingers round the place. We feel unconsciously that the age in which he labored was a great one. Christianity was then in its youth, and in the fulness of its heroism it longed to perform some deed worthy of its cause. It was the lofty idealism of its teaching which then drew the sword, and not the gloomy fanaticism which, five centuries later, plunged the world into the horrors of the Thirty Years' War!

The open place or square on which the Cathedral stands is spacious and handsome, its most beautiful object being the ancient Town Hall, erected in the fifteenth century, which stands almost immediately opposite the south door. This is built of red sandstone, and is of only moderate height, but its open arcade, adorned with shields, its handsome balcony and Gothic windows, give it a highly-characteristic and original appearance. The statues which are placed between the windows are of about the same period as the building itself; they represent the Emperor Max, the last of the knights, and Charles V., upon whose empire the sun never set ; and between them Philip I. and King Ferdinand.

As we stroll leisurely through the streets, we find many relics of the time when the House of Haps-

Marketplace and Kaufhaus,
Freiburg, Germany.

Marketplace and Kaufhaus,
Freiburg, Germany.

burg ruled in Breisgau ; many an antique gable rises boldly beside the flat roof of a modern house, and the fountains in the High Street still murmur in the same tones that greeted the ears of the princes of the arch-ducal house when they rode forth to the tournaments. But the feeling of the citizens has totally changed since those days ; they are no longer moved by the traditions of imperial dominion, but by the magic charm of Freedom, which, having been latent in the name of the town, sprang to life in the hearts of the people, and Freiburg became unexpectedly one of the most powerful and enlightened towns of South Germany.

On the Kaiser-Strasse stands a granite pedestal surmounted by a bronze figure of Victory. It is a war monument, erected by the Austrian Government in 1876 to the Fourteenth German Army Corps and its brave leader, General von Werder.

Intellectual progress went hand in hand with out-ward development, and the population and the extent of the town increased rapidly. An observer looking down upon the town from the renowned Schlossberg, could hardly imagine it to be the same place in whose colleges he had sat, perhaps forty years before, at the feet of Rotteck and Welcker. A long avenue planted with chestnut-trees leads us at last to the gate. Stately houses, built in the style of the modern villa, stand right and left of us, for quite a colony of dis-tinguished foreigners have settled here within the last few years.

Again we catch the sound of running water, and we see before us a well, with a broad basin made of red sandstone. On the pillar, which rises out of the water, there stands the stone figure of a monk holding a Bible in his right hand, while his left is thoughtfully supporting his chin. What ominous thoughts are working beneath that overhanging brow! It is Berthold Schwarz, who was a native of Freiburg, and the idea—the Danäe gift which he left behind him for mankind, was—Gunpowder!

His real name was Konstantin Anklitzen, but Berthold was the name he took on entering the cloister, and Schwarz (black) was a sobriquet given him in consequence of his occult pursuits.

How he must have started up affrighted, in his quiet cell, when the first report crashed unexpectedly out of the mortar! Since then whole towns have been reduced to ruins and armies stricken down; for a few grains of his magic powder suffices to shatter the strength of the boldest body, and the power of the noblest mind! The stone monk muses, half-troubled, half-wondering. How many ideas has his idea destroyed!

CHAPTER VIII.

THE VOSGES COUNTRY.

A SHORT time only has elapsed since the Rhine, flowing under the walls of Breisach, separated two great nations, two noble countries, two mighty foes. The Rhine was the visible type of the great political gap which separated Germany from the rest of the world. For two hundred years, since Louis XIV., the office of the Rhine has been—to separate. Now that the old communion between mother and daughter has been re-established, it will assert its uniting influence, and the Rhine will help us, more than any human instrument could do, to promote a mutual understanding between the races which had, unfortunately, become strangers to one another.

We will now pass over to the other side of the river, to that district which is known as Upper Alsace. In olden times, when the sons of the Carlovingian king divided their inheritance, it was called Sundgau.

We have already seen from a distance the broad street that leads over the Rhine to Colmar. This is the road along which we have now to go, between the lofty poplars which stand on either side. We soon come within sight of New Breisach, with its deserted trenches which surround the fortress. Fort Mortier projecting far out commands the flat plain, and we rattle through its gate. Freshly cut in the sandstone is the imperial eagle, and underneath it the word " Germany, 1870."

Breisach is a small and unpretending little town, although it possesses its *Grand Café*, as may be seen from its signboard; the houses are seldom more than one story high, and the grass grows plentifully between the paving-stones. There is an absence of bustle in the place and its inhabitants.

The road which leads from here to Colmar goes straight through the wood; it may be seen lying for a couple of miles in front of us. Sometimes we have only low bushes on either side, then green firs with their slender trunks, and then we have meadows and pastures. Here the last load of hay is being carried, and the reapers are eating their supper under an old nut-tree by the roadside, and a little village peeps out from among the trees. Nearly all the houses are cleanly whitewashed, so that they have a very bright appearance, with their pointed roofs.

The inn is distinguished by the sign of a great star, and is the principal one in the place. Wagons stand before the door, and the drivers are gathered together in a noisy chattering crowd. All is cheerful bustle; but the time for tarrying is short. A glass of beer is quickly ordered, and as soon disposed of; each man exchanges a few words hurriedly with the nearest group, and then sets off with his powerful team, making way for the next bird of passage to take his place.

It is about two hours' drive from Breisach to Colmar, and then we rattle noisily through the streets of the old town. Every minute we turn a corner; all the houses have gables and balconies, and in the streets the idle lads stand gaping at us as we pass.

Colmar, with its thirty thousand inhabitants and its picturesque and historical reminiscences, has become a very quiet place, and appears to have stood still for ages. It once had its time of prosperity, but that was six centuries ago, in the days of the great Hohenstaufen, when Frederick II. was Emperor of Germany, and the old walls, which had once been only a Frankish manor, were elevated to the position of an imperial city. The citizens have never forgotten this fact, and have always prided themselves on being truly imperial. At the worst time they stood by the Empire with unswerving courage.

No other town in Germany showed such fidelity as Colmar. In 1474 it courageously forbade Charles the Bold to enter its walls, when he attempted to enforce his purchased rights with the sword; and when Louis XIV. seized upon Alsace it resisted the incorporation with France with an energy which bordered on despair. Colmar also bore its banner aloft in the intellectual struggle for Art and Learning, and men whose memory is still honored by the world were at that time proud to be its citizens. Martin Schön, the greatest German artist of the fifteenth century, was born and died here.

The annexation to France was a turning-point for both sides—for the moral power is greatly influenced by the political—the German imperial city became a French provincial town, and the "Great King" Louis XIV. seemed to imagine that subjugated countries estimated the greatness and power of their conquerors in proportion to the severity of the treatment they received at their hands. The persecutions which were soon heaped upon the Reformers were received in deep dejection, and even by the French it was asserted that the reconciling of Colmar to its fate was retarded for nearly a century by the harshness with which the people were treated.

But what did that matter to the all-powerful ruler at Versailles; his answer to every question was, "Tel est notre plaisir." So the town mourned: the "Sovereign Court of Justice" which was bestowed upon it was but a poor substitute for the glory of its old freedom; and Voltaire, in deep mockery, recalls the fact that once the works of the great Bayle were burnt in the market-place at Colmar. The proud Corsican also thought no better of the town, for, although two of the most brilliant leaders of the French army, Bruatt and Rapp, came from here, he repaid it with the deepest contempt. His merciless sentence was "Colmar is a hole." Monuments to

Admiral Bruatt and General Rapp, designed by Bartholdi, now stand in Colmar.

Walking through the streets and looking up at the houses, it seems as if we had plunged into the middle of the old German period: the Town Hall, with its slender spire and the graceful perforated stone gallery which runs along under the roof; the Pfister House, and many other buildings, are monuments of architecture as fine as any to be found even in Nuremberg and Augsburg. A touch of grace is given even to the police station—a building rarely associated with pleasure—for over the ugly façade there is a balcony of wonderful elegance.

We have only to turn to find ourselves opposite the Cathedral, which was built by Master Humbert; his monument stands under the east door. Although the exterior possesses a certain crudeness, the effect of the whole is imposing and harmonious; and simple as the interior appears, it is not wanting in sanctity. The broad choir, dating from 1350, is particularly beautiful and calm, with its old dark-brown woodwork. The carved door which leads into the sacristy hides one of the noblest treasures of mediæval art—"The Madonna Among the Roses," which Martin Schön bequeathed to the town.

No one disturbed us as we made our tour of the spacious aisles; here and there a blind beggar stood in a corner and muttered a petition for alms, close by two or three children whispered, and one old woman sat nodding in a chair. Before every seat was a white card bearing the name of the owner. By looking through the rows of names it could be determined how far the German element still survived; the result showed it to be a large proportion of the whole. It is true that many an honest citizen had added an accent grave or an accent acute, but the greater number of the names had German endings, such as *bieder, müller, hauser, bauer,* etc.

We now ascend a winding stairway not far from the gate, and find ourselves in a little turret room; we step out on the dizzy parapet of the tower, and the vast prospect stretches before us. On one side we see the chain of the Vosges rise in the clear morning light; villages stud the valley, and many a lordly castle stands on the heights. Over yonder, where the horizon almost vanishes in the haze of the distance, we can just distinguish some towers. They are the walls of Schlettstadt, and they point the path we are to follow.

But before we turn northward in order to continue the course of the Rhine, the adjacent neighborhood offers many attractions which we must not forget. Here the Alsatian saying first becomes true—

> " Three castles on one hill,
>   Three churches in one church yard,
>   Three cities in a row,
>   By these you may Alsatia know "

The number is still true, for not far from Egisheim

we see three towers on a wooded hill, which appear to stand in a line, and bear the curious name of "The Three Axes." Actually they stand obliquely behind one another, and are the towers of one and the same fortress, each of them bearing its own special title, namely, Weckmund, Wahlenburg, and Dagsburg, names which remind us of bygone days.

Egisheim is one of the numerous castles which claim the honor of being the birthplace of Pope Leo IX., who was a Count of Egisheim and Dagsburg, and it was formerly well worthy of such a son, but the noble walls were reduced to ruins in quite early times, during a war which was stirred up by a miller of Mülhausen.

The two beautiful lakes which represent the artistic climax of the Vosges chain are best visited from Colmar; the road thither passes through Kaiserberg. That name sounds familiar to our ears, for it was given to the town by the great preacher John Geiler, who spent his youth here. The present importance of the town does not depend upon learning, or any kind of curiosities; but in that charming simplicity, that picturesque originality, which brings it pleasantly before the eyes of strangers. It is conscious of an active Present and a renowned Past, of which we are reminded on all sides in word and form; on the Town Hall, built in 1604; on the fountain, on the wall even round the church-yard, and, in fact, everywhere we find mottoes, in the form of old rhymes, full of meaning. Some are severe, and even coarse; some are tender and poetic, some are gay, some are sad, according to the occasion and circumstances in which they were first used. This town was strong in its fidelity to the Emperor, to whom it belonged, as its name naturally indicates; and in the Confederation of the Ten Cities its voice was heard, and its counsel held in considerable respect.

The road now goes farther into the green depths of the Vosges; we have left Orbey behind us, and are making for the wooded ridges of the mountains, sometimes following a narrow path, and sometimes trampling through luxuriant heather. It is not long, however, before the landscape begins gradually to grow wilder, gray boulders lie scattered about, short scanty Alpine grass covers the ground, and only a few weather-beaten firs are visible on the distant ridge. We hasten once more through the solitude, and suddenly a new view opens before us—the waters lie motionless between bare white rocks, which rise precipitously to a considerable height, and are clearly reflected in the lake below. This is the White Lake, and it is a remnant of that icy period which once covered the face of this country.

Its deep basin is only parted by a broad solid ridge of rock from another sheet of water equally deep and motionless, though much smaller. It is not surprising that the character of the two lakes should be somewhat similar, though at one time this was not the case, for the banks of the last we have referred to were bordered with dark primeval firs. Then the name of "The Black Lake" was appropriate to it. But the devastating axe has penetrated to this spot and robbed it of the dark wood covering, so that nothing now remains but the inhospitable rock. Its declivity, however, towards the bank is less steep than that of the White Lake, and the form of the mountains is less grotesque.

In spite of this, however, we still feel ourselves in the true uncultivated mountain world, and only at the mouth of the lake we are willingly reminded of the existence of restless human ingenuity by the dam which regulates the outflow of the water. In this way is the stream made of service to the manufactories in the valley below. They entice the clear bright water to their noisy workshops, and when it would run cheerily under them it is suddenly seized upon and tortured by their jagged wheels.

The neat little town which we come to on the road from Colmar to Schlettstadt is called by the Germans Rappoltsweiler, though it is better known by its French name of Ribeauvillé. It is one of the most cheerful little cities in all Alsace, and it was here that the old Piper kings had their day.

The Count of Rappoltstein was the "King" of all the musicians and minstrels of the Upper Rhine. They recognized him as the head of the brotherhood, and paid him an annual tax; in return for which he took them under his protection.

Every year, on the 8th of September, these wanderers assembled at Rappoltstein to celebrate a joyous festival—and to settle their disputes. When the last Count of Rappoltstein died, in 1673, this remarkable jurisdiction, together with the title, " King of the Pipers," was conferred upon the Counts-Palatine of Birkenfeld, who were in the service of France, and it was held by them until the French Revolution. Even now, on the 8th of September, the inhabitants of Rappoltsweiler celebrate a local festival in memory of the old times.

The thick shady trees of the suburbs have now been made into pleasure gardens, and on the hills, which are overgrown with vines, the ruins of the castles of the old rulers stand. The more lawless the period, the higher the bold knights placed their dwellings, and it was only as men became more peaceable and opposition less decided, that they moved slowly down into the villages and towns. This fact is forcibly illustrated here. The highest of the three castles which command the town is called Rappoltstein. It was built in the fourteenth century, and is considered one of the oldest castles in Alsace; it was the ancestral seat of a renowned race. Later, however, though still as early as the time of the Hohenstaufens, the second castle was erected lower down on the rocks. This in its turn was soon followed by a third, in the style of the Renaissance, and named after St. Ulrich. The middle ruin is called Girsberg, and was held by a family of the same name.

As we follow the road which leads from Rappoltsweiler to Markirch we meet with another venerable fortress which stands on a gray rock in one of the cross valleys. The ruins now look down only on the quiet country. Once when the high bay windows shone in the sunlight, there stood here a renowned old abbey of the name of Dusenbach, and three chapels which were subject to it.

Pilgrimages were made to this shrine, for the Holy Virgin, to whom it was dedicated, was the patroness of the musicians who frequented the roads of merry Alsace. Now all is silent, and the little stream, the Dusenbach, ripples in solitude over moss-grown stones, and without the echo of human voices, the boughs of the old trees rustle, which at one time formed the green arcade up to the cloister door.

We would willingly stand awhile and think of those who formerly wandered here, but they and their retired home fade from our minds as we approach the great masterpiece which now looks down on us from the lofty summits. That is Hohkönigsberg, the noblest stronghold in Alsace. Nothing is known of the origin of the castle, but as early as 1462 it was partly destroyed by the Archduke Sigismund and the Bishop of Strasburg. It was again burned by the Swedes in the seventeenth century.

The road now goes steeply upwards, passing a very picturesque forester's house, until we see before us two enormous towers and the reddish walls of the fortress, which once enclosed many a comfortable chamber and many a noble hall. One of the latter is so well preserved that the staircase, which in olden times led up to the watch-tower, appears to be still accessible, and our footsteps as we approach re-echo under the great "Lion Gate."

How many bold footsteps have sounded here before folks of the present day came with their "curious eyes"—how many lordly races have here meted out rigid government and cheerful hospitality! The Lords of Rathsamhausen and the Counts of Dittingen, the Sickingens and the Fuggers, have all at different times called this fortress their own. Many a merry feast has the Bishop of Strasburg held within its walls, and many a highwayman has waited here on a dark day, ready to fall suddenly upon the caravans of merchants on their way to Basle.

But good and bad, conqueror and conquered, have all long since gone to their rest, and young saplings of fir and larch grow unmolested in the dilapidated court-yard. The commune of Schlettstadt now possesses the venerable ruin, and is responsible for its care. It fulfils its trust with commendable fidelity, for Hohkönigsberg is its pride and its jewel.

The impression which Schlettstadt itself makes on the traveller is much the same as that of Colmar; the environs are flat, the streets are empty, and land appears to be valueless and consequently unused. Involuntarily we feel the oppression which seems to be an essential part of all fortified towns, and hinders the development of unrestrained prosperity.

If we approach the town from the side near the railway, we see scarcely anything except a few bare towers which rise above the roofs, and it is not until we enter the interior of the town that this confused mass of houses resolves itself into its parts and we see many charming details. There is the venerable Cathedral of St. George, founded in the fourteenth century. It is one of the finest specimens of Gothic architecture in Alsace, with its clock-tower standing up conspicuously among the pile of masonry. On some of the houses are brown wooden balconies shaded by high roofs, but the character of the whole place nowhere rises above quiet mediocrity.

During our tour of the town we will pay a visit to the principal hotels of the place. The two most important which Schlettstadt formerly possessed were the Goat and the Eagle. These two have now, however, combined (a sad *mésalliance*, by-the-bye, for the Eagle), and though the present hostelry is but of moderate pretensions, a traveller may make himself very comfortable under its shelter. Schlettstadt has in its time entertained many distinguished guests within its walls; as early as the year 775 Charlemagne celebrated the feast of Christmas here ; and, like

Colmar, it was one of the most faithful cities of the empire at the time when France took possession of it. Its fidelity was proved by many serious sacrifices, for the town, which had become attached to the Emperor in 1216, was repeatedly besieged by the Bishop of Strasburg. His mercenaries, under the Hohenstaufen, Frederick II., and under Louis of Bavaria, stormed its walls, in order to chastise the citizens for defending their town against Rome for the Emperor.

Schlettstadt held an important position in the Union which was formed by the ten cities of Alsace, and its alliance was always sought and its enmity was much dreaded by each of the contending parties. Sometimes, indeed, the shadows of lawless deeds overclouded its history. The citizens took part in the atrocious cruelties of the Jewish persecution in the sixteenth century, and they also were active in those disturbances which were the prelude to the Great Peasant League. It was, indeed, one of the former burgomasters of Schlettstadt who marched at the head of the wild mob which, under the banner of the Bundschuh, declared war on "knight and priest," in order to win freedom for the peasantry. This righteous object, which was to be peaceably obtained a century later, was then sought with dreadful cruelty, and the effect was accordingly unsuccessful, the last decisive struggle taking place almost under the very walls of Schlettstadt.

The real influence of the town, however, and that

which spread far beyond the limits of the Empire, did not lie in force of warlike arms, but in the intellectual qualities which were cultivated here. Schlettstadt possessed a college as early as the fifteenth century, in which teachers of European renown labored, and to which scholars flocked from all the countries of Europe. Their number often amounted to many hundreds, and it was at this time that the splendid library, which the town still possesses, was founded. This is unfortunately about the only relic which learning has left.

As the twilight begins to fall we take a last quiet walk through the streets. Behind the Minster a lively scene presents itself before us; numbers of noisy boys perched up in an empty wagon, and an audience of little girls, sitting on the stone steps of the houses, are singing snatches of "Madame Angot," and one of them, with queer harlequin jumps, shouts the hackneyed couplet:

> "Vaut pas la peine, vaut pas la peine,
> De changer le gouvernement."

Thoughtless childhood should not be deprived of any harmless pleasure; but when these boys have grown to be men, and the little girls have become their wives, they will of themselves think of other things, and possibly they may have other opinions on the subject of the change of government.

CHAPTER IX.

STRASBURG.

WHOEVER would know a man thoroughly, should see him under a variety of circumstances : in the sunshine of good fortune, when happiness unfolds and elevates his nature, and in the depth of distress, when the power of necessity lays bare his weakness. What applies to individuals applies also to collective bodies of men, that is, to great towns, and their true nature is alone revealed by the study of that mirror of endless vicissitudes which we call History.

Three times has the writer of these pages seen Strasburg, the " fair," the celebrated in song, and each time under totally different circumstances, varying from the highest glory to that of the deepest misery.

The first time was nearly thirty years ago, when she stood in the brilliant train of Paris, her queen. Paris stood at that time among the Cities of the Earth, fatally beautiful, like Cleopatra, fascinating all the world. She had summoned the Cæsars of Europe to her court, for the Great Exhibition of 1867 was opened. All the provincial towns surrounded their mistress with homage, as noble ladies surround a queen, and in their circle stood Strasburg.

What a different picture was presented on the second visit! War lay on the land, and on all sides men were struggling for victory. Nightly the sky was red with fire, and the day was darkened with smoke, in the midst of which the sacred Minster reared its head. Deserted by France, cut off from Paris, Strasburg lay behind her walls on the Rhine and mourned. Gradually, piece by piece, almost inch by inch, her walls were worn away by shot and shell; all the agonies of hunger and thirst were borne by the inhabitants; she was unable to save herself, but she would not capitulate. But from the camp yonder the conquerors sang a song of welcome to her:

> "You stand in the garb of sorrow,
>   Unhonored and full of grief,
>   But your old love will come to-morrow,
>   And his good sword shall bring relief."

It was the end of September; the bombardment, which had ceased for a few hours, began afresh, for evening was not far distant. When it had become quite dark we took a carriage and drove out to the batteries. The night was cold, and the loose stones of the uptorn streets rattled under the horses' hoofs. Every now and then the animals reared and plunged when a more than usually loud volley thundered forth. We passed through one or two little villages where the people stood and peered out of their garret windows. As we drove between field and forest single dark figures occasionally passed us on the road, and all the while the lurid reflection on the other side of the Rhine grew brighter and clearer. There was fire in Strasburg—Strasburg was the torch that lighted us on our dark road. Presently the driver refused to proceed, and we descended and followed on foot a path across the fields until a broad building barred the way. This was a brick kiln with extensive out-buildings, and from the spot where we were standing to the town was hardly more than half a mile in a straight line.

What an awful sensation we experienced as we stood there in the midst of this wild destruction! All day the firing had been violent, now it raged. Not only the power but the fury of the enemy blazed out in every shot, and the thundering sounds seemed to be wild imprecations uttered by the whole force of the passion which had been let loose by War! We stood, watch in hand, counting the shots as they fell. They were like fearful pulse-beats, and as the fever of a sick man increases towards evening, so did this firing become wilder as the night dragged on. One shell after another rattled against the fortress, followed almost without an interval by answers dashing against the German batteries; their course could be traced through the air—though it was a mile long, they travelled it in a few seconds. Afar off was heard their angry hiss under the silent canopy of heaven.

City Gate, Strasburg.

Such is the picture that we gazed on then, at that anxious time, which is still associated in our memory with the name of Strasburg. But how completely it has changed now!

Four years elapsed, and the days of affliction had passed away on the occasion of the third visit to the old town on the Rhine, to the German Strasburg. Traces of many wounds, it is true, were still visible, and many shadows passed over the lofty brow at the recollection of bitter sorrows, but, on the whole, there was a feeling of calm reconciliation and of new and joyous power in the heart of the town.

What a load has fallen from our hearts as we walk through the Strasburg of to-day! We look upon a resurrection; the rapid foot of Time, which we so often deplore, has here exercised its power of healing and of blessing, for incredible things have been done in these last years.

The very first impression of the streets, which so frequently has a lasting effect on one's mind, is extremely pleasant. In one place, we are struck by the grandeur of the buildings; in another, by their homelike comfort. Thus we remain equally free from the oppressive effect of a great city and the confined feeling of a small provincial town. It is, indeed, just this which gives that peculiar charm to a sojourn in Strasburg.

It is a town in which a stranger does not long feel strange. This is specially the case with visitors coming from the other side of the Rhine; for, in spite of all the opposition which stirs the heart of Alsace, the German nature of the place cannot be denied. Recollections which the last two centuries have not washed away are still extant; whenever we have relations with the people themselves we meet with German manners. In the new intellectual circle, too, which has been brought into Strasburg by the government, and more particularly by the establishment of the University, the German guest is received so kindly that he feels himself at home in the best sense of the word.

The University was founded in 1621—and many celebrated students were gathered within its walls. Goethe was graduated here as Doctor of Laws in 1771. In 1794 it was suppressed by the National Convention, and in 1803 it was turned into a French Academy; this lasted until the Franco-Prussian war. In 1872 it was reopened as a University, and now has many students.

We will therefore go on our way, disturbed by scarcely another discord, and wander at our leisure through the beautiful town and examine its treasures and curiosities.

The noblest of these treasures, the pride and wonder of Strasburg, is its Cathedral: a building whose dumb stones are more eloquent than language. At first the bulk of the huge masses almost overpowers the eye; but into what grace and delicacy these masses are developed! how light the ponderous stone becomes in the combinations and harmony of the whole! What gigantic power the spiritual has here won over the material! As we stand before the Cathedral we cannot help thinking of it in connection with that period out of which it grew. What must have been the blossom of an epoch which could bear such fruit! what the consciousness of power of a town that could rear such a temple for its faith!

The early history of the great building dates many centuries back, and is, consequently, somewhat confused. The present structure represents the labor of nearly five hundred years. The first beginnings of a Christian church in Strasburg were made in Chlodwig's time, but they and all the decorations that had been added by the Carlovingians became a prey to the flames and were entirely destroyed. Bishop Werner accordingly had to commence a completely new work when he laid the foundation of the present Cathedral in 1015. He himself was of the noble house of the Counts of Hapsburg, but the names of those whose hands embodied his thoughts and designs have been lost in the great gulf of Time.

It is only in the third century after its foundation that we meet with the name of that master whose memory is now inseparably connected with the Cathedral of Strasburg, namely, Erwin von Steinbach. Whose heart does not leap at the thought of the glory that surrounds that name! The stately building rose before his enlightened spirit and under his creating hand, as the rich branches of a tree grow in the light of the sun; it became not only his tomb, but also his imperishable monument.

The façade is covered with delicate tracery and numerous sculptures. The three portals, representing scenes from the Creation and the Redemption, are among the finest specimens of Gothic work in existence. The niches in the lower story contain equestrian statues of the Emperors Clovis and Dagobert, Rudolf of Hapsburg and Louis XIII. (this last erected in 1823). During the Revolution many of these statuettes were thrown down, and the spire of the Cathedral escaped a like fate only because it was protected by a red republican cap made of metal, which served as a protecting badge!

As is well known, one only of the two towers has been built, up which a winding staircase has been placed. The site which the other tower should have occupied runs out into a platform, and has been made to serve the watchmen for a dwelling. More than fifty times has the building been threatened to be destroyed by lightning. Once it seemed doomed to destruction by a terrible earthquake; and, lastly, the roaring waves of the Revolution, with the shot and shell which have whistled past it, rendered its fate almost certain; but still the old sanctuary stands firm and unmoved, indifferent alike to the storms of ages and to human passion, both of which have fallen powerless before its silent majesty.

As the view from the Cathedral tower extends for many miles, so do the memories of this place reach back for hundreds of years, and include many races and innumerable individuals whose names are famous. The Minster tower is like a stone book in which visitors from all parts of the world have carved their names—princes, beggars, nobles, and many others are included among the number; and even Voltaire, Herder, Montalembert, Goethe, Baumann, Meier, Schulze have gazed upon this scene.

Not only is paper patient, as the German proverb says, but stone is so also, and the swallows, quite unconcerned as to who gives them shelter, settle first on one pillar and then on another, and do not ask in whose memory their twittering song is raised.

Everywhere we turn, whether we go outside the city gates or lose ourselves in the confusion of the streets, we see the Cathedral towering above all; its spire rises to a dizzy height above the roofs, and the appearance of every open space is affected by it. There is a curious legend concerning the laying of the corner-stone of the Cathedral of Strasburg. Bishop Werner, in full pontifical array, had just blessed the stone and given the signal to have it lowered into place when two men, brothers, who stood in the front row of spectators, accidentally jostled one another. The elder, furious at what he considered an intentional rudeness, turned on his brother and stabbed him to the heart, the blood splashing the bishop and dripping down on to the corner-stone, which had been put in place.

The murderer was seized and led away to be put to death; but as he passed the bishop he fell on his knees, exclaiming: "My lord, my lord, I deserve death—I know it—I have slain my brother, who was innocent; only let not my death be in vain! Under the stone which you have just lowered there flows a spring of water which will, in time, undermine the foundations of the Cathedral. Now, if you will bury me—a murderer—under the stone, the spring of pure water, rather than come in contact with my polluted bones, will shrink away from me and work its way to the surface elsewhere, and thus will I protect this holy place and help it to endure through the ages."

The murderer's request was granted, the stone raised again, and he, stepping down, gave the signal for it to be let down. Thus, the stone lowered upon a living man, forms the foundation of the tower, and popular superstition avers that the murderer's bones have had the desired effect of keeping the foundation firm.

Strasburg is rich in squares, which are frequently adorned in the centre with a handsome monument. One of these—the Kleber-Platz—is adorned with a bronze statue of General Kleber, who was born in

Strasburg, and murdered in Egypt in 1800. The buildings which surround these open spaces have a lofty, spacious appearance, and when this is not the case they are distinguished at least by their age or their artistic value. It is this that gives its original character to the Pig-Market, which certainly is not in a select quarter of the town; and it is this also that makes the Cathedral Square itself so charming. In the latter stands the so-called "Old House," with its high gables and brown beams; it is a building of the thirteenth century, and forms as picturesque a corner as it is possible for a town to possess.

The street through which we now proceed leads to the Gutenbergplatz. In the midst of the hubbub of the market there stands, surrounded by green trees, a pedestal, and on it rests a bronze figure of a man with flowing beard and lofty brow, holding in his hand a sheet covered with ornamental letters. One sheet? oh, it is far more—it is the symbol of the art of printing, the greatest gift which man ever gave to the human race; it is the testimony of the victory of light over darkness which he holds in his hand.

It was in Strasburg that John Gutenberg invented the art of printing. He dwelt here for nearly twenty years as a citizen of Strasburg, and whatever may have been done elsewhere, it was within his own room that the idea of this great discovery had birth. The Gutenbergplatz stands, as it were, as a symbol of the intellectual power which the middle ages possessed in their great free cities.

As the former German period of Strasburg history has eminently a burgess character, so during the French epoch did the military element gain the ascendancy, as well as that pretentious, intriguing policy which had its school on the polished floors of Versailles. After this came the omnipotence of the first Bonaparte; and all these different periods are, more or less, embodied in the outward appearance of Strasburg. Even the names of places lift us into the French world as we step across the Broglieplatz, or the Paradeplatz, where General Kleber's monument stands.

The Broglieplatz (or Bröhl, as it is familiary called by the townspeople) is without doubt the handsomest and most frequented of all the squares. Here is the fine residence of the mayor; the great cafés under the trees are in the French style, and, in fact, there is everything required by the fashionable world. Totally different, indeed, from these parts of the town are those old confined districts where the artificers work and the poorer classes dwell; there the odd corners of the old free town have been preserved with all the original peculiarities which the architects of that time possessed.

Many such houses may be seen on the Ill Canal, and the whole tanners' quarter near which the old "Vine" stands presents that picturesque mixture of styles which only an old town can offer; the eye, indeed, loses itself in rich architectural details of gables and windows, balconies and bays. Doors with beautiful iron-work and broad steps carved in massive oak are frequently found in plain, simple houses; and even in the narrowest streets magnificent houses are unexpectedly met with. These are all relics of the old free-town period, and they give to the place the same kind of quaintness that we meet with in Augsburg or Nuremberg.

Thus the architecture of the town possesses a threefold element: palaces in the style of the Renaissance and the Rococo period; dwellings built during the old prosperity of the imperial town; and, lastly, that mass of modern buildings of no particular style which sprang, as it were, out of the earth as a compensation for those destroyed in 1870. In a word, everywhere the Old is contrasted with the New—the Past with the Future—and everything struggles, either consciously or unconsciously, towards the assimilation of these two opposite elements.

CHAPTER X.

THE CONVENT OF ST. ODILLE.

On leaving Strasburg and driving towards Barr we come upon a large mountain covered with dark wood, and the white building which we see near the old ruins of the Heathen Walls is the Convent of St. Odille. The road leading up to it is remarkably beautiful and varied in its scenery.

We first come upon the little village of Ottrott, with its long row of houses, where we rest before ascending further; as we go a lad clad in a blue blouse passes along the street beating a drum, and announcing that on the following day there will be a sale by auction. Heads appear at every window, and in the village inn for the next few hours, nothing but the sale is spoken of.

Almost immediately behind the village we plunge again into the forest, and lest we should lose our way we take one of the merry boys who are playing in the street for our guide. For a few minutes, before we enter into the depths of the wood, our way lies through a cornfield. On passing this, a narrow path takes us upwards, and the green boughs rustle above our heads. Here and there among the luxuriant brambles stands a half-decayed monument raised to some one who has met with an accident in his work ; now and again, a weary woman with a great bundle on her shoulder meets us, and passes us with a pious greeting, but otherwise no sound is to be heard except the tapping of the crossbill in the thicket. The world around us seems lost in solitary beauty.

All at once we come to an opening, and through the trees we see the convent looking down on us. It lies opposite and quite close to us, but the road takes a circuitous route over the top of the ridge. We then reach the first remains of the Heathen Walls, which have come down to us like an heirloom of centuries. The thick clambering ivy spreads itself over the huge stones, as if to veil the gray sanctuary from our curiosity. But the present generation has a keen eye, and with its restless spirit of inquiry has penetrated here in order to unveil the mystery which surrounds this wonderful building. All is not yet known, it is true, but we have got far beyond the domain of mere conjecture.

It was at first supposed that these huge walls, which extend for about fifteen miles, were of Celtic origin, and that their purpose was to divide the sacred dwelling of the gods from the dwellings of the human race. Who has not read of the sad blood-stained worship which was performed in the obscure solitude of the woods ? The altars were high as mountains, the sacrificial victim was slaughtered on a block of stone, and there the festivals were celebrated with wild splendor.

Such was the first idea which the sight of these walled heights raised in the minds of archæologists. They have, however, since descended from the world of deities to the human race, and found that men built this fortress for their own protection and defence. These walled enclosures occur more than once on the heights of the Vosges, and whole races took refuge within their spacious circumference when an enemy overran the land. This opinion gave rise to another, namely, that the builders were the Romans. They undoubtedly ruled the races which these walls availed to shelter, and, taking this view, it is probable that the origin of the whole immense work, including the castle which was joined to it, dates from the third or fourth century. It seems likely, indeed, that it may be put down to the time of the Emperor Valentinian, who is known to have fortified the entire course of the Rhine as far as Holland.

In making a circuit of the walls, which are several miles in extent, the method of building can plainly be seen. Oaken stakes have been used to join the stones firmly to each other, but what most attracts the eye and gives an appearance of originality to the whole mass is the expert way in which the wall is worked into the rocks, and which, as it were, indicate the foundation of the building.

We mount higher and higher out of the forest into

the open country, between flat-worn stones where the heath grows luxuriantly. We pass another green meadow, when once more the trees form an arched roof above us, and we proceed until we stop on the threshold of the venerable Convent of St. Odille.

St. Odille was the patron saint of Alsace. Tradition says that she was the daughter of Eticho, Duke of Alsace, who ruled in the seventh century. She was born blind, but gained her sight by being baptized. She founded this nunnery, and died here in the odor of sanctity.

What joy and what misery has this roof covered during the course of centuries! It has stood on its lofty rock not only as a watch-tower looking down on the country at its feet, but it may also be said to have been as an instrument to register the course of time. Barbarossa was once a guest here; and it was here that the Abbess Herrad composed her religious work, "The Garden of Delight." These old walls, it is true, have been more than once reduced to ruins, but they have always risen again out of the wreck, and are still the favorite resort, not only of the pious, but of everyone for whom the beauty of Nature and the charm of ancient association have any attraction. All visitors are made equally welcome, and enjoy a kindly hospitality which they must always remember with gratitude.

As we pass through the convent yard with its old lime-trees, we see the lady superior standing in the doorway. Everyone, both old and young, visitors as well as the inmates of the house, call her "Mother;" and, indeed, she is worthy of that expressive and beautiful name—always thoughtful for others, always gentle, so that the very place itself over which she rules seems to be influenced by the kindliness of her nature.

Fresh nosegays of wild flowers are in the simple dining-room, and, indeed, every corner; even the passages and the little garden on the narrow slope where the rock declines into the valley is carefully tended. The children belong to the families who are spending the fine weather here, and they romp about without restraint in the spacious halls. Inside we see two visitors playing chess, for people come and go as they will, and always find a kindly welcome.

On the occasion of our last visit it was astonishing to find how great the preponderance of the German, and especially the North German, element was among the guests. There were, however, French visitors also. Once the door flew suddenly open and a swarm of twenty heads appeared in the opening. "Bonjour, ma sœur; nous avons faim, nous avons soif, nous sommes énormément fatigués!" We were all somewhat astonished at this theatrical manner of asking for supper and lodging, but the good "Mother" only smiled softly, and in an hour all were noiselessly provided for.

The most precious relic on Mount Odille is the chapel, which bears the name of the illustrious patroness of the convent, and several hundred feet lower is the spring of sacred water which is said to be a cure for blindness. The little chapel, though it is more homely than sublime, must yet raise some feeling of reverence even in the mind of him who knows little of that form of devotion which, centuries ago, gave rise to such places of worship. Here are no lofty stalls whence the thunder of an inspired discourse carries away the hearts of thousands of hearers. It is more like a private chamber for the soul, where the heart is silently overwhelmed with the knowledge of itself, and can gaze into Heaven undisturbed by the presence of others. We pray here free from that grandeur which makes us at times half-timid and reluctant to approach the shrine of modern ecclesiastical structures. It is a church eminently fitted for women, whose piety depends less on sense than on the instinct of divine feeling.

What different influences surround us when we leave the peaceful circle of the convent walls and pass out into the wilderness of the mountains, over the rocky plateau to Wachtstein, where the stony ruins almost overhang the rock. Here let us stop and gaze down upon the country lying below us—the ancient Wasgau spreading before our eyes with its dark woods and golden undulations of corn-laden fields. Here and there old villages and towns dot the landscape, stretching away into the distance to where the horizon is lost in blue haze. Far off we see the lofty tower of Strasburg Cathedral. Then our eye returns from the distant prospect to our own immediate surroundings, and to the plateau on which we stand. At its foot lie scattered ruins, a winding path leads down through the bushes, and the rain-worn boulders stand about, and look like huge deserted altars. A pagan atmosphere seems to surround us, and we are in the presence of such a wilderness that we seem to feel almost as if the old creating elements were at work once more.

Presently the wind begins to rise, and our eye thoughtfully follows the trace of the crumbling "Heathen Wall," which here stands again before us. A kite with outspread wings hovers over us, and then slowly descends to the summits of the woods. Not a human soul is near. The genius of the Past takes possession of us; for the two great powers, namely, Paganism and Christianity, which once struggled for the possession of the earth, were never nearer to one another than they are here—the one which, let us hope, has now expired, and the other that new Christian faith which brandished its sword and built its cloisters throughout all Germany.

CHAPTER XI.

THE BLACK FOREST.

WE now begin a beautiful, quiet journey; the loftiest summits of the Black Forest range before us in a long blue chain, and lovely spots, through which we are to pass, are shaded by the mountains. The deep defile through which the road goes is called the Kappeler Valley, and here the Acher runs between bare rocks to the Rhine, though in our immediate neighborhood we are surrounded by meadows which border the feet of the wooded slopes.

This is the land where Hebel's old German poems and Auerbach's village stories had their origin, and here is still found that picturesque distinctive costume without which no purely national life can be imagined. Under the long black coat is seen the brilliant red waistcoat, and the blue trustworthy-looking eyes are shaded by a large broad-brimmed hat.

The Black Forest, or Schwartswold, extends for eighty-five miles almost parallel with the course of the Rhine, from which it is distant in places not more than twenty miles. The Black Forest is about twenty-five miles wide. Its highest point is near Freiburg; from there it descends steeply to the Rhine. The

summits of the Black Forest are covered with snow
for eight months out of the year; consequently,
agriculture is of little importance to the inhabitants.

The Middle Ages have left many traces of their
history in this district, among the most notable being
the ruins of the Castle of Yberg, ill-famed in the
mouths of the people because an impious and rapa-
cious knight had there exhumed the bones of his ancestors to find treasure; also the Castle of Roeteln, in
the vale of Wiesen, the home of the poet Hebel.

Near the foot of the mountains the villages are
large and handsome, and in the white house which we
entered we met with plain but hearty hospitality.
Newspapers were lying on the table, and the peasant
was able and willing to converse on all that was going
on in the world. He showed us his stables and barns,
and told us about his ancestors and his children, and
when we at length asked him to whom we were indebted for so much kindness, he said proudly, " I am
called Michael Kobel the Fifth !" We doubt whether
Charles V. was more proud of his title than our friend
Kobel the Fifth !

A short cut brings us to the inn, which is the centre of life in every village. Nearly all the inns on
the Baden side of the Black Forest, and, indeed, beyond in the plain of the Rhine, bear one of the ancient signs of the Lion, the Eagle, the Black Horse,
or the Swan. They generally also have a picture of

one of these well-known creatures placed conspicuously over the door instead of an inscription.

The host, who receives us, himself carries our luggage into the comfortable sitting-room, where we find numerous guests. The walls are hung with tapestry, and mingled with the pictures of the heroes of 1870 we find occasionally portraits of Schiller or Goethe. From the ceiling hangs the inevitable carrier's sign, for that must have its place of honor—the carrier being, indeed, the embodied symbol of progress.

The guests who are seated at the host's table are of various ranks and conditions, though all seem persons of intelligence. There are wood-carvers and peasants, tax-gatherers and parish officials, watchmen, and other local dignitaries. At their invitation we seat ourselves at the table, and find that they are just discussing an official enactment; and the way in which it is criticized, the sharpness with which the weak points of it are observed, surprise us not a little.

The great events of the last few years still form the staple of all public conversation, and they engage the attention of the two carriers who sit apart from our table, each clad in a blue smockfrock and carrying his whip. They get to high words respecting the fortifications on the Moselle and the Maas; and as neither will yield they ask the host for a map, which he soon produces, and on which they continue their endless arguments.

Those features which we have described as being common to the large villages of the Kappeler Valley are found in the large, handsome village of Ottenhöfen, which lies in the middle of the valley. The hamlet of Seebach belongs to it, and though unimportant in itself, it is celebrated for the ruins of Bosenstein, which tower above it, and for the following legend which is connected with it, called "The Legend of the Lady's Grave."

In consequence of a curse which a starving woman had called down upon the wife of one of the knights of Bosenstein, the lady bore seven sons at a birth during her husband's absence in a distant land. The mother, horrified at what had happened, instructed a servant to drown six of the children; but it so happened that just as the dreadful deed was about to be perpetrated, the father accidentally returned and rescued the infants. By his order they were reared in the depths of the woods, unknown to their mother, and when they were strong, handsome knights their father invited them to his castle. A splendid banquet was prepared, and in the midst of it the lord of the castle suddenly asked: "What punishment ought to be given to a mother who, herself, doomed her children to death?" "She should be buried alive!" cried the Lady of Bosenstein, with feigned indignation. She did not know that she had pronounced her own sentence; but the knight started up, and with terrible mien announced to her her doom. She was

Cottage in the Black Forest.

at once hurried away from the banquet, led down into the valley, where the stream springs from the rock, and there may be seen in the stone a deep hole which appears to have been hewn out by human hands—this is known as "The Lady's Grave."

The path, as we proceed, takes us still deeper into the forest. Here and there a steep foot-path leads up through the thicket from the broad circuitous road. The masses of wood lie below, with their green summits swelling in dark waves like a green sea. What profound rest! what holy silence! nothing but the rustling of the wood is heard around. Such is the spot where the venerable monastery of All Saints stands. It is no longer, indeed, a monastery, but only the ruins of one; for the weather-beaten pillars stand desolate, and for many years past the transept with its pointed roof has lain shattered on the ground.

Even in the ruins, however, there is a kind of rhythmical beauty which, with such surroundings as it possesses, exercises a sort of fascination on the beholder; it is a picture of rare poetical power—a stone elegy. The history of the monastery is old and interesting. Its foundation reaches as far back as the time when the great Barbarossa sank in the floods of the Calycadnus, for it was at that time (1196) that Uta von Schauenburg gave the rich estate to the Præmonstratensian monks, and it was not long before their institution became the most powerful of that region.

In the seventeenth century it was raised to the dignity of an abbey, and, in spite of many calamities, it maintained its ancient renown till the year 1802, when it shared the lot of other religious houses, and its property was secularized.

But a worse fate than even this lay in store for the sacred edifice. One year after the event above referred to the roof was set on fire by lightning. Strange to say, this misfortune happened on the anniversary of the foundation of the church, on the day of the year when the bells had formerly been accustomed to ring out proudly to assert the glory of the lordly abbey. On this occasion they sounded an alarm, and clanged despairingly for help. But help was of no avail; the stately buildings which surrounded the monastery soon lay a heap of rubbish, only the blackened stone pillars of the church remained standing. The beautiful ruin now lies among the green pines like the tomb of departed splendor, and we almost seem still to hear the echo of the *Memento Mori* which used to be sung here!

We pass the old monastery garden, where the wind plays among the rustling limes, and soon we find the valley becoming narrower as we proceed. All at once it sinks to its lowest depth, and the valley has become a ravine full of crevices and rocks, which lie in slabs like steps, over which the river rushes angrily, as if to secure possession of the path; these are the Büttenstein Falls, some of them fifty feet in height.

The beauty of this woodland picture was for centuries unknown and unseen, but the searching eye of the present day has brought it to light. A secure path now leads the traveller over to the seven falls, and by the same route we come down the Lierbach Valley to Oppenau.

Another point of interest lies near us on this journey if we take the road out of Ottenhofen which leads up to the Hornisgrinde. There lies the Mümmel Lake, that expanse of water which the pregnant superstition of the peasantry peoples with a hundred hovering sprites. It is a dark, melancholy mirror, framed in fir woods, through which the wind sighs almost inaudibly. No fish are found in this lake, and the water is black and mysterious. It is said to be the abode of the water-god Mümmel and his seven beautiful daughters, the Mümmelchen.

Tradition says that a desperate poacher once killed a gamekeeper in the nearby forest, and threw the body into the Mümmelsee, thinking that the black water would keep his secret; but as the murderer stood watching the ripples made by the body as it sank, the water-god, who would allow nothing to be thrown into his domain, rose up in wrath, caught the poacher by the legs, and drew him down under the water, where he was drowned.

The daughters of the old water-god rise up out of the lake every moonlight night, dressed in green and white, with diamonds in their hair. They dance all the night through on the shore. As the first glimmer of dawn appears their father rises up out of the lake, beckoning them back to their native element. As they touch the water they are transformed into water-lilies, and they lie all day lazily rocking on the bosom of the lake.

One night a young shepherd met with one of the water-sprites, who had strayed far from her sisters. They sat together on the soft moss; they sang, they embraced, and never in his life had he seen so beautiful a creature. He himself was one of the handsomest lads in the country round, with bright golden hair and pink and white cheeks, so that the Black Forest had never contained a happier or fairer pair of lovers.

One request alone she made, and that was, that if by chance she should at any time not come to the border of the lake, he was on no account to call her, as his doing so would cause the destruction of them both. For two days, during which she did not come, he heeded the warning, but on the third, being driven by a powerful impulse to the border of the lake, where he could see the water roses blooming in the depths, he called beseechingly on the name of his beloved. He called! he listened!—suddenly darkness fell on the mountains, the water of the lake began to foam, and, driven by irresistible terror, he fled into the depth of the woods, and was never after seen by human eye.

The immediate surroundings of the lake harmonize with the gloomy legends which are associated with it.

On the south bank, where Seebach seems to steal out of the dreary wilderness in order to hasten to the cheerful valley, there stands a rough stone hut; it is uninhabited, and its bare rooms lack that charm which the presence of man breathes into dead walls. For all this lonesomeness it has had a friendly aspect to many, for it is placed where it is as a shelter for stray travellers who are overtaken by storms; it belongs to everyone and yet to no one.

The scenery becomes wilder as we ascend the jagged footpath; there are no more huts, but the overhanging wall of rock protects us from wind and rain. A weather-worn finger-post nailed to one of the fir-trees points us out the road, from which we look down upon the dark lake. The ancient Romans must have felt the fascination that lies in these depths when they called the place *Lacus Mirabilis*.

We have now reached the summit of the Hornisgrinde, and find it gloomy and desolate; the keen wind sweeps over the plateau, on which short heath and brown rushes grow plentifully, for the ground is marshy and poor. A pointed tower on the summit, in which we vainly seek a door, shows the four points of the compass; and here we see the beautiful world lying beneath us for an immeasurable distance. We look from Höhgau on Lake Constance to the Taunus—from the source of the Danube, over the plain of the Rhine, as far as the summits of the Vosges.

CHAPTER XII.

BADEN-BADEN.

ALTHOUGH the renown of Baden-Baden is of modern origin, a knowledge of the place existed in very early times, for here, as elsewhere, the Romans took possession of the warm springs and made them the centre of a town called *Civitas Aurelia Aquensis*. After the fall of the Romans the place suffered much in various wars; but when it had risen slowly out of its ruins not a few abbots and knights strove for its possession, until at length Barbarossa gave it in fee to the Margrave Hermann, who died in the Crusades in 1190. Under his family the town reached a position of great prosperity, and a fine new building was erected in the early part of the sixteenth century, in addition to the old castle which stood high up on the mountain. The new edifice was placed lower down, almost on a level with the cheerful, busy town, but it was at last destroyed by the fire of the French soldiery. After lying for a long time in a state of ruin, the castle was rebuilt, and now serves as the summer residence of the reigning family.

A handsome road with a broad rampart leads up from the town, and the outer wall is surrounded by ancient, rustling trees. While the old building, which was burnt in 1689, was so remarkable for its architectural features as to be frequently compared with the Castle of Heidelberg, the present structure is plain and unpretending, all the rooms being designed rather for domestic comfort than for the display of regal splendor.

The only relic which recalls to us the primitive times of this stronghold are the mysterious dark dungeons which extend far under the castle, the precise use of which have not yet been ascertained. The guide descends to them with a flaming torch in his hand, and we grope after him through a labyrinth of passages; on one side we hear the creaking of a prison door, on the other the noise of an iron bolt. If we examine closer we find that the door is composed of a single slab of stone, and that the bolt is nearly ten feet long, and runs from one chamber to another.

For a long time the prevalent opinion was that this was one of the centres of the ancient *Vehmgericht*, and if this is not the true historical explanation, the first impression of the place is so horrible that it is easy to understand how the idea arose. What a fearful and pitiless time must that have been when hammer and chisel were plied to furnish such a shelter for the enemies of the builder! What is imprisonment in our days compared with this entombment?

The old castle stands much higher, about three miles above the town itself, and consists of picturesque ruins, which lay hidden for centuries in the green depths of the wood before the curiosity of man found a path to its heights. Now it is all carefully arranged and made easy of access, for man soon brought the luxury of Baden-Baden hither. The huge masses of rock which rise in all their wild ruggedness behind the castle give an idea of what the character of the place was when Hermann and Bernhard, Jacob and Christopher, dwelt at Hohenbaden. From this spot we have a fine and extensive view of the country below.

The town lies partly in the green valley and partly on the slopes of the hills on either side; beyond this we see open meadow-land and wooded heights, and through the valley the clear waters of the river ripple merrily. Truly we gaze upon a little earthly Paradise. After leaving Hohenbaden we soon come upon another citadel, which stands upon a steep point of rock, and was once the castle of the Counts of Eberstein. They themselves have long ago disappeared into obscurity, but legend still winds its tendrils about the rugged walls, and though it is long since any bold knight added to its renown, there was an observant poet who many a time paid it a visit. The beautiful ballad which Uhland sang to the Counts of Eberstein is well known.

Not far from the castle are two great rocks, known

Entrance to the Old Castle, Baden=Baden.

Entrance to the Old Castle, Baden=Baden.

among the peasantry as the angel's and the devil's pulpits.

The legend concerning them tells how the devil, getting tired of the lower regions, came up to the surface of the earth one day, through the springs of Baden-Baden, which have tasted of sulphur ever since.

He was very much in need of new victims to roast, so he stationed himself on one of these rocks and began to preach. The passers-by, knights, priests, and peasants, curious to hear what it was all about, stopped to listen to his eloquence, and soon he had them so fascinated that they could not tell right from wrong, nor black from white, so plausible was he in his arguments.

Just when it seemed that Satan would return to his kingdom with a goodly number of converts, the heavens opened and an angel floated down, and taking his stand on a rock opposite, began to preach with a still small voice, but in a very different strain.

The devil, enraged, raised his voice and tried to drown the low voice of the angel, but one by one his hearers left him to gather round the heavenly messenger and listen to his words of peace. The devil, finding himself alone, began to swear and tear up the grass and shrubs, and he stamped his red-hot feet on the rock so hard that the prints of his hoofs can be seen to this day.

But we must now bid farewell to the reminiscences of legendary times, and descend from the solitude of the woods to the active bustle of the present which prevails in the valley below. The large number of fugitives who fled from France during the terror of the Great Revolution, and who populated the German towns from Lake Constance to Coblentz, considerably influenced the whole character of Baden, and continued to do so until the events of 1870 broke through these traditions.

Since that time the number of foreign visitors has rapidly increased, for while forty years ago they scarcely amounted to five thousand, at the present time they reach the number of sixty thousand a year. The establishments which are appropriated to the amusement of this avalanche of visitors have obtained a degree of perfection which justifies the inhabitants in considering their spa the first in the world.

This is true from a social rather than from a hygienic point of view, for the complaint for the cure of which Baden-Baden is most efficacious is *ennui*. For that old craving which goes through all humanity, and appears and reappears on thousands of lips, if it also dies on thousands—that craving for pleasure and parade, for splendor and delight, is met with here in its most concentrated form.

Busy hands have brought together almost all the

good things of this world; the merchant has brought his stores, the gardener his flowers, the goldsmith his costly treasures, and the artist his art. Music sounds over the polished floor, horses fly over the green course, shots whiz through the air, and golden-haired sirens crowd round the spring which once was hidden in the deep recesses of the wood. Unceasingly is heard the sound, echoing, roaring, singing, ringing in our ears, "Live, enjoy life!" Still, as all these enjoyments created only satiety and not happiness, there came another holding a shining ball in his hand and saying, "Here is something which is the essence of happiness—try this!" Then he set the ball rolling, and thousands of gleaming eyes followed it. Thousands also rolled their glittering gold after it, as at every throw and every fresh turn in the game, the haggard croupier repeated his monotonous formula, "Messieurs, faites votre jeu; le jeu est fait, rien ne va plus!" Thus Baden-Baden has become what it is, and though public gambling has been abolished since 1872, something seems to remain even now of the feverishness of that time, and of that eager pursuit of fortune which was then a characteristic of the place.

It would be unjust to look upon all this as the real nature of the lovely spa, for many live there in the quiet round of every-day duties, and many find their enjoyment there solely in a pure sense of the beauty which Nature spreads before them. But it is also true that thousands come to drag through their weary days with the help of this copious supply of excitement. They feel nothing of the fresh, fir-scented breeze; they appreciate nothing of the idyllic beauty of a happy, sheltered home; they seek the fever that consumes, the excitement that destroys, and they exhibit all their wealth in order to conceal their real poverty. It is of them only that we have spoken here; the harmless guests, who also assemble from all parts of the world, shall not be mentioned with them, but only that community which appears, more or less, in every fashionable watering-place, and which has its own peculiar physiognomy. For these the word Baden-Baden means something quite different, and the disappearance of the gaming-tables and of the French element is indeed a serious loss.

The Friedrichsbad is the principal bath-house. It was erected about twenty-five years ago, and rises on terraces from the Stein-Strasse, quite close to the springs. The internal arrangements of this establishment are unsurpassed. There are hot and cold baths, plunge-, vapor- and sitz-baths; large swimming-pools, with warm and cold water; and one floor is set apart for curative gymnastics and massage.

Though each individual is at liberty to select that part of the town which he fancies will suit his health best, the social pleasures of the place are decidedly centralized, and the centre is that lovely park in which the Conversation House stands. The long drinking-hall is shaded by handsome trees and surrounded by gay flower-beds, and has lofty open corridors, which are decorated with illustrations from the most interesting of the legends of the Black Forest. We see the dancing nixies of the Mümmelsee, the Emperor Otto encamped before Eberstein, which his men are besieging in vain, and the gipsy woman watching her treasures beside the splashing waterfall of All Saints. Such were the forms which passed over these spots when the miraculous spring, to which thousands now make their pilgrimage, was still a hidden forest secret, known only to the lofty pines and to the silent rocks.

So we muse. But we must leave the fascinations of bygone days and step into the circle of the busy exulting life of the present day, for indeed we stand on the spot where the life-pulse beats loudest. Music crashes out from the kiosk which lies opposite the Conversation House; the countess in her long silken train bows graciously to the prince, who offers her his arm. What caprices of humanity are exhibited in all these garments! What caprices of Nature in all these forms, which range from the truly noble to the basely criminal! The crowd becomes thicker and thicker; rattling equipages fly past.

It is now twilight, and the branched candelabra are lighted, and a great display of fireworks is prepared for the evening. As the air is mild and warm the folding-doors of the rooms are thrown open, and forms of fairy-like beauty stream in and out, making a constant movement like the flowing of a river. There also is the rustling of the ladies' dresses, the noise of endless conversation, and that predominating hum of life which pervades every room but one. In this strict silence reigns, so much so that one can hear the very breathing of the men who sit there and who brood over the newspapers of all countries. It is this reading-room which is decorated in the richest style of the Renaissance.

Presently the shower of fireworks outside attracts even the tenants of this silent apartment; the old castle is already illuminated by Bengal lights; thousands of rockets burst, and people from all parts crowd to see the beautiful display. It is midnight before the crowd on the Kurplatz begins to clear away; and then the jeweller, who comes in the season from the Palais-Royal, shuts up his ebony case, and the fair moths who flutter round his glittering treasures slowly disappear. Baden-Baden retires to rest, and there is silence in the houses and in the streets, and no sound is heard except that of the splashing waters of the Oos, which murmur through the town as they pass under the gray iron bridges.

The season is, naturally, at its height in the autumn, at the time of the great races, which are among the most important of those on the Continent.

Conversation House, Baden=Baden.

Occasionally not less than from one to two hundred horses are entered, though only about half the number actually go over the course; the total value of the prizes reaches nearly a hundred thousand marks. The course is about eight miles distant from the town, in the plain of the Rhine, near the village of Iffezheim. Iffezheim is, at this season, the most brilliant of all the brilliant spectacles that Baden has to offer.

Pigeon-shooting is also practised on the same course—a cruel sport, the introduction of which does not add to the credit of Germany. The number of live pigeons yearly required for this purpose amounts to many thousands.

But the special and the greatest attraction which life in Baden-Baden offers is not to be found in the brilliant crowd; we must seek it in those charming retired villas which lie along the banks of the river in the Lichtenthaler Allee. The gardens which surround each house are laid out with the greatest care. More than a thousand cartloads of the best forest mould are often brought for a single garden, and fifteen or sixteen hundred of the most costly plants are used to fill one small bed.

But we must pass on, away from modern Baden-Baden, back to mediæval times. A mile and a half from the town is the village of Lichtenthal. We pass through it, cross the bridge, and, turning to the right, find ourselves at the Nunnery of Lichtenthal.

It was founded in 1245 by Irmingard, the granddaughter of Henry the Lyon. The convent has escaped destruction in some miraculous way, and is still occupied by Cistercian Nuns. In the church adjoining is the tomb of Irmingard.

In strong contrast to the mediæval character of the place, a war monument of 1870–71 rises directly in front of the nunnery.

But it is growing late; we must hasten back to Baden-Baden. As we near the town the lights twinkle out from the Conversation House and we hear the strains of the band. Looking on this enchanted scene we wonder that we can ever leave it; but is there any spot on **earth so lovely that we could enjoy it forever?**

CHAPTER XIII.

THE PFALZ.

A BRIGHT, sunny picture lies before us when we set foot upon the soil of the Pfalz. Life surges round us, like a pulse which beats more rapidly here than in the other countries of Germany. The speech is loud and cheerful, and there appears in labor, as well as in pleasure, a sort of energy which compels our sympathy. The secret of this local characteristic, perhaps, exists in the fact that the vine flourishes here most luxuriantly, and covers hill and dale, and clambers even over the poorest cottage.

A district which proves itself so useful, and is so well cultivated, cannot, perhaps, be called exactly beautiful, but it bears that stamp which careful industry never fails to imprint. There are, however, parts of the Pfalz where the hand of man has never interfered with the fine, bold, natural forms, and where the charm of picturesque beauty is added to the fertility of the soil. It is through such a portion of the Pfalz that our road leads us.

We pass through the Rockland of Dahn, with its long undulations of dark pine-wood interspersed with rugged red sandstone, and then through those remarkable districts where from the steep mountain-

summits scattered ruins look down into the valley below.   Those ruins are the remains of strongholds
within whose walls the weal or woe of the Empire
was once decided.

The coach carries us out of the little town of Berg-
zabern, with its partly ruined fortifications, towards
the mountains.   The road continually leads us upwards, and runs between thick fir-trees; it passes an
old mill, several solitary crosses, and occasionally a
wagon drawn by a weary team.   But in spite of the
quiet surroundings we feel the bodily and mental activity which is at work in the inhabitants, and small
as the place is, its people are overflowing with energy.
Every child can give us what information we require
concerning the road.   When we ask which way will
lead us up to the steep rock called the " Maiden's
Leap," we obtain an intelligent answer.

In the inn parlor, where the dignitaries of the place
assemble to take their evening glass, every guest is
welcome, and we are favorably impressed by the
modest neatness of the room and the eloquence of
its inhabitants.

The following morning we ascend to the two great
strongholds, Trifels and Madenburg, which are united
by a long dark spur of rock.   Nothing remains of
either except wild ruins, which indicate the splendor
of past times.   Madenburg is the grandest ruin in
the Rhenish Palatinate, but Trifels is especially rich
in reminiscences; it was not simply a princely strong-

hold, but an imperial castle in all its splendor. The inhabitants of the Pfalz have almost forgotten its existence in the daily bustle of their everyday work, but great, eternal Nature has laid her protecting hand upon this relic.

The path leads up to the castle through a beech wood with its shining branches, and when we gain the summit a vast world lies before us studded with meadows and streams, towns and castles. It was here that the Emperor Henry IV. sat in the deepest anguish, when the German princes vowed to renounce him if he did not remove the interdict within six months; and it was to this place that the costly treasures of the Empire were brought, and here they remained for years in safety.

Now nothing but waste ruins are left; princes dwell here no longer; songs no more resound and echo through these walls; gold no longer adorns its chambers, except the glorious light of the setting sun. Merry children now play and romp where princes wept, and the beech-trees with their rustling branches alone stand in lofty pride, with dark moss growing on their trunks, and birds singing overhead. The imperial citadel of Trifels is now dumb forever!

During the Third Crusade Richard the Lion-Hearted and Leopold of Austria were besieging Acre. Both were noted for their courage, and they vied with one another in performing many valiant deeds of arms. Leopold, jealous of Richard's superior glory, finally gave up the siege and returned home, vowing that he would make the English King bitterly regret having overshadowed him by his superior prowess.

Leopold soon had the opportunity of fulfilling his vow; for Richard, returning from the Crusade, was shipwrecked on the coast of Illyria, and was forced to make his way back to England alone and on foot. He exchanged his garments for a pilgrim's robe and scrip, and proceeded on his way, passing safely through the greater part of Austria.

One day he found himself obliged to part with his signet-ring to procure him food and shelter. This ring betrayed him to his enemies. He was seized and imprisoned in the Fortress of Durrenstein, and kept there until Henry IV. of Germany took him into custody, and transferred him to this castle of Trifels.

While Richard was pining in captivity, wondering why his faithful subjects made no effort to find him, his brother, John Lackland, had usurped the throne and was reigning in Richard's stead. The people hated John, and longed for the return of their rightful king, but only one man thought of going in search of him. This was Blondel, the King's minstrel; he felt sure that Richard had been taken prisoner by the Emperor of Germany. So he started to find his master, and wandered from town to town, and from castle to castle, questioning all whom he met, and singing, under the walls of every stronghold, a peculiar air known only to the King and himself.

After months of weary wandering Blondel came to Trifels, and under the tower he began to sing his little song. Imagine his joy when he heard the refrain taken up by the voice of his dear King! Richard, his long-lost master, was found, and his weary search was ended.

But Blondel could do nothing alone to deliver his King, so he hastened back to England, told the English nobles the result of his quest, and they gladly undertook Richard's release. His ransom was paid and Richard came home in triumph, ousted his traitor brother, and ruled over England for many years. He died in 1199, and was buried at Rouen, where his tomb may be seen to this day.

The present capital of the Pfalz—if one may speak of the capital of a province—is Speyer. It is adapted for this position neither by its size nor by its outward appearance, but for this very reason its past history is the more important, for it belongs in an eminent degree to the historical cities of the Empire. Its growth began early, like that of the other Rhenish towns; it was first fortified in the time of the Romans, and called Augusta Nemetum; a bishop held his court here under the Frankish king in the fourth century, and two hundred years later a Carlovingian emperor chose it as his favorite dwelling-place.

Numerous imperial Diets have been held in Speyer, but the most important was that of 1529, under Charles V., after which those who had espoused the cause of the Reformation received the name of *Protestants*, from their protest against the hostile majority.

From the sixth century Speyer is more bound up with the traditions of the Empire than any other German town; and though it was often but a temporary dwelling-place for the Emperors, it was an eternal resting-place for many of its great rulers. It was not only when their hearts longed for brilliant pageants or the assembly of their vassals at the imperial Diet, that their eyes turned towards Speyer, but their thoughts followed the same path when those great hearts were weary and they felt their end approaching; Speyer was the dying thought of the German emperors. "Bring me my charger," said the Emperor Rudolf, when weary and bent under the burden of his mighty life; and he rode to Speyer to die, close to the tomb which was to contain his ashes. Where was this tomb? It was the Cathedral, which even from a distance may be seen, with massive walls and towers.

This structure Conrad II. began to build as a burial-place for himself and his successors, and it was continued by his son Henry II., and finished by his grandson Henry III. After these had been finally laid to rest here, a whole line of German emperors and empresses were buried in this imperial sepulchre, including Henry IV., who was burdened with Pope Gregory's excommunication, Henry V., Philip of Swabia, Rudolf of Hapsburg, the false emperor Adolf of Nassau, and Albert I. of Austria, the Empress Gisela, wife of Conrad II., Bertha, wife of Henry IV., and Barbarossa's wife and daughter, Beatrix and Agnes. So the solemn honor of being the burial-place of emperors was added to the glory which the town had already gained from its populous and renowned character; and it was not desecrated by any strange hand for upwards of six centuries.

The old imperial city fell a victim to the consequences of the disasters of the year 1689, a year which set its brand so pitilessly on all the districts of the beautiful Pfalz. It had suffered severely in the Thirty Years' War, but through all its vicissitudes its existence was preserved, and even the wildness of those times retained some slight remnant of veneration for the royal tomb and for the sacred imperial name. It was reserved for the marauding hosts of "His Most Christian Majesty" to efface even this remnant, and to cover themselves with that shame from which the serf and the Swede had shrunk.

It was the soldiers of the Great King who, under the leadership of Louvois, Montelar and Mélac, broke open the consecrated graves in the Cathedral of Speyer, and there, before all the people, amused themselves by playing bowls with the heads of the German emperors.

Not content with this, they then set fire to Speyer at every point. They seemed to wish, indeed, to substitute another and a still larger sepulchre for those they had laid waste, and to convert the city itself into a grave and the country round it into a desert. One stone was not left upon another. The Cathedral alone withstood their devastating rage, and although they tore the ornaments from the walls, the walls themselves remained firm.

The French Revolution brought fresh woe. The soldiers of the Republic used the consecrated building as a magazine in which was stored all the necessary supplies which the war incessantly consumed; and in the place where the organ had pealed forth solemn *Te Deums* the " Marseillaise " was roared from savage throats. Indeed, at one time the whole of the material of the magnificent temple was about to be sold by auction for a few thousand francs!

We are often amazed when we hear how at times the greatest and noblest lives have hung upon a thread, and we shudder at the very thought of what would have been the consequence of so irreparable a loss; so it is here, as we gaze at this wonderful work, the destruction of which would have been an irretrievable loss to German Art. To have possessed the Cathedral of Speyer, and, after preserving it through all the storms of history, to have lost it for a despicable sum of money, the value of the mere stones and bricks, would have been an enduring sorrow and disgrace for the German nation.

The merit of restoring the Cathedral to its present splendor is undoubtedly due to the Bavarian kings, and especially to Louis I., who combined all the arts in order to make the restoration as brilliant as possible.

The huge size of the building is not realized from without. When standing before the principal entrance, those portions which lie behind are hidden from view, and on every side are seen fresh traces of modern work. This may at first have a somewhat disturbing effect, for age and dignity are almost inseparable ideas, and the subdued weather-stained coloring is always associated with the thought of the great well-known cathedrals of the world.

The façade has three portals. Over the middle one is the imperial double-eagle; over the side-entrances the lion of the Palatinate. The rose-window above has a gold ground, on which is the head of the Saviour, crowned with thorns. The interior (which is adorned with Schraudolph's beautiful frescoes) presents the idea of the light additions of modern work, besides conveying an impression of power to the whole style of the building with its fine proportions.

We have, perhaps, not clearly expressed what we mean, for nothing is farther from our thoughts than a wish to imply that its architectural beauties are not of a very high order. It is, however, not quite easy to state exactly the idea we would convey. A visitor we met once in the Cathedral indicated our impression in one word, better than any long explanation could have done. Looking round on walls and ceiling, he said: "The Cathedral of Speyer pleases me better than any other in the world—better than Strasburg, Milan or Cologne." "Indeed!" was our astonished rejoinder; "and pray what gives it such decided pre-eminence in your eyes?" "Oh! it is so neat; it is the *neatest* cathedral in the world."

We descend to the dark crypt, and after carefully inspecting it come up again to the light, and pass through all the smaller chapels. The last of these is dedicated to St. Afra, and here let us stop for a moment. This is the place where the body of the Emperor Henry IV. was laid when he died under the ban of excommunication, and the priests refused to lower him into the grave of his ancestors. The coffin of the man who once begged for mercy in the Castle of Canossa lay unburied for five years before the resting-place of his fathers. The fate of his body in death resembled that which it had experienced in life.

Such are the invisible shadows of the olden time which fall upon these lofty sacred walls when on the holy Sabbath the choristers pass between them with tapers and fragrant incense. No brilliant colors ever have erased or ever can erase those shadows; they are the gloomy inheritance of these places. Henry IV. at Canossa is an eternal grief in the remembrances of the German nation, the immovable shadow which hangs over the old Empire at Speyer.

In 1813 Napoleon had concentrated all his forces at Leipsic to overwhelm the allied powers. Then Speyer was deserted, except for its women and children and a few old men; for the people of Speyer were loyal, and none who were able to bear arms stayed at home.

All was quiet at the ferry, for the hour was late, and the old ferryman was dozing over his oars when he heard a loud call from the other side of the river where the city lay. He quickly rowed across, and as his boat touched the landing a tall figure stepped silently into it. This person was followed by others, who, emerging from the shadow of the Cathedral, came silently down the street, their military cloaks muffling their faces.

When the last passenger had embarked the ferryman pushed the boat from the shore, but before he could begin to row he felt that the boat was moving swiftly through the water, apparently by itself. Shivering with fright, the boatman dropped his oars and began crossing himself, feeling sure that the boat was propelled by some supernatural power.

Soon they reached the opposite landing, and the tall figures stepped ashore, revealing, as they did so, a glitter of armor and swords. The last passenger, telling the boatman that if he watched for their return he should have double fare, stepped swiftly after his comrades, and they were all swallowed up by the darkness.

Three days passed, and the old ferryman looked in vain for the return of his mysterious passengers; but at midnight on the third day they again appeared, and were rowed silently back to Speyer. Each man as he stepped out of the boat dropped a coin into the ferryman's outstretched palm, then disappeared among the Cathedral shadows.

The old boatman marvelled much who these strangers could be, and the next day he marvelled more when he found that, instead of the usual penny, each of his midnight passengers had given him a golden coin, and on each coin was stamped a different effigy and a different date.

He took the coins to the priest, who examined them carefully, and declared that they bore the effigies and dates of the emperors lying buried in the Cathedral of Speyer.

On the morrow came tidings of the defeat of the French at the terrible three days' battle of Leipsic. Then the boatman knew that the old legend was true, and that the German emperors had risen from their tombs, and had gone forth to battle, to deliver the beloved fatherland in its hour of need.

CHAPTER XIV.

HEIDELBERG.

THERE is an ideal among places as well as among persons, and favored forms exist which are beloved of all; among these, few will deny that Heidelberg may claim a place. It stands bright and clear along the river-side; the mountains which surround it have shadows of a delicate blue tint, and on every side are running springs, balmy air and happy human faces. This characteristic, which is constantly interwoven with intellectual work and cheerful enjoyment, is now so closely bound up with the name of the town that we can scarcely realize through what shame and sorrow it passed before such days dawned upon it.

The heights above the Neckar were fortified as far back as the time of the Romans. On them stood the citadel which the Bishop of Worms built. It consisted of rude solitary towers, which were given in fee first to one noble and then to another, till at last Conrad founded the little town, the city of the Counts-Palatine of the Rhine. Its beginnings were tedious and difficult; all the elements conspired against it, and yet its vitality was indestructible. It rose with fresh glory out of the ashes to which it was reduced, out of the flood by which it was covered, and strengthened itself with those weapons which must ultimately prevail, namely, the weapons of intellectual power.

The University of Heidelberg, which was founded in 1386 by the Count-Palatine Ruprecht, is reckoned one of the earliest in Germany. The effect of its establishment was not long in giving a peculiar character to the whole town. No longer was its chief source of pride the splendor of a royal court, or the unapproachable beauty of its environs, but it raised its head in the full consciousness of intellectual superiority; it became a Minerva among the cities which stand in the broad plain on both sides of the Rhine. In its heart there stirred the great idea which was later to become a familiar watchword, " Knowledge is power !"

And, indeed, a powerful and joyful period commenced; the Prince-Palatine Frederick had victoriously prevailed over all his opponents, the noblest of guests were received in the great castle, the noblest men of the time studied at the University; and renown, wealth, beauty, pleasure, all united to adorn the life of the place. Heidelberg became the pearl of German cities, and stood shining beneath the banner of free thought.

A little later and all changed once more. The same banner which had been the emblem of peace and progress became the standard of war—a war which

The Court-yard, Heidelberg Castle.

The Court-yard, Heidelberg Castle.

was contested for thirty years, and which seemed as if, at any cost, it would wrest the town from the hands of the Germans.

Another period began. Minds were divided, the hosts stood opposed one to another, and the greatest and most horrible war which the world has ever seen broke forth. The prosperity and peace of the city declined. The first leader that appeared before the walls was the gloomy Tilly, a monk in soldier garb. He invariably sent his messengers into each town that he approached and called on the people to surrender, giving them only the alternative of fire or sword. Heidelberg also received such a warning. It was beleaguered, stormed and burnt; but the literary treasures, the splendid library of the Palatinate, was presented by Tilly and the Prince-Palatine Max to the Holy Father, who carried away these pearls of German intellect to the Vatican. About one-third of this collection was returned to Heidelberg in the early part of this century. The library now contains nearly five hundred thousand books, manuscripts and ancient documents—but that is only a small portion of the treasures that were carried away to Rome and are still there.

After Tilly came the Swedes, and after the Swedes the Imperialists, each in their turn working further destruction to the town and its inhabitants; fire and sword were the watchwords of those days.

But the worst of all the sorrow that passed over

the town came from the hand of Louis XIV., who not only conquered and laid waste the districts of the Rhine, but also disgraced them. The castle was destroyed, the tombs of princes were defiled, and the inhabitants were filled with despair. It required many years to efface these misfortunes, and the following century passed silently and wearily at Heidelberg.

Many calamities still befell the town, but it was like a man who having gone through the heaviest and most indescribable sorrows bears patiently whatever else may come. Its prosperity, its glory were broken down; it was no longer looked on as a prize for the ambition of war, and no longer a fitting stage for the mailed foot of History.

It was in the beginning of our own times that the town first woke out of the deep swoon of exhaustion into which it had sunk, and its features acquired a new living charm. The power by which it was renovated was again the power of knowledge. "And new life blossoms out of the ruins." If ever this consoling creed of history were true it was fulfilled here; this same town which had seen all the abomination of desolation became a plantation whose creative blessings spread all over Europe. The greatest achievements of science had their cradle here. The greatest names of science found here their home. In this way there reappeared in the physiognomy of the inhabitants that bright cheerful character which influences our first impression as we now enter its gates.

The town of to-day smiles at us like a man who has never known a sorrowful hour; but we know through what anguish these walls have passed. Earth and history have their martyrs, as well as Heaven, and Heidelberg stands among these silent sufferers.

We rarely analyze that mysterious something which constitutes the individuality of a town, or ask ourselves what it is that particularly attracts us to it. Heidelberg possesses nothing of what are called "sights." The number of its inhabitants is moderate, and their manner of life simple and devoid of distracting pleasures; but the deserted castle with its ruins attracts us more than a thousand palaces with all their treasures.

We cannot leave this labyrinth where the paths are full of violets and every wall has some great associations. In the fragrant woods which surround it the sun flecks the intricate paths with spots of light. We cannot tear ourselves away from the fragrance and the coolness of these woods, and from the enticing secrets chirped to us from every bough. In the cool shade there lies a pool, where the murmuring streamlets rest awhile before they run down towards the valley. The place is called Wolfsbrunnen (the wolf's well), because it was here that a fortune-teller named Jetta, who lived near this place, was torn to pieces by a wolf. There lies the Devil's Hole, and

yonder the King's Chair, and there, where the
wood opens, we look down on the straggling wonderful ruins.

We leave the green foliage and return to the town
with its cheerful life, where the glory of intellectual
pre-eminence is found combined with happy careless
youth. We ask again, who can tear himself away
from all these attractions?

Now we will ascend leisurely to the castle, for that
is always the first object to which a stranger is attracted. How many times have pen and pencil
essayed to describe this pearl of beauty! How many
thoughts full of poetry have awakened at the sight—
thoughts which have never found utterance, but have
flashed through the soul as a falling star rushes
through the vaults of heaven! Thousands have
stood here, and still the old charm works afresh for
each one. The original power of these walls has long
ago been shattered, but the power it exercises over
the minds of men has constantly increased, and no
destroyer has been able to subdue it.

The Castle of Heidelberg, as is well known, was
not the work of one hand nor of one period, but is a
complete square of palaces, in which the ideas of a
century and the supremacy of long generations are
embodied. It was a little town in itself, with castles and towers, with galleries and gardens, built as
a counterpart of the old palaces of the Roman Empire.

Imperial hands have been busy here also, and the imperial eagle stood above the portal; but the emperors were none of them of that effeminate yet savage type which we have seen in Nero and Galba, Heliogabalus and Caracalla—they were men of iron frames and harsh names. The Emperor Ruprecht built the wing which first confronts us as we approach the court-yard by way of the bridge and gateway. The building which is now named after him is by no means the oldest part of the castle. This goes back to the time of Rudolph, having been completed a century before, and within its ruins lie the oldest and gloomiest legends.

We go farther, and reach a corridor where the well of the castle is; the four syenite pillars near it are a legacy of the Empire, having once stood at Ingelheim, in the territory of Charlemagne. They were brought to Heidelberg by Count-Palatine Ludwig.

Every one of the palaces which we pass has its own history, its own beauty, its own legends; the most beautiful of them all is that which is named after Otto Heinrich, built in 1556. Here we stand before one of the finest masterpieces which the early Renaissance produced. This also bears the scars of that frightful period of war, and has become a ruin; but what irresistible beauty still speaks to us out of the dumb lifeless limbs! Truly a thousand palaces of the present day could not outweigh this one—this torso of a palace!

It has been said that Michael Angelo designed it, and whether or not this supposition has any historical foundation, the fact that it ever existed is the most perfect testimony to the beauty of the work. It was built at a period when the slumbering powers of antiquity were again slowly awaking and penetrating every artistic production; the Greek classics were held next in esteem to the Bible, and next to the youthful energy of the Reformation the indestructible beauty of the antique seemed part of the very condition of the people. Princes began to feel like the Olympians, and made the Olympians the companions of their homes. This train of thought, this tendency of the time, is to a certain extent impressed on the façade of this splendid palace, which is like a stone mirror of those glorious days. In the open niches stand the figures of Hercules and Samson, Joshua and David, the representatives of strength and courage—the foundations on which a kingly house ought to stand. On the one side the Christian virtues, on the other the enthroned and newly-revived gods, Jupiter and Saturn, Mars and Venus. Motionless and intrepidly these figures succumbed to their fate in those frightful days of war. Sometimes the hand of a hero, sometimes the crown of a king or the limbs of a goddess fell to the ground. They were but of stone; but there is a soul in these shattered stones which makes us feel even now the pain of their wounds.

Was all this glory then created for destruction? Who were the masters that built these wondrous walls? Their very names are unknown, and no man any longer calls these splendors his own. The wind rustles through the open doorways, the swallow brushes the window-frames with its slender wings, and the stars look down from above into the roofless chambers.

The existence which these walls now lead is mournfully silent; passionless and actionless, everything here speaks only of the past. The men of the present day pass by in hundreds without understanding anything of its meaning. Only now and then some one comes whose imagination carries him to the past, and who feels some sympathy and veneration for what has gone before. Under the glance of such a one the old red walls spring once more into life; for him the scenes of bygone ages are mysteriously re-enacted. He hears the mailed footstep of princes re-echo through the halls, and the ringing laugh of lovely women once more enlivening these silent chambers. Could he, however, awake all the forms and bring to light all those whose names are associated with these walls, the array would indeed be endless.

Every corner is full of images, from that of the regal figure on the battlements to that of the dwarf who crouches in the cellar to guard the great cask. The latter is one of the wonders of Heidelberg which no visitor omits seeing, and which many gaze on with more enthusiasm than on the shattered splendor of kings. It is said to be capable of containing two hundred and thirty-six thousand bottles; but the cask is empty, and is only a remnant of that time when princes prided themselves on the size of their belongings, and had lost that finer and more spiritual charm of possession which had departed from them.

The original cask was built in 1591. When it fell to pieces in 1662 it was replaced by another; that lasted until 1728, and the present tun was erected by the Elector Charles-Philip in 1751.

The dwarf Perkio, the court-jester of the Elector Charles Philip, was very small in stature, but a veritable giant where drinking was concerned. The castle and his master's wealth were as nothing to him in comparison to the mighty Heidelberg tun. He was so in love with it—and what it contained—that he finally refused to leave the vault where it was kept. He spent all his time beside it, drawing and drinking beaker after beaker of its contents.

For fifteen years he sat beside his beloved tun, jealously guarding the wine which he alone had the privilege of drinking. At the end of that time he discovered, to his consternation, that he had emptied the cask; not a drop of wine was left within its mighty bulk! Then, proudly comparing himself to David, and declaring that he had conquered a Goliath, and feeling—the cask being empty—that life was no longer worth living, he laid down beside it and quietly passed away, requesting that he might be buried directly beneath the faucet that he had turned so diligently, and that his statue might be placed where he was wont to sit.

Of all occupations and amusements none was wanting in Heidelberg. Lions' dens, orange gardens, brilliant feasts abounded, to say nothing of sanguinary encounters. Everything! and of all there remains now nothing! A ruin covered with green ivy stands before us—it is not the ruins of a castle, but the ruins of an epoch.

Down below, at the foot of the castle, the current of the gay student life runs merrily along full of vivacity and brightness. The period when Heidelberg belonged to the Counts-Palatine of the Rhine has long since passed away. Now it belongs to the students, and it is not the castle but the university which is the centre of its glory and of its importance.

Heidelberg now has over a thousand students. In 1886 the five hundredth anniversary of the founding of the university was celebrated with much ceremony.

Heidelberg has completed its mission in political history; its place lies henceforth in the intellectual history of Europe. We have, therefore, only to depict in a few lines the joyous, stirring description of the student city, as given by an old student:

"I can picture to myself, as if it were yesterday, my departure from home. The carefully-counted bank-notes lying on the table with the passport, the good advice and good wishes from relations and friends, the long journey with its rapidly-changing scenes, and the beating of my heart when the guard came to the door of the carriage and said, 'Now, gentlemen, tickets for Heidelberg.'

" It was not without a feeling of veneration that I entered this seat of the Muses. Even the road from the railway is an interesting walk for a stranger. At such a moment, however, as I am describing, the mind is a blank sheet on which are swiftly sketched the first impressions, to be afterwards slowly corrected and completed. The Rhine life reigns on all sides. I saw people who are accustomed to transact all their affairs with open doors; girls with brisk step and bright eyes, lads who rushed romping by; noisy fellows in blue blouses were in every corner, and hackney-coaches rattled by, filled with stoutly-shod students. Now and then a figure passed which I felt must be that of a professor."

If we compare Heidelberg with other places in South Germany, and especially with Munich, we are astonished that two places geographically so near to one another should in point of culture be so far removed; in this respect the distance between the old Bavarian nature and that of the Rhenish Palatinate is three times as great as the actual distance between the two principal towns.

When hiring a porter at the railway station at Heidelberg it would seem that all of them are æsthetically inclined, and that each of them had been to the university. They speak of Bunsen and of the late Vangerow as if they were their best friends. Thus there continually rises to the surface an impression of the special character of the town, which naturally has its root in university life. This character is announced not only in the popularity of the Heidelberg celebrities and the respect which even the porters have for "their" professors, but also in a thousand little particulars. It lies before the shop-windows where colored caps and ribbons are exhibited, it is met with in the bookseller's stall, and even in the beer-shops.

Whatever happens to a Heidelberg student, he manages to adapt himself to circumstances, whatever they may be, or whatever they may be called; and this characteristic is stronger here than in the great towns where the extent of the foreign element obstructs the natural development of the students. Many, however, are said to belong to the student class who pitch their tent in the coffee-house and come in contact with the beadle oftener than with the professor, and who spend even more time on their pet dogs than on their own toilet. But there are great temptations, even for such as intend to work honestly, for few universities offer so enticing a field for the gay enjoyment of life as Heidelberg. The true German student life is developed more thoroughly here than elsewhere, and the beautiful neighborhood attracts excursionists into the open country on the bright summer days; the little towns of Neckargemund and Neckarsteinach are thus especially popular.

Below on the river lie swift boats, the wine sparkles, and the castles look down from the rocks full of martial memories on many a lively scene. The Neckar Valley, though much smaller and more unpretending, perhaps shows the most intimate relationship to the Rhenish life; and the pulse which pervades that life is cheerfulness.

That yearly festival which is held in the golden autumn on the banks of the Neckar is well known. It is celebrated at the time when the grapes are ripe on the hillsides, and when every one gathers in the harvest on his own land and from his own vines.

Mannheim also is a favorite walk for the students of Heidelberg, especially those who like to see the ways of the world as they are represented on the stage. When a novelty is announced on the theatre bills, the news of such an event travels in no time for miles around, and the curious come to Mannheim in long caravans to see the show. But the frivolous student may also learn here what is meant by hard work, and what is achieved by unremitting toil; for it is to the results of work that Mannheim owes the position which it holds among German towns. It was work also which, within a few centuries, called the neighboring town of Ludwigshafen into existence as if by magic.

Valley of the Neckar from Heidelberg.

Valley of the Neckar from Heidelberg.

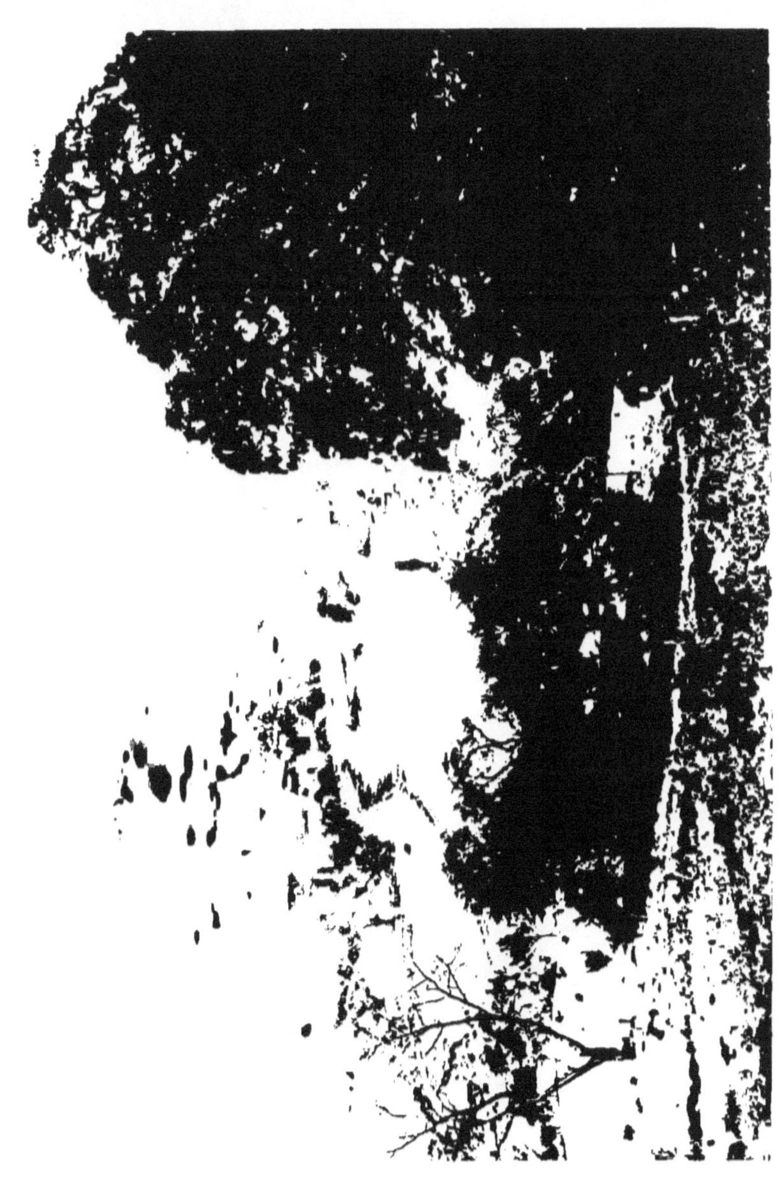

But who can think of anything serious while the gay-colored cap still covers the young and thoughtless head? He who would flee abroad must have an easy mind; the time of care comes soon enough of its own accord. Then it is no longer a question of enjoyment, but one of toil. The sultry hour of the examination comes nearer and nearer; that hour when we must pay toll on the thorny road of knowledge. We only really go through an examination properly when we are young, for it is only then that we have the courage to fail; later in life we remark that old Socrates was right with his theory that the beginning of knowledge was to know that we know nothing.

Ah! in what a condition we were on the occasion when we made our first visit to the examination-room. We kept ringing the bell, and making our landlord's pretty daughter run about the passage even more than usual. As we went out she cast a compassionate look on the victims adorned for the sacrifice. She well knew what our humors signified, for she had seen them very often, and understood what was about to happen. Such were our college days at Heidelberg.

Heidelberg itself is almost like a blooming garden, but if it is not sufficient to satisfy the ideas of some, there is for those who prefer the addition of Art to Nature another garden at Schwetzingen, the fame of which reaches throughout Europe. Of the town itself there is little to be said; it was formerly only an appendage to the summer palace, and is at the present time just a little fussy official place, as noisy and lively as was once the nature of the district of the Palatinate, and yet as quiet as is becoming for a town of four hundred souls. It is a curious fact that of the numberless strangers who visit the place, no one asks for the town, that being simply an approach to the castle and garden.

The view which we have here is not beautiful in that free unconstrained sense in which nature presents her loveliest forms. Its value rests upon the high degree of cultivation in its exact reproduction of what was at one period held for beauty. The period of which we speak is embodied in the names of the later Bourbons. The kings of the Maintenons, the Pompadours, and the DuBarrys were the patterns of royal taste; the castles of the nobles grew up everywhere in the form which prevailed at Versailles. Not only the dumb senseless stone was subject to this constraint, but also living, blooming Nature, which vainly resisted the power of human hands. Gardens in the style of Louis XIV. were added to the castles, and such a garden do we see here.

It covers an area of nearly two hundred acres. On reaching the dazzling white wing of the building we look through the arched gateway and see before us a flat surface on which not a single mound relieves the monotonous level. The stiff geometric treatment is repeated also in the long lime avenues, and in their running fountains and gray statues.

We enter and walk slowly onward along the gravelled paths. All around us we see large flat flowerbeds with thousands of fragrant buds crowded together in one heap, the whole having the effect of a variegated nosegay on a huge table. Above the water in the stone basins rise dolphins and dragons, of damp stone or dark metal, bearing upon their backs gay cupids. Then the path branches out on both sides on to the turf, and thick avenues open right and left; the ivy clings round those trees which have been allowed to grow wild.

There is something almost mysterious and world-forgotten in these deep shadows. The stone figures which we meet with share this characteristic, and acquire a mystical significance. Old Pan looks down from a high rock, the water drips and trickles in the stony grotto, the fir boughs whisper to each other— it seems almost as if we might hear the sound of the instrument which the god holds to his lips, or see the forms which the music from his pipe attracts, or meet a nymph rising from her bath and looping together the tresses of her streaming hair. Such images are inexhaustible on our way through the park and garden. We meet with temples and " ruins," artistic bridges and lakes.

In all this place there seems to be but one thing wanting, namely, the human beings who once took pleasure in these splendors. All these stone memorials, these flowers, this turf, look as though they stood upon a huge immeasurable grave, beneath which sleeps a vanished century.

CHAPTER XV.

THE BERGSTRASSE AND THE ODENWALD.

THE country between Heidelberg and Darmstadt is covered for miles with thick forest. Beneath the lofty branches the lurking deer finds shelter, and within its rocky walls many olden glories have decayed. The objects in the landscape here do not raise before us anything of historic importance, nor as we gaze upon them can we picture to ourselves that we stand before a theatre of stirring deeds—it is simply a national pleasure-place.

On our road a slightly-built lad passes us, and gives us a pleasant greeting; the girls who sit at the cottage-doors we notice wear black coifs over their fair plaits, and unconsciously the old song rings in our ears:

> "There stands a tree in the Odenwald
> With many a bough so green,
> 'Neath which my own true love and I
> A thousand joys have seen."

Yes, we are wandering through the Odenwald, a district covering more than forty miles, which is bounded on the south by the Neckar, and descends on the west in a long, sharply-defined line towards the broad plain of the Rhine. In primitive times, the great high-road called *Platea Montana* passed through here, and we still find the lovely green tract which is now known as the Bergstrasse or mountain-road.

Right and left of us appear charming little towns and snug villages full of original architecture. The air is soft and the soil fruitful; but, besides this abundance of the earth and the tranquillity of the people, there remains something which is indescribable, namely, the charm of poetry. Even the railway, which rushes close to the slope of the wood, has not been able quite to destroy the charm. It is still the old Odenwald with its green branches, its powerful forms, and its sweet melancholy song.

Such being the state of this beautiful tract of country, we care but little whether the place took its name originally from the silent solitude (*Oede*) which in olden times must have hung over these woods, or whether the memory of old Odin is preserved in its title. We only now seek and are satisfied with enjoying the dusky verdure offered by the boughs, and the beauty which smiles upon us from the hills.

The most celebrated among the latter is that one the summit of which bears the somewhat curious name of Melibocus, the highest point of the Bergstrasse. The way to it leads through lofty beech woods, on emerging from which we see a great tower with open battlements, and under its shadow we gaze over a broad expense of country unfolding itself before our eyes. At our feet hamlets and villages lie among rustling woods.

Among them are Alsbach, the little town of Zwingenberg, and many others. Beyond these come wooded hills, the serene Taunus and the rugged Spessart, which stretch far away in pleasant undulating forms. The Schwarzwald are darkly indicated in the distance, and farther away still are the blue Vosges almost hidden in the haze of the horizon. Between them lies the broad plain of the Rhine, and out of it rise majestically the old cities with their towers and churches whose names are the pillars of German history, Speyer, Worms, and Mayence the Golden! Let us rest here in the green shade and think over the memories of times long gone by, from the doings of the wild race of the Chatti who once dwelt here to the days when the German army passed over the Vosges yonder.

A picturesque road leads from Melibocus to the Felsberg; a lonely forester's house opens its hospitable doors to us, and when we have taken a short rest we make our way to the "Felsenmeer." Long before the end we seek is in view the path to it has something mysterious and ghostlike which suggests the old pagan times. On every side are shattered rocks overgrown with damp moss, and only now and then do we catch a glimpse of the blue sky through the lofty beech-trees. Nature alone is dominant here.

But all at once a huge square block of stone lies before us. This is not the work of Nature, human hands have evidently been at work here thousands of years ago; though the secret of the race and period to which it belonged is not yet solved. We proceed, and penetrate still farther into the forest, when our steps are again suddenly arrested by a gigantic pillar, almost grown into the earth. This also must have been formed on the spot out of the rock. The open forest was the workshop in which it was fashioned—but who was its master, and what was its purpose? Was it destined for one of the old pagan gods which were so soon laid low by Christian swords; was it part of a palace of a Roman prefect, or did Charlemagne have it fashioned for his palace at Ingelheim? Who can tell? The powers of those who made it were either exhausted in the work, or they were scared away by new times which brought other rulers and other altars. Be this as it may, they left behind them the uncompleted pillar in its original place, the forest. The luxuriant foliage soon spread its protective shelter over it, and time cast round it the veil of mystery till a new race arose who found it out and in vain attempted to solve the problem of its history as they stood before the silent stone.

Not far from this is the " Felsenmeer," or Rock Sea, a huge plain in the midst of the forest which seems to be strewn over with shattered rock—"fragments whose origin is not more enigmatical than their appearance is remarkable." How may the spirit of the people have animated these places in the Dark Ages when proud nobles lived up here in their castles, and the enslaved peasants existed in the villages below!

The Odenwald, like all forest districts, is rich in legends, and the groundwork of all these myths seems to be the noises and the doings of imaginary and invisible wild animals. Not far from the Felsberg itself, which we have just reached, lies Schnellert and the stronghold of Rodenstein; at the foot of the latter there used to stand a primitive farm-house, and the owner was acquainted with all the dark secrets of the mountains; he told us the tale of the Wild Huntsman.

Centuries ago the castle was occupied by the Lord of Rodenstein, a champion of the German fatherland; one who swore to fight for his country against all foes and to love it forever.

Wishing to give his whole life to his country, he refused to marry, and lived in his castle quite alone; so there was no one to mourn for him when one day he vanished and failed to reappear.

It was reported that he had been killed in battle, but the peasants insist that he did not die, but withdrew into the vaults of the castle, only to reappear when danger threatens his beloved fatherland. They declare that whenever a war has broken out a tramp of mailed steeds is heard in the ruins, and at nightfall a shadowy army, led by the Lord of Rodenstein,

is seen sweeping across the sky in the direction from
which the danger comes.   As peace is proclaimed the
ghostly band returns to Rodenstein, and re-enters the
castle, singing a hymn of victory, there to lie quiet
until another danger urges them forth to the defense
of their country.

But the peasant has yet another tale.   He tells us
that the Lord of Rodenstein and his ghostly band are
not the only tenants of the castle.   Deep down below the walls there is another sleeper—the Emperor
Frederic Barbarossa.   He sits motionless in front of
a huge marble table, around which his fiery beard
has twined itself, patiently waiting for the time when
his country will have need of him.

The Emperor's slumbers are broken only once in
a hundred years, when he bids his page go up to the
mountain and see if the ravens are still circling overhead.

> "O, dwarf, go up this hour
> And see if still the ravens
> Are flying round the tower.
> And if the ancient ravens
> Still wheel above me here,
> Then must I sleep enchanted
> For many a hundred year."

The page returns and reports that the ravens are
still flying, and Barbarossa, sighing because the time
of his release has not yet come, sinks again into the
slumber which must last another century.

But when the red beard shall have twined itself

for the third time around the marble table the trumpet *must* sound, and the Emperor, rising from his enchanted sleep, will hang his shield on a withered peartree, which will burst into bloom at his touch; while the Germans will gather once more about their old Emperor, and the fatherland will be free forevermore!

> "In some dark day when Germany
>   Hath need of warriors such as he,
>   A voice to tell of her distress
>   Shall pierce the mountain's deep recess—
>   Shall ring through the dim vaults and scare
>   The spectral ravens round his chair,
>   And from his trance the sleeper wake.
>   The solid mountain shall dispart,
>   The granite slab in splinters start
>   (Responsive to those accents weird)
>   And loose the Kaiser's shaggy beard.
>   Through all the startled air shall rise
>   The old Teutonic battle-cries;
>   The horns of war, that once could stir
>   The wild blood of the Berserker,
>   Shall fling their blare abroad, and then
>   The champion of his own Almain,
>   Shall Barbarossa come again!"

The castle which stood on the summit of Schnellert was built in an unusual manner. It presented a hexagon, of which each side measured sixty feet; within this came a strong wall, a deep ditch, and another stone wall. But the walls have all fallen to pieces centuries ago.

Amongst the ruins, it is said, there once dwelt three sisters, who were doomed to live there by some fatal enchantment, and they were guarded by a wild huntsman in the form of a black dog. They often prayed for release; and one day the most beautiful of them appeared to a young acquaintance and told him that she would come to him in the form of a snake and kiss him three times; if he remained brave and steadfast it would remove the curse, and she would give him her love and all her wealth. When the slimy serpent appeared on the following day, and coming towards him darting her forked tongue, wound herself in thick coils around his body, his heart failed him, he staggered back, and from his lips escaped the cry, "Lord, help me!" The snake vanished, and with it the lady's love and her gold.

Of the other castles in the neighborhood, Schön-berg and Heiligenberg are remarkable in an historical sense, but without doubt the castle of Auerbach is the most noteworthy. There still remains, even in the ruins of this colossal building, something of that mighty power which formerly held dominion here; for fire and sword have not been able entirely to destroy these massive towers and battlements.

The origin of the stronghold takes us back to the time when the Carlovingian kings were its masters, before it occurred to the spiritual power to take possession of the lordly castle. The next banner planted on these walls was that of the princely abbey of Lorsch, one of the oldest in the whole empire; then came the Archbishop of Mayence, the chancellor of

Neckarsteinach.

the empire and Prince-Palatine, and later the lesser nobility.

How often the waves of battle have surged against these walls! But the fortress held out bravely and faithfully, till it surrendered to the treachery of the mercenaries of Louis XIV. in 1674. The man who reduced the noble castle to ruins was Marshal Turenne, the leader of that war from whose wounds the Rhine has not yet wholly recovered.

If we descend from the hills into the valley, we soon find in the place of the lonely forest depths active, cheerful movements, for the Rhenish character even here affects the disposition and the whole nature of the inhabitants. Every one we converse with gives us friendly and cheerful answers, we constantly hear the rushing of the mill-stream and the merry whirl of the wheel, and here and there we come upon little houses leaning against the rock wall, with the blue smoke rising from their chimneys straight into the air.

At the mouth of the Stettbacher Valley, immediately under the Heiligenberg, lies the smiling little village of Jungenheim, the name of which is widely known, even as far as the Ural and the Volga, for the cheerful little village in the Odenwald was a favorite resort of the mighty Czar. This imperial patronage attracted many strangers to the village, and now handsome villas have sprung up among the thick beechwood, so that Jungenheim has rapidly become a favorite and fashionable resort. The pleasant habits of the people in showing kindness to strangers considerably helps to attain this end.

Hitherto Odenwald has offered us little except idyllic pictures, though we must not forget the attractive little towns which are situated along the Bergstrasse. They, indeed, are almost idyls themselves—which is no detraction from their merits. The first we meet with on the road from Heidelberg to Darmstadt is the old town of Ladenburg, the *Lupodunum* of the Romans, who established here one of the most important of their settlements on the Upper Rhine. The ruins of a Roman bath and other remains bear witness to the period.

The position of Ladenburg was no less important in the Middle Ages, when it was the capital of the district named Lobdengaus, a territory first in the possession of the French king and afterwards in that of the Bishops of Worms. It was in the name of the town that the Counts of Lobdengaus held to the so-called " Stahlbühel " and the Gedinge or public tribunal.

In the twelfth century the Bishops of Worms, having been driven out of the episcopal city by an insurrection of the citizens, took up their residence in Ladenburg and kept up a brilliant court there. The street called Saalgasse recalls the palace of its former protectors, the Frankish kings, for the royal palace here, as elsewhere, was called the Saal or Hall. The church, which is very old, contains monuments of the Barons Metternich and Sickingen.

A convent which was built by the Barons von Sickingen is still standing, and is said to have had the following origin: A young lady of the family once lost her way in the neighboring forest and wandered about until quite late at night, when she was guided home by the sound of the church bells of St. Gallus. The grateful family founded the convent, in order that the bell should sound every night at eleven o'clock, and that every week two measures of corn should be baked into bread and distributed to the poor. A similar story is met with in other places.

The Church of St. Gallus above referred to is said to have been founded by King Dagobert. In the history of Ladenburg, which is rich in sieges, we meet constantly with traces of Lorsch, that renowned mighty abbey which was a sort of magnet for all the property in the neighborhood. The Spanish, the French, and the Swedes lay before these gates during the Thirty Years' War; but now that the times have grown more peaceful, the fragrant trees, whose valuable fruit is celebrated throughout Germany, bloom undisturbed.

Continuing our road a little farther, we come to Weinheim, which reminds us of what Karl Simrock says in his "Picturesque and Romantic Rhineland:" "He who always sits in the railway carriage must not boast of having seen the Bergstrasse. He must

take a carriage of his own, and must, at least, get
out at Weinheim in order to pay a visit to the old
Windeck. Standing near the slender tower, over the
stables supported by pillars he must have looked down
into the moist valley of Gorxheimer, where the Wech-
nitz runs through beech-grown meadows, and have
raised his eager eyes to the light-blue distance of the
Odenwald, which opens right and left before him.

"On the Hessian frontier, at Unterlandenbach, which
yields the most renowned wine of the Bergstrasse,
he must have looked well before him and behind him,
and on either side of him, for here the mountain-
chain describes a semicircle, and the Oelberg at
Schrieszheim comes into view with its beautiful combinations of form. Nowhere else does Melibocus,
the king of the Bergstrasse, appear in such sublime
majesty. At Heppenheim he must have visited
either the ruins of Starkenburg, from which the
whole province is named, or the neighboring town
of Lorsch, to which not only the Bergstrasse but the
whole country round is indebted for its culture and
and its old historical traditions.

" He should have skimmed through a few chapters
of the history of the country, and have learnt at
least enough to know that Starkenburg was built by
the monks and vassals of Lorsch in 1064, in order
to preserve for their abbot Ulrich the possession of
the wealthy abbey, which the Emperor Henry IV.
had given away to his favorite the Archbishop Adel-

bert of Bremen; he must know also that if Lorsch was founded early, it also degenerated early, so that Pope and Emperor gave it over to the Archbishopric of Mayence for the reformation of its discipline, and, if necessary, for its complete incorporation—a step by which Mayence drew down upon itself the war with the Palatinate.

"He must, at least, have paid a visit to Auerbach in order to try to release the Meadow Maiden, for who knows whether the cradle wherein he was rocked might not be woven from the twigs of the tree on which her deliverance depends; for this youth who is to win her must have been rocked in a cradle made of the twigs of a cherry-tree beneath whose shade she had been wont to linger. If he fails, the Meadow Maiden must wearily wait once more until a cherry-tree has grown in the meadow and a cradle has been made out of its twigs, for she can only be set free by a child who has first been laid in that cradle.

"He must have visited Zwingenberg and Melibocus, —yes, even to the far-shining tower that adorns its summit, and marks the highest point of the mountain-chain. When he has done all this, then he will feel himself monarch of the Odenwald and of the vast Rhineland at his feet."

After leaving Heppenheim we come to Bensheim —and, in passing, we may remark that on the Bergstrasse all the names end in *bach* or *heim*.

Many of the finest examples of architecture in

Bensheim were destroyed in the frightful conflagration of 1822, but we still find towers and gables, galleries and gateways, which will bear comparison with the original buildings of the Schwarzwald. Bensheim is also closely connected with the traditions of the old abbey of Lorsch, which is situated hardly four miles from it. In the highly-decorated little chapel there Louis the German and his son found their last resting-place; and Pope Leo IX. laid his hands in benediction on the grave which the people held sacred, in spite of the lawlessness of the time.

Poetry and legend twine their golden threads around these spots, which have become associated even with the song of the Nibelungen. It is to Lorsch that Chriemhild brings the body of the noble Sigfried, and the verses of that great poem lament in telling lines how the " bold hero lay in his long coffin " before the Minster.

We wander on past the ancient town of Zwingenberg, past Seeheim and Eberstadt to Bessungen. At Bessungen we leave the forest, which up to this time has been on our right, and we turn out of the celebrated road bordered with fine fruit-trees, which has led from Heidelberg hither. The associations also which have accompanied us now grow faint, the country becomes flatter, and the moral atmosphere which surrounds us is more modern. Our gaze no longer rests upon green summits and fallen citadels, but on the varied bustling life of the present day.

We are in Darmstadt, the capital of the beautiful country of Hesse.

We see here the same contrasts which meet our eyes in nearly all towns which have succumbed to modern ideas of progress. The interior, the kernel of the town, is still built in the old style which drew all the houses and streets as closely together as possible; but the new town which presses out beyond the walls and the gates requires vast dimensions, the roads are broad and straight, and the houses high and handsome. The genius of the present rules here, though in but few towns is this principle of extension older than a few decades.

The Grand-Duke Louis I., who died in 1830, is the prince to whom Darmstadt owes its growth. His monument consequently very properly stands in the centre of the modern quarter. Art lent its consecrating grace to the affection which erected this memorial, for the figure, which stands upon a lofty pedestal, was fashioned by no less masterly a hand than that of Schwanthaler.

The palace where the Grand-Dukes of Darmstadt reside is called the Castle. It was begun by the old Landgraves of Hesse, and every century since has added something to it, according to its own taste. The most important part is, without doubt, that wing which belongs to the first ten years of the last century, and was finished by French hands. Its fine façade looks down on to the market-place, and it contains the

noblest treasures of art and science which the country
possesses. The value of the picture gallery, of the
antiquities, and of the other collections is well known.
The theatre enjoys an honorable reputation throughout Germany, and is constantly patronized by the
reigning Grand-Duke, who in this respect follows the
example of his predecessors. In short, the little
capital well knows how to detain the strangers whom
the beautiful scenes of nature in its neighborhood have
attracted to it.

CHAPTER XVI.

WORMS.

THE whole of the road over which we have just passed runs along the right bank of the Rhine, and the green forest was so enticing that it drew us far into the cool shadow of its branches. But this is the last time that such leafy companions accompany us in our course along the great river. We now return to the bank in the broad plain through which it flows, and to which it has carried fertility and prosperity for thousands of years. The town element naturally predominates again here, and the first of the great cities which we meet with on the left bank is Worms.

Worms is not beautiful in that ordinary sense which considers only attractive colors and attractive forms. There is another kind of beauty, however, which is grave and self-contained, and almost disdains to be criticized by every passing gaze. Such is the beauty which is peculiar to the places in this part of the country, and to the environs of the ancient town of Worms.

The landscape is flat, the colors are subdued, and the Rhine flows calmly, but strongly, between the meadows. Thick willow-bushes stand on both sides of the river, where a deserted bed is separated from it by a wide sandbank, on which now and then a heron may be seen. Nothing interferes with the broad expanse of sky which offers free play to the sailing clouds, while the spires of the cathedral in the distance rise in silent majesty. We shall at once feel, as we look on the scene before us with observant senses, the inner meaning, the historical character of this landscape. The spirit which animates it is one of calm energetic power, that characteristic which demands great and historical figures for its consummation.

Worms is one of the most ancient of the cities of the Rhenish provinces. The Rabbi of Tudela refers to it as the primeval abode of emigrant Israelites. A legend is connected with this ancient Jewish colony which tells how, when better days had come, and they were summoned back to Jerusalem by the high-priest, they were loath to go, and lingered in the blessed land of the green Rhine, saying, in reply to the call: " We live in the promised land ; Worms is our Jerusalem, our Synagogue, our Temple !"

They felt justified in giving this reply by the circumstance that when they were driven forth from the Holy City they carried with them some of the consecrated soil, and intermixed it with the earth of their burying-ground, and with the soil in which the foundation of their new Synagogue was laid. So this became to them the land of promise, where they prayed and where their bones were finally laid to rest.

It is a well-known fact that in the persecutions of the Middle Ages the Jews of Worms were often spared when other colonies were persecuted. This was owing to the fact that the members of the Synagogue at Worms spread the report—incredible as it may seem to us—that when the Saviour was about to be crucified, and the other Jewish communities of the world had assented to it, the Worms Synagogue alone withheld its consent!

Another explanation of how the Jews came to Worms is given in the family chronicle of the Dalberg family, whom we find mentioned in old deeds as "Chamberlains of Worms." The chronicle relates how their primitive ancestor was a "cousin of the Virgin Mary and, at the same time, a centurion in the twenty-second Roman Legion."

He, when this Legion was stationed on the Rhine, brought Jews with him to Worms from Jerusalem after its capture and destruction by Titus—and, indeed, in the capacity of slaves; then, with true Christian magnanimity, he gave them their freedom, and by them the Synagogue was founded.

It was in the old fallen Camba here that the German princes used to assemble to choose a king, and it was also in the same place that the quarrel between the two Conrads was ended:

> "And as the throng stood waiting all around,
>   And the great hum of men was so allayed
>   That the Rhine's quiet flow could be observed,

> They saw how suddenly the two great knights
> Grasped one another's hands with hearty grip,
> While cheeks and lips met with a brother's kiss.
> Then did they know no jealousy remained,
> And each to other willingly gave place."

Thus may be rendered the description given by Uhland, in his "Duke Ernest of Swabia," of the election of a king in the year 1024. Concord having gained the day, the princely train and the rejoicing people proceeded to Mayence for the coronation.

All these are pictures of events which have long since passed away, but the landscape, the ground on which they were enacted, still lives, and the actors in them re-awake for him who looks deeply into the features of the place. Such a one hears still the noisy hum of the people, and sees the gigantic form of the mighty king towering over the shoulders of the rest. This force of historical association, this invisible reanimation of historical figures in a certain spot, is the sign of an historical landscape.

In Worms we can dispense with that which is, but no one would willingly be without the stirring thoughts of what has been. Here is the spot where the great Cæsar once stood ; it was here that Attila, the gloomy hero of devastation, drove his cavalry across the Rhine. Before the Cathedral of Worms we are inflamed by the quarrel of the two queens Brunhild and Chriemhilda, and it was over this same Cathedral

that that mighty cloud arose whose lightning gleams
for ever for us in the song of the "Nibelungen."
Indeed, the southern side of the Cathedral is richly
decorated with statues of the fourteenth century,
representing the characters of the Nibelungenlied.

The Cathedral is still the greatest of all the monuments of the city; it is one of those splendid stone
giants which the church has stationed along the Rhine
as guardians of its power. There is apparent throughout the building, with its round towers and pinnacles,
a sort of defensive character; the stately edifice presents itself to us as it were fully armed. The entire
style is Romanesque. The ground-plan is that of a
Roman basilica, but enriched with every decoration
which a creative lavish period possessed. The unity
of the whole is nowhere destroyed by an inconsist-
ency.

"Being built in the early years of the ninth century," says Simrock, "it is one of the oldest and
finest monuments of the rounded arch style. From
the eastern choir, and the northern side of the nave,
hideous masks and grim beasts look down on us,
the production of dark paganism which the Christian church of the eleventh century had not yet been
able completely to get rid of or suppress. The western choir shows somewhat later forms, and a tran-
sition to the pointed arch. This is explained by a
necessity having arisen in the fifteenth century for
the rebuilding of the one western tower. But a west-

ern choir hardly lay within the plan of the first architect. According to fixed law, the principal entrance should have stood opposite the eastern choir. The present beautiful entrance on the south side, which is pure Gothic, must have been added three hundred years later."

These rough walls look down on us, mighty as the times from which they sprang, and the impression they make is not weakened when we step with muffled tread within the sacred walls. There are the stone tombs of the old ecclesiastical princes of Worms, and over the altars pictures with golden backgrounds. In one of the chapels is the great stone font, and in another the last resting-place of queens. We stand within the magic circle of a masterpiece, and our consciousness tells us at every step we take that the air we are breathing is historical.

How many assemblies, imperial diets, and other councils weighty with the fate of Germany, have been held within reach of these walls! In the year 772 war was declared here against the Saxons. In 1122, at an imperial diet here, a treaty was made between the Emperor Henry V. and Pope Calixtus II. respecting the investiture of the bishops with sceptre, ring, and staff.

In the year 1495 a great diet was held, under Maximilian I., at which club-law was abolished and public peace established. Later still came that most famous diet,—the Diet of Worms—when a bold, determined man, the "world-shaking monk of Wittenberg," stood before the walls of the sacred old Minster, and tore that great cleft in the globe which divides two eras, and created those two spiritual hemispheres into which the world is divided—"Here I stand, I cannot do otherwise. God help me!" Such was the effect of these words that men wept, men who scarcely knew what a tear was, and paved the way for the Gospel.

The legend of the Luther-tree at Worms dates from these days. It is a huge cork-elm, which has been noted for centuries. As Luther, seated in an open carriage, neared the town he was surrounded by the townspeople and nobles, who had come out to meet him.

Near the carriage rode the knightly Captain von Frundsberg, talking to the honored guest. As they neared the city gates he said: "Little monk, dost thou verily believe that thy teaching will prevail?" Luther pointed to a weak sapling of cork-elm which grew by the road-side, and filled with exultation and trust in God, answered: "Yea, Sir Knight, so truly as yonder sapling may become a mighty tree and vie in height with the towers of the city!"

And the mighty cork-elm which withstood the storms of centuries is the Luther-tree of Worms.

But the period when Worms was the centre of historical events, when the mighty Charles V. and all the princes came into the imperial city, is long since past; and deep degradation has followed the days of prosperity. The Thirty Years' War visited it with desolation, but in the marauding wars of Louis XIV. it was not only desolated but destroyed. When the regiments of the enemy had lain long enough within these walls, the citizens were informed that it was the will of "the most Christian king" that Worms should be burned to the ground. Only a short respite was granted them, and then the consuming flames mounted towards heaven. It was a gigantic struggle between the two great elements. The earth and its stone would not yield, and the restless flames would not quench themselves till they had destroyed the last house.

At that time Worms was populous and powerful, as became an old imperial town. A double wall ran round the city; it had seven gates, and the Rhine tower was so strong that thirty mines had to be laid under it before it could be overthrown. Piece by piece the old magnificence fell into ashes, and while the people outside were wringing their hands, the town was levelled with the ground on which it had stood.

All was dead and silent: only the walls of the Cathedral remained amid this burnt wilderness. Every human possession perished: God only had preserved His house!

Men built again; walls can be replaced, but no future race can supply the spirit of the great past, that was destroyed with the ancient battlements. A quiet, dull time began ; grass grew in the streets, and the new race grew up depressed and weary. The population hardly numbered a third of what it had once been ; and they lived on the remembrances of the past more than on any belief in a great future.

This meaningless and objectless life lasted for some time, and even in the middle of the last century a chronicler tells of the many "barren places and wastes" which were to be found in the interior of the town. Even as late as 1840, Victor Hugo calls Worms "une ville qui meurt," and depicts, with gloomy eloquence, the impression of agony which he had received when visiting it.

In our own days, life has all at once re-appeared. It is not the old powers which have awakened after long slumber, but the spirit of the present, the modern ideas, which on being circulated through the old petrified limbs, has brought into existence thousands of busy arms who fill the great factories and thousands of laden wagons which fly over the railroads, up and down the Rhine as far as Holland.

In the Luther-Platz we see an imposing monument to the great Reformer, erected in 1868. A bronze statue of Luther stands high on a pedestal, surrounded, lower down, by the four precursors of the Reformation, Savonarola, Huss, Wycliffe, and Petrus Waldus. Lower still are allegorical figures of the towns, Magdeburg (mourning), Augsburg (making confession), and Speyer (protesting). Between these are the arms of the twenty-four German towns which first embraced the Reformed faith.

We enter a handsome house on the Lindenplatz; green vines clamber over the porch, and within there reigns that cheerful hospitality which is the prerogative of the Rhine. Everything is comfortable and handsome. The father sits in his broad arm-chair at the table and tells of the old times; the amiable smile which now and then flits over his countenance evidently comes from his heart. He gazes on his beloved and ever-cheerful wife with as much pleasure and affection as he did five-and-twenty years ago. A thousand recollections are revived for the youthful guest, while the golden wine, which is found only at Worms, sparkles in the great green glasses.

In the background there moves the sweet daughter of the house, quietly occupied with the business of the table; prudent and lovable she is as Elsie in the fairy-tale, and as every true child of the beautiful old city ever has been. She understands her work thoroughly, and still remains always modest. Her brown hair droops over her smiling face, and she performs the duties of the house unknown and unembarrassed, so that in watching her we do not wonder that the district in which Worms is situated was once, in the splendid days of old, named Wonnegau, or "the district of delight."

Worms appears to us in more than one respect to

be the first town on the Rhine which exhibits purely Rhenish life. This characteristic of the inhabitants seems to us to increase as we go farther down the river, until we reach Cologne. And this life is not wanting in that lovely characteristic of female beauty: pure amiability and pure modesty meet us here. There is a complete world of local customs, ideas, even of names; and in every heart there flows Rhenish blood. We recall with gratitude the hospitable day we spent in Worms, in the powerful old imperial city of the past, in the quiet city of to-day.

We meet with no large town between Worms and Mayence, for which reason the country is all the more rich and blooming. It is covered with fruitful vineyards, and is full of that gladness which seems to be inseparable from the vine. Such is the picture upon which we gaze as we glide down the blue stream. In the midst of this smiling country we are free from all the sadness which is, more or less, always associated with the walls of towns, and from all those fierce struggles whose gloomy memories make the Rhine the stream of history.

We first stop in Oppenheim, and here we recognize once more the signs of stormy days gone by, for above the expanse of vine gardens there stands a bold and commanding stronghold. This, in its time, has seen many an Emperor within its chambers, and many an enemy within its walls, for it was an imperial fortress, and was worthy of the proud name which described it as the " crown of the country."

The little town which crouches at its feet is much older, and was built upon the ruins of what is supposed to have been a Roman settlement. Though unpretending and modest, it once possessed the finest church which the Gothic style ever created in Germany, and it required all the vandalism of the war of the Palatinate to give up this masterpiece as a prey to the flames. More than half of the renowned Church of St. Catherine was destroyed in 1689, but in 1878–89 it was entirely restored from the designs of the late architect Schmidt, of Vienna. Not only is it a monument of faith, but we feel that the grandeur of ancient times and the history of past races lie covered by its stones. We feel this deeply when, walking quietly along its aisles, we come upon the great names which are written on these tombs. They are not names of individuals only, but they bring before us whole pages of history. The corner-stone of St. Catherine's is said to have been laid with great pomp and rejoicing in 1262 by King Richard.

Outside, in the quiet churchyard which surrounds the building, rest thousands whose names and fate are known to none; and, according to ancient custom, a charnel-house has been built in which are collected the skulls that have been dug up from time to time. What horror would thrill through us at the picture, if while staring through the grating at these bleached bones, the thoughts which once beat beneath these brows were suddenly to become embodied —thoughts which were untold, unfulfilled, and lost for ever!

Even here we find traces of war, which several times visited the cheerful little town, for many of the bleached heads are splintered at the temple and bear the mark of a bullet. Who has sent him to his death? was it a Swedish knight, who lay before the town during the Thirty Years' War, a mercenary of the French army which Turenne brought to the Rhine, or a Spaniard from the Basque Mountains?

But who thinks now of such forgotten woes? On the hills that once drank in the blood of warriors, the vines are waving and the clear wine sparkles in the green ringing glass. It is here that we first meet with the name of "Rhine wine," and all that lies yonder towards the Pfalz belongs no longer to the map, but to the wine chart. "Niersteiner" and the wine of Laubheim and Bodenheim have attained, far and wide, a well-deserved reputation, and with them we will fill our beaker to the brim while the boat bears us over the blue Rhine to Mayence. Already we see the Cathedral towering over the broad roofs of the city, and seem to hear the sound of the church bells of the old royal city on the Rhine. So we once more fill our glass in honor of "Mayence the Golden!"

CHAPTER XVII.

MAYENCE THE GOLDEN.

Now let us continue our way along the " Priestly Highway of the German Empire," as it has been called from the number and the celebrity of the ecclesiastical sees which we shall pass. We are now at " Mayence the Golden," and we shall go as far as " Cologne the Holy," along the lovely banks with which God has blessed the great German river.

This town, so often sadly memorable in history, and yet so indestructible, was once situated farther up on the softly-sloping hills. In the course of time it has sunk down to the river-banks. It has also sunk from the height of its classic origin, when the Romans built their stone bridges here, and made a yoke for our German forefathers ; and also it has descended from its ecclesiastical height, when the bishops turned the crozier into a temporal sceptre. But in spite of all, though power and wealth have been lost under a thousand calamities, it still remains " the Golden."

The inhabitants of Mayence have also preserved their character for pleasantness and good humor, and wherever the traveller wanders in this romantic val-

Marketplace, Mayence.

PFARRER.
LOEWEN-APOTHEKE
Jos. Strohschneider
MANUFACTURWAREN
HANDLUNG

ley, up stream or down, along the fine silver surface
as far as the Mouse Tower, he finds the men of Mayence to be "Father Rhine's" happiest and pleasantest children.

The situation of Mayence, if not the most beautiful, is at all events most open and pleasant. From
the heights of the Kästrich or the "Anlagen" (at
the feet of which is the handsome railway bridge),
the eye sweeps over the river Maine and over
the many-tinted spurs of the Odenwald and the
Taunus.

The airy fragrant heights of Hochheim and its
vineyards overlook the confluence of the Maine and
the Rhine, and from the high bank on the other side
rise the massive contours of the red-brick Backstein
barracks, now the Prussian cadet school of Bibrich.
The little local steamers pass briskly backwards and
forwards past the low island; the tugs of the Rhine
Boat Company go panting through the clear waters
at the head of a whole flotilla; the express boats
move majestically along, like the traditional stately
swan—in the style of the Mississippi floating palaces;
and between the steaming passenger-boats filled with
people the Rhine stream flows lazily on.

On the other side we see dimly rising out of the
mist of the horizon, or shining in a direct ray of the
sun, the faint outline of the Platte, the hunting castle
of the Duke of Nassau; the white temple of Neroberg, like a great forest mushroom; and the gilded

pinnacles of the Byzantine Greek chapel shining between the trees.

Farther down the stream we see the Niederwald springing high above the terraces of Rudesheim. It is still of the same capricious yet soft gradations of stone color, and forms a kind of gate to a bend in the Rhine, shutting it in so as to open out an entirely new panorama on the other side.

If the sunlight is favorable the observer may see from the hills of Mayence a little piece of the pearly track of the Rheingau spread in the fragrant little Eden, where God has so favored men that He has caused the seltzer spring to issue from the earth close to the vineyards. Here everything sings " Glory to God in the highest "—the crosses and crucifixes between the vine gardens, the juicy golden grapes, the swelling chestnut-tree, the villas and cottages scattered among the dark-green foliage, the little town which bathes its feet in the sparkling river, and, finally, the glad and grateful hearts of men.

But beautiful as the scenery is all round us, history has harshly visited this part of the Rhine Valley, particularly the left bank, and Mayence especially has felt its heavy hand.

The origin of the first warlike disturbances are lost among childish legends. It is said that there lived in Trier, fourteen years before the Christian era, a sorcerer named Nequam, whom the people of Trier drove out of their town on account of his evil arts.

Nequam swore to be revenged on them by building another town, and he came to the place on which Mayence now stands, and raised a town out of the earth by magic.

Another legend ascribes the building of the city to a fugitive from the siege of Troy named Moguntius. This might, perhaps, account for the name of the town, but the authority is hardly to be relied on. Authentic history begins with the fortified Roman station which stood here, and although it seems unlikely that no German settlement should have been formed before that time in so particularly favorable a situation at the confluence of two great rivers, yet absolutely no trace of any such previous settlement is to be found.

The two great epochs of Mayence were the Roman period and the ecclesiastical period. The stone annals which yet remain tell us of both of these epochs. The oldest of them informs us that Agrippina caused a fortified winter camp to be formed at Moguntiacum in the year 38 B.C., and Caius Sertorius was at that time named *Curator civium romanorum Mog.*

The real fortifier of the place appears to have been Caius Drusus, who, in 14 B.C., also built a camp on the other side of the river at Castellum—the present Castel—and erected a stone bridge across the Rhine in order to enable his legions the more conveniently to cross over to their German families who dwelt in the woods.

We are reminded of him at the present day by the "Eichelstein," which stands above the "Anlagen," or gardens, and was once a handsome building erected for him by his legions, but is now a ruin, as are also the aqueduct which he made, and the Roman bridge, of which the stone pillars remain only to be used as anchoring-posts for the well-known floating water-mills, which may be seen here in some considerable numbers. The value of the culture which the Romans brought into the country is inestimable; when the twenty-second legion came, on their return from Jerusalem, they also brought Christianity and Bishop Crescentius with them; both were objects of hatred.

Crescentius is described in local history as a pupil of St. Peter. He is said to have suffered martyrdom in the reign of Trajan about 103 A.D. Mayence seems to have been one of the most Christian cities of the Roman Empire of that time; and Alexander Severus was murdered here by his soldiers for the new faith.

The prosperity of the town again declined until Rando fell upon it and mercilessly destroyed it and both its Roman and Christian inhabitants. After it was rebuilt, Mayence fell a prey to the Vandals and their allies on Christmas Eve of 406, and was totally destroyed by fire. Attila destroyed it again in 451, and it was only after the expulsion of the Romans in 622 that the permanent rebuilding was begun again under Theodobert and Dagobert.

Mayence was the seat of the East Frankish duchy. It was, however, not till the time of Charlemagne, when he built his palace in Lower Ingelheim and introduced the cultivation of the vine, and when St. Boniface became archbishop of Mayence, that the town rose to importance and was well known throughout Germany. This continued until 893, when the Emperor Arnulf conquered the town.

But from the time when the bishops, those pious servants of the church, constituted themselves counsellors of the German Emperor and temporal rulers, an endless period of dissension began which it would be impossible to relate fully here. Monasteries overran the country, and the church was dominant under the protection of the Pope.

A man like Bishop Hatto seemed a necessary result of the state of things, and he gave the world a specimen of the basest misuse of power in the cruelty which was imputed to him. Even the archbishop Willigis, a son of the house of Wagner, who was about the best of all the bishops, had the ambition to be chosen Elector, and introduced into the arms of the town the well-known wheel with the legend:

> " Willigis, Willigis,
>   Forget not this,
>   That thy father a wheelwright is!"

thus modestly denoting his origin.

The Cathedral, the Church of the Holy Virgin,

was commenced by Willigis, and under him harmony at length reigned among the citizens. This soon ended, however, under his successors, and Henry IV., the penitent of Canossa, set a limit to the power of the bishops and protected the constantly contested privileges of the citizens, until, in 1104, the Diet of Mayence declared him to have forfeited his throne.

During the life of Archbishop Ruthard—and apparently encouraged by him—the persecution and massacre of the Jews took place, the wealth of these people having long roused envy and vexation. The public pawning-houses, which were in the hands of the Italian Jews (whence the present name of "Lombards") did a large business. This brought great wealth to the owners of these establishments and the banking-houses, who provoked the anger of the people by the ostentatious display of their luxury. At last the smouldering fire broke out in massacre and spoliation ; and even the bishop himself shared the booty with the robbers—an act which he had to expiate by seven years' banishment to a Thuringian monastery.

It would, as we have already said, take us too long to follow the long succession of archbishops, with all the good and evil with which they are associated, and which culminated with Arnold, who was robbed, murdered, and horribly mutilated by the citizens, whom he called "dogs."

Before this, however, the lawlessness of the people and of the clergy had reached a critical height.

Frederick II. himself incited the people of Mayence against their archbishop Siegfried III., whom they drove out of the town. Siegfried collected an army and besieged Mayence, which was forced by hunger to open its gates. The citizens in revenge attacked him one night while asleep in his castle of Eltville, and forced him, with the knife at his breast, to sign a fresh charter. They sent him again into banishment, drove all the clergy out of the town, and determined to do without religion, so that for several years no religious services whatever were held. However, friendship with the archbishop was restored under Matthias; who, nevertheless, eventually died by poison.

Avarice and a marauding nature were usually the causes of the misfortunes of the archbishops, who but too often preferred making war or carrying on some lucrative trade, to concerning themselves about the spiritual welfare of the people.

In the year 1254 the citizen Arnold Walpoden, of Mayence, founded the League of Rhenish Towns. Mayence became the leader of this powerful association, and was soon strengthened by more than a hundred neighboring towns, from Basle on the south to Bremen on the north. Mayence, as the centre of the Rhenish towns, received the flattering name of "the Golden." About this time the Robber Knights became a menace to safety.

In the thirteenth and fourteenth centuries Mayence became the favorite resort of the Minnesänger, or Troubadours. In 1318 the most celebrated of them, Heinrich Fraunlob, the pious minstrel who sang the praises of the Holy Virgin and of female virtue, died here and was buried in the Cathedral.

In the year 1462, Adolf of Nassau took the town by treachery, plundered it, killed five hundred of its citizens, and deprived it of its civic freedom. In 1552 it fell into the hands of Albert of Brandenburg. Then came the Swedes, under Gustavus Adolphus, who laid under contribution the monasteries to which the clergy had fled. Later, in 1644, the town was occupied by the French, who left it in 1648, after the Treaty of Westphalia. They returned in 1792, under Custine, to whom Mayence surrendered through treachery and cowardice. It was retaken by the Prussians, under Kalkreuth, in 1793. The French again blockaded the fortress a year later, and it was recovered by the Austrian Marshal Clerfayt.

By the Treaty of Luneville, Mayence passed into the hands of the French in 1797, and remained in their possession until the fall of Napoleon. In 1814 the Vienna Congress gave the town, whose fortifications had gained greatly in importance during all these varied fortunes of war, to the Grand-Duke of Hesse. This duke held it as a fortress of the League until, in 1866, the League itself became a thing of the past.

Such are the main points in the history of the old

Electoral city—a continual struggle with conquerors and oppressors from without, and with priestly political supremacy from within.

None of the spirit of that old oppressive period remains among the present population, though traces of French character are still to be met with in the people of Mayence. French regiments, French fashions, the frivolity of the French colony so long established in the neighboring town of Coblentz, left behind much light blood in Mayence. It could not be expected that French nature and French *chic* should be readily eradicated, and the trace of it remains at the present day in the graceful women of Mayence.

It is difficult now to believe, when we meet the splendid religious processions in the streets, that there were many years during which no public worship was held ; though it is true that to-morrow we may meet in the very same street Prince Carnival and all his motley court.

With such a history as that indicated above, Mayence is necessarily rich in antiquities, and especially such as are of Roman origin. Much also that is interesting, belonging to a later period, has survived the destruction and calamities that have visited the town.

The Cathedral, the great work of Willigis, the best of the bishops, which was begun in 978, was six times destroyed or partially destroyed by fire, and in war it has seen wild hordes break into its interior. It was totally destroyed by fire in the year 1009, but was rebuilt, and had approached so near completion in 1024 that Conrad II. was able to be crowned there. In 1024, in 1137, and 1191 it was again a prey to the flames.

Gustavus Adolphus, on one occasion, even commanded it to be blown up. During the bombardment of the town in 1793 it again suffered by fire, and in 1813 it was turned into a French forage magazine. Modern times have done their best to restore and complete the beautiful church.

It does not lie within our province to act as cicerone; but we would rather refer our readers for all details to Heyl's book of "The Rhine Countries." We will only mention the numerous tombs and monuments in this Cathedral, and especially the marble tablet inscribed with the year 794, just at the entrance of the church. There is no doubt that this was the tomb of the beautiful Fastrada, the ardently-loved wife of Charlemagne. The monument is not at all destroyed, nor is the above-mentioned stone, which is the original one.

The objects of greatest interest are the chapter-house with the Chapel of St. Ægidius, and opposite it the bishop's throne and two rows of stalls; behind these are the cloisters and the garden. Among the monuments is a modern one to the minstrel Count Henry of Meissen, called Heinrich Frauenlob. According to the inscription, it was raised to the pious

The Cathedral from the Marketplace, Mayence.

songster by the women of Mayence, in the year 1842.
The sculpture on it is by Schwanthaler.

" In Mentz 'tis hushed and lonely, the streets are waste and drear,
  And none but forms of sorrow, clad in mourning garbs, appear ;
  And only from the steeple sounds the death-bell's sullen boom ;
  One street alone is crowded, and it leads but to the tomb.

" And as the echo from the tower grows faint and dies away,
  Unto the Minster comes a still and sorrowful array,—
  The old man and the young, the child, and many a maiden fair ;
  And every eye is dim with tears, in every heart is care.

"Six virgins in the centre bear a coffin and a bier,
  And to the rich high-altar steps with deadened chant draw near,
  Where all around for saintly forms are dark escutcheons found,
  With a cross of simple white displayed upon a raven ground.

" And, placed the raven pall above, a laurel-garland green,
  The minstrel's verdant coronet, his meed of song, is seen ;
  His golden harp, beside it laid, a feeble murmur flings,
  As the evening wind sweeps sadly through its now forsaken
    strings.

" Who rests within his coffin there ? For whom this general wail ?
  Is some beloved monarch gone, that old and young look pale ?
  A king, in truth,—a king of song ! and Frauenlob his name ;
  And thus in death his fatherland must celebrate his fame.

" Unto the fairest flowers of Heaven that bloom this earth along,
  To women's worth, did he on earth, devote his deathless song ;
  And though the minstrel has grown old, and faded be his fame,
  They yet requite what he in life hath done for love of them."

The Church of St. Stephen is also said to have
been founded by Willigis in 990. Within it is the

tomb of the good man, with his skull and his mass vestments.

The image of the Virgin in the Cathedral is said to work miracles. A story is told of an aged musician who, finding that no one would listen to his old-fashioned tunes, stole into the Cathedral, and, after praying for aid, stood before her shrine and played a hymn upon his violin in honor of the Virgin Mary.

The Holy Mother, touched by the old man's poverty, raised her jewelled robe and deftly kicked one of her golden slippers into his hat, which was lying on the floor in front of her. Falling on his knees, the old musician humbly thanked the Virgin for her charity, then hurried off to a neighboring goldsmith to sell the shoe in order to buy bread.

The goldsmith questioned the old man as to where he got the shoe, and not believing the miraculous story that the minstrel told, he had him arrested. It did not take long for the court to find him guilty of sacrilegious theft, and to condemn him to death.

As he was dragged past the Cathedral door on his way to the place of execution, he begged permission to say a last prayer before the Virgin. He was permitted to kneel before the shrine, with his hat and violin beside him. Tremblingly the old violinist begged Mary to open the gates of Heaven for him. And when he had ended his prayer he again played a little hymn, declaring that his last music on earth should be in honor of the Blessed Virgin.

While he was playing, the Virgin, in the presence of the multitude that had followed the old musician into the Cathedral, deliberately lifted her gown, for the second time, and kicked off her other golden shoe into the tattered hat of the old man.

This second miracle convinced the people that the old minstrel had been unjustly condemned, so the priests stepped forward and offered him a pension for life if he would return to the church the two golden shoes. The old violinist accepted the offer, and the priests made haste to lock up the golden shoes in a safe place for fear that the Virgin should again be tempted to bestow them upon some other poor suppliant at her shrine.

In the course of the Franco-Prussian war, Mayence was one of the principal depôts for the French prisoners, whose great camp formed a splendid spectacle. Mayence was at the same time the embarking-place for the transports and commissariat ships. Time, which levels all things, has left here little that is characteristic. Life and its business in Mayence is exceedingly brisk, active, and prosperous.

At every season of the year the traffic on the banks of the Rhine is very great, as well as over the bridge at Castel, which forms a favorite rendezvous in the fine summer evenings for the lively people of Mayence. The beautiful "Anlagen" is another favorite resort. This was the case especially at the time when Mayence was still a fortress of the League, and when the alternate performances of the Prussian and Austrian bands collected the fashionable inhabitants for miles round. In winter the ice in the trenches attracts a great many of the nimble young Mayencers.

We leave Mayence with a few rapid glances at some of the points of interest in the interior. The only historical interest which is attached to the citadel is that the Eichelstein was within it. The Eichelstein was a monument said by tradition to have been erected in the year 9 B.C. by the Roman legions, in honor of Drusus, who was killed by a fall from his horse.

Thorwaldsen's statue of Gutenberg announces that a new light rose upon the world from Mayence. The inscription on it informs us that this monument was erected to Johann Gensfleisch of Guten by his fellow-citizens, aided by subscriptions from all Europe. Gutenberg sprang from a patrician family of Mayence. The whole world knows what it owes to his discovery, but the year of his birth and the house where that event occurred are unknown.

He was a goldsmith by trade, and he threw himself blindly into the mania for gold-making, and spent long months in hunting for the " philosopher's stone." He spent enormous sums of money in his vain experiments, and at last was forced to some practical work to earn his bread. He chose wood carving, and through the cutting of separate letters, and arranging them into words, came the idea that later led to the art of printing.

The Elector's palace, on the Paradeplatz, was built from 1627 to 1678. In the year 1792 it was the residence of the Electors; in the time of the revolution it was the meeting-place of the members of the Mayence clubs. The bishop's palace dates from the year 1666. In its neighborhood is the convent for English girls, where Ida Hahn meditated over the vanity of the world and her own folly.

The monument of the immortal Schiller stands in the Schillerplatz. It is said that the syenite pillar of the fountain, which was built in this square in 1760, came from Charlemagne's palace at Ingelheim. The German House which lies opposite the castle is worthy of notice. It was erected in 1716, and was formerly the house of the German Order; it is now the occasional residence of the Grand-Duke.

The numerous strangers who visit the town in summer congregate chiefly by the shore in the Rhein-strasse, where there are a large number of hotels facing the railway, which is uncomfortably squeezed in between the shore and the street. All day long we hear the clanging of the railway bell and the shriek of the engine, as much as to warn us that we have not a minute to spare. Owing to the constant movement of the engines and the shunting of the carriages, we are so detained as to have but a few moments to reach the landing-stage, from whence we embark on board the local steamer; which, ploughing through the water and scattering the spray, sparkling like myriads of diamonds, bears us between the green islands dotting the river, to Biebrich—to the land of Nassau, which is one of the finest jewels of the German Empire.

CHAPTER XVIII.

BIEBRICH.

THE Castle of Biebrich rises on the right bank of the Rhine. It is built of red sandstone, and has a light and open situation. It is still the property of the prince who governed the most beautiful little country of Germany, but who, in an anxious, critical hour staked this crown, this diadem of all Germany, upon a doubtful throw, and lost it, as so many have lost their all at the fatal gaming-table. Its fine situation makes it one of the most beautiful of castles.

In front of it, immediately on the bank of the river, is a shady avenue which, like the Villa Reale of Naples, is frequented by the lazzaroni of the shore, the so-called "Rheinschnaken," or "loafers," who hang about here waiting for the arrival of the steamers in order to offer their services at a cheap rate to passengers.

In the distance, behind the castle, rise the woody heights of the Odenwald and Taunus, forming a chain —a green screen—round the valley lying at its feet, and breaking off abruptly towards the river, as if frightened back by the Rhine, and falling almost precipitously towards the shore in steep terraces opposite Bingen.

Vol. I.—16

From the windows the eye travels far from the flat roof of the castle out into the beautiful Rheingau, from whose heights the Johannisberg peers over the dark ruins of Rudesheim and all the celebrated little wine towns, while on the farther side of the bank the heaped-up clouds shine in the dark-blue distance.

It is a wonderful scene: the banks on both sides of the river apparently closing in under the Nieder-wald; on this side there are sloping vineyards with their little houses, villas, and shady parks, which form a girdle round the bank; on the other the citadel of Klopp, the chapel of St. Roch, commanding the valley from the heights—the old Ingelheim of the great Frankish emperor—Ehrenfels, and the retired Mouse Tower. In the river between are scattered the green islands, towards which the busy steamer hurries, to vanish behind the lofty rock of Rude-sheimer.

In the distance, again, are the towers of Mayence and Hochheim, and between them the light arch of the railway bridge and the perforated casemates of Castel. Finally, there is the varied active human life on both banks, the lading and unlading of the bulky Dutch trading-ships, the Rhine skiffs, the lofty minaret-like chimneys of the factories which pour out their smoke in clouds into the blue ether. There can hardly be a pleasanter, brighter picture than this place offers to the eye, although the bank opposite the castle is so insipid and monotonous.

Many things unite to produce the charm which it exercises: there is the distant view on all sides, the wonderful reflections of the green wooded hills in the golden mirror of the river, the poetic force of the ever-moving water, the sunlit poetry which rests upon it all, and, lastly, the unresting, pulsating life ever pursuing either business or pleasure.

Although Biebrich is not important—Mayence on the opposite bank seeming to have grown at its expense—it is a busy little place, with numerous iron, cloth, and glass manufactories, and a population of eleven thousand souls.

Near Biebrich lies the island of Peters-Aue. Here centuries ago the Emperor Louis the Pious, son and successor of Charlemagne, died at his summer palace on the island.

There seems to be no doubt that Biebrich owes its name to the number of beavers that formerly used to find a suitable situation for their buildings in the islands which lie opposite the town. At the present time proofs are not wanting that these animals were once very numerous in the Rhine. Since the beginning of the last century they have been greatly destroyed and driven away by thoughtless trapping, and more especially by the increasing population of the banks, so that at the present day the name of the place is nearly all that remains of them.

Formerly the flesh, bones, and skin of the beaver caused him to be eagerly hunted by the inhabitants of the Rhine banks. But as the forests along the river were cut down the beaver became more and more scarce; yet even in the beginning of the present century the animal was occasionally seen on the banks of the Rhine.

In 1720 there was such danger of the beaver becoming extinct in the north that Frederick William of Prussia passed stringent laws for his preservation. Beavers are still found, though rarely, in the Elbe, the Weser, and other rivers; and in the province of Magdeburg they are said still to have a quiet resting-place, where they are protected and preserved.

There is a legend that a beaver was discovered in the foundations of the palace of Biebrich, but for that I cannot vouch.

The castle, which is built in the style of the Renaissance, was finished in 1706 by George Augustus of Nassau. The sandstone figures which adorn the roof, otherwise valueless, have a somewhat mournful appearance, for they were very harshly treated in 1793, at the siege of Mayence, when the French planted their guns on the Peters-Aue.

A large and beautiful park with fine trees is situated behind the castle. Duke Adolf of Nassau cultivated this with the greatest care, until his country fell to the share of Prussia. At the last hour he could not save that country, when the choice was placed before him after the battle of Königgrätz. He decided for Austria, less perhaps from his own inclination than from that of a blind counsellor. The obligation which was imposed on him to maintain a public road through the park, his private property, and the numerous abuses of this privilege, cooled the interest of the absent prince for his favorite spot. He sold the splendid palm-house to the town of Frankfort, which replaced its palm-garden by a rare orangery. The park is still beautiful, for its fine shady trees are uninjured, but its former cultivation has vanished since the castle lost the princely household.

Deep in the park lie the ruins of old Biburk, also called Moosburg. It stands on other ruins which formed the castle of Louis the German in 874. Its history is obscure and lost in conjecture. The statues at the entrance came from the tombs of the Counts Katzenellenbogen, in the abbey of Eberbach. The sculptor, E. Hopfgarten, formerly made himself a studio in the interior of this castle, and had a commission from the duke to carve a sarcophagus for the Greek chapel at Wiesbaden. Hopfgarten died in 1856. Some of his works, among them a model of a Lorelei, were preserved in this studio till 1874, when they were sold by his heirs and carried away.

Since Biebrich has lost its interest as the residence of the Duke of Nassau, its commercial importance, as well as that of the parish of Moosbach, has declined. The State established a military cadet school in the barracks built by the duke, but the court was wanting. Mayence, lying opposite, absorbs all the business, and that jealousy of its neighbors which is found in small towns still exists. It was once great enough to induce an attempt to frustrate the intention of building a harbor at Biebrich by sinking a whole fleet (of which Heine has sung) with stones.

CHAPTER XIX.

WIESBADEN.

LEAVING the river and passing the Mosbach railway station, the road, which is shaded by a double avenue of trees, rises gently to Adolf's Hill. On one side we get a charming glimpse of the islands and a part of the Rheingau; on the other, quite as attractive, of Mayence, Castel, and the mountain-chain.

Before us lies the Taunus, from the plateau of which the hunting-castle, the Platte, and the chapel look down through a break in the woods; whilst to the left the forester's house on the forest-road to Schlangenbad peeps through the rising wood, and to the right, on the ridge of hills, the watchtower of Bierstadt commands the whole of the Rhine Valley.

Even before we reach Mosbach, we meet with the first of those country houses which are, as it were, the outposts of that community that has sought comfortable seclusion in the loveliest of the Rhine valleys, in the "city of idlers," Wiesbaden. On both sides stretch the pastures of fertile green intersected by the Taunus and Nassau Railway.

In a few minutes we reach the plateau, and at our

feet lies the little paradise which was once the residence of the Dukes of Nassau, the " Mecca " of all those who make a pilgrimage to its warm springs, and the " Nice " of Germany. It is protected from the north-east wind, and is a favorite resort of those who, tired of the whirl of the great towns, wish to end their days under the Rhenish sun and in the mildest climate. Indeed, it is difficult to find another place so highly favored by heaven as this.

Up the slope of the valley, surrounded by wooded hills, are country houses scattered among luxuriant gardens, and parks environing the town, where the warm vapor of the medicinal spring—like the geysers of Iceland—always emits from the peculiar " Kochbrunnen " a thick column of steam to invigorate and shower its benefits on all who come within its range. Everything here speaks of comfort, wealth, and contentment. A tall chimney, here and there, ventures to creep in between the villas; and the numerous golden-tipped flagstaffs on the roofs announce the readiness of the inmates to avail themselves of every occasion for a holiday.

In the last few years the rage for building has brought the country houses even as far as Adolf's Höhe. They are on each side of us as we stroll down the Adolf Avenue into the neatest and most elegant of German towns, which, fifty years ago, was little more than a village, but has now attained a population, good and bad, of more than sixty-five thousand souls.

We say of good and bad, for, like Baden, Wiesbaden originally owed its pleasure-gardens to the gaming-table, and it was only when gambling was prohibited by the government that private families began permanently to take up their residence here. What therefore the evil spirit of play commenced has been finished by the good genius of enterprise, and scarcely did the Wiesbadeners perceive that they could get on better without the former, than speculations in houses and land began. The Electoral town became a miniature cosmopolitan city, its society became a mixture of all nations, a neutral settlement of people from all parts of the world, in which every language is understood, and every coinage is current.

The history of Wiesbaden, about which the present mixed society troubles itself but little, begins with the time of the Romans, who built the old *Mattiacum*, and it was the existence of the warm spring which led to its erection. Pliny speaks of it, and the remains which have been found on Heidenberg and Römerberg are said to date from the time when the fourteenth legion, which was afterwards relieved by the twenty-second, was stationed in these parts.

The name Wisibad, Wisibadum, appears in records of 843. The Rhenish "Robber-Knights" ran riot here, and once completely laid the city waste. In 1815 Wiesbaden was the capital of the Duchy of Nassau. In 1866 it was occupied by a Prussian militia company, who met with no opposition, and since then it has been the seat of a Prussian government.

The Kurhaus, finished in 1810, with its beautiful gardens, naturally forms the centre of the town. The ascent from the railway-station through the Wilhelmstrasse is quite imposing, bordered as it is on one side by lofty plane-trees, and that part of the Kurgarten named the "warm bank," with its beautiful lawns, ponds, and music tents, which are seen between the trunks of the plane-trees. Next to the open place before the theatre is the garden of the Kurhaus, richly and artistically arranged with flower-beds, and between them are cascades which are illuminated in the evening. Right and left are repeated the avenues of great plane-trees, which lead the fashionable world into the private gardens behind the assembly-rooms. Opposite to these avenues are two rows of very beautiful red-thorns, and behind them again colonnades of shops. This open place presents a gay and busy scene, particularly in the afternoon and evening, when the beginning of the concert summons everybody to the back of the Kurhaus under the shady red chestnuts.

The company sit closely packed together under the trees, or wander at will by the banks of the fish-pond, on which a flotilla of white swans swim round and round, though much disturbed at times by the gondolas with their gay-colored streamers, which move over the still surface with more ease and greater

speed than the limited space would seem to warrant.
This place has a wonderful effect when, during the
concert, the fish-pond is illuminated with Bengal
lights, and the fountain is made to throw its column
of water higher than the tops of the trees. Bengal
lights are in great force at Wiesbaden; with them
and fireworks and music, the energetic director keeps
his patrons amused and in constant circulation.

The rooms in the Kurhaus are imposing and richly
decorated, especially the great assembly-room, with
the little conversation-room and refreshment-room.
In four of the saloons at the left side of the house
might once be heard the chink of gold and silver and
the rustle of bank-notes on the fatal green cloth.
The intermittent "rouge gagne et la couleur" and
the clear click of the roulette ball has here made
many hearts beat anxiously or joyously. All this,
however, has long since ended. No one thinks of it
now, and the hangers-on who used to gather about
the gaming-tables have departed to Saxony and
Monaco.

Wiesbaden has become a steady town. We own
ourselves to have been in error when we said elsewhere that the demon of play was like a wall-fungus,
and could not be destroyed, for even if—which
Heaven forbid—Wiesbaden should be swallowed up
by an earthquake, the words " faites le jeu !" would
only sound from the depths like the bells of the buried
city of Vineta from beneath the waves of the Baltic.

The Wiesbaden Gardens extend for a considerable distance, reaching to the village and ruins of Sonnenberg and to the Dietenmühle, the much-frequented hydropathic establishment. On one side of the gardens is the Sonnenbergstrasse and on the other the Parkstrasse, both of which are bordered with villas.

These gardens possess great attractions on account of the shade they offer, especially in the spring, as the sheltered situation of the place, protected as it is from keen winds, allows the most delicate vegetation to flourish luxuriantly. The abundance of the *Bignonia catalpa* and the trumpet-tree, with its candelabrum-shaped white blossoms, give the pleasure-gardens a peculiar charm. The effect of the gay flower-beds in the neighborhood of the private houses is also very agreeable.

At the end of the Wilhelmstrasse, past the Kurhaus and Theaterplatz, we come upon the Taunus road, and at the same time the Trinkhalle. On the right of it, at the beginning of the Sonnenberger road, the Pauline Palace may be seen on the heights of the "Schönen Aussicht." The palace is the property of the duke, and was formerly the dwelling-place of the widowed duchess. It crowns the summit of a somewhat steep ridge, which is covered with park-like trees and flowers, and was built in 1841–43, in a quasi-Alhambra style.

At the end of the Trinkhalle the road leads on the right to the Geisberg, which, with the Agricultural

Academy and numerous villas, forms one part of the town. Going straight on, there is a shady avenue of limes, and the Elizabethstrasse, bordered with country houses, after a short distance opens on to the beautiful Nero Valley.

Here, in this valley, we are confronted with that great forest on the Neroberg, on whose slopes, which are dotted with vine-dressers' cabins, grows the noble Neroberger, with which the increasing houses seem to contest the costly ground.

From the Kapellenstrasse, which passes over this mountain, the villas on the edge of the forest look down into the valley. This is the road to the Greek chapel, which may also be reached by a footpath that winds between the vineyards and hop-gardens.

This chapel is built in the form of a Greek cross, and has a curious effect with its five gilded pinnacles, the highest one hundred and ninety feet from the ground, to each of which a double cross is attached by chains. In dull weather it has almost the effect of a ray of sunshine on the valley. It is built of bright sandstone, and was completed in 1855, and dedicated by the Duke Adolf to the memory of his early-lost consort, the Princess Elizabeth Michaelovna of Russia. The interior is built entirely of marble. A magnificent altar screen, with figures of saints on a gold ground, separates the body of the chapel from the choir. An exquisite monument to the Duchess Elizabeth is in a recess on the north side of the chapel.

The road leads farther up the mountain, through a strong and thickly-grown beech wood, to the plateau of the Neroberg, eight hundred feet above the sea. Here stands the Belvidere, a temple from which may be obtained a splendid view over the Rhine, including Biebrich, Mayence, Darmstadt, and the mountain-chains. Beautiful walks and promenades lead through this wood, which is a mile in extent. The hunting-castle, "the Platte," built in 1824, and belonging to the Duke of Luxemburg, lies still higher and more exposed, being nearly fifteen hundred feet above the sea. It commands the Neroberg and has an extensive view over the Rhine Valley.

The Wiesbaden spring, the most precious possession of the town, supplies about a dozen bath-houses. The waters are drunk in the morning at the hall and in its immediate neighborhood, the inhabitants being roused early by a concert of choral music. After that the visitors retire to their baths, and profound silence reigns on the promenades, which is only disturbed by the children and their nurses, and the melancholy wheel-chairs of those invalids who have escaped early from their bath.

The Kurgarten is also quiet in the forenoon. At the pond the children feed the swans who come waddling clumsily up to them. Among the trees sit a few visitors reading novels, and under the shady chestnuts the waiters loll idly against the trunks, dozing, with their napkins on their knees, and isolated groups of chess-players sit silently round the tables. The morning is claimed entirely by the waters, the afternoon and evening are given up to pleasure and diversion, which are sought, not only in the concerts and festivities of the Kurgarten, but also by making excursions into the beautiful environs.

The favorite resorts of visitors to Wiesbaden are Schlangenbad, to which the road leads through the shade of the thick beech wood, and Schwalbach, two bathing-places lying in the cool valley-side between wood and meadow, in which ladies who are disposed to nervousness often attempt to seek restoration to health.

Schlangenbad especially was, about twenty-five years ago, quite a little female Republic, in which the occasional visit of a husband to his wife caused almost a sensation. But there was another period much farther back when the little valley used to collect within the walls of the one building which had been erected and embellished for the purpose a pretty lively assembly of both sexes. The higher clergy and a number of canonesses looked upon Schlangenbad as their own peculiar domain. About the same time also the little place received the noble Prince Eugene (1708) as a guest. The baths of Schlangenbad have been known for centuries, the old Kurhaus having been erected as early as 1629.

The very simple history of Schlangenbad relates that shortly after the discovery of the spring it was sold to a doctor of Worms for a puncheon of wine. It lately passed from the possession of Nassau, to which it had belonged since 1816, into the hands of Prussia. There is no doubt that the place owes its name to the great number of snakes which abound in the woods, and are caught by the boys of the neighborhood and exhibited to the visitors.

One of the most charming and easy excursions is to the Georgenhorn Hill, over which the road from Wiesbaden passes. It presents to the observer a vast panorama of the Rhine, with a distant view of Frankfort and the environs of Worms. The advantages of the situation have induced several enthusiastic lovers of nature to establish themselves in the villas here which command a view of the broad Rhine Valley.

The pleasantest point in Schlangenbad itself is the gallery of the Nassau Hotel, from which we look over the little splashing fountain to the valley yonder. On the left is the Kurgarten, rising in terraces, where a very modest choir is performing its afternoon concert, and a band of jugglers turn their somersaults.

Before us lies the promenade, constantly enlivened by the most elegant toilettes; behind and near us, steps hewn in the rock lead to romantic shady spots, for almost everywhere arbors and clear springs offer such poetic resting-places to the nervous visitors. A pleasant stillness hovers continually over wood and valley, and this is only broken occasionally by a

Kurhaus Gardens, Wiesbaden.

Kurhaus Gardens, Wiesbaden.

merry party mounted on donkeys who approach near us, or by the arrival of a coach from Wiesbaden loaded with merrymaking tourists.

The discomfort of this place, when the whole valley is covered with snow and everything is wrapped in its winter sleep, is amply atoned for when spring unchains the ice-bound springs in the woods and strews the meadows with tender blossoms, adorns the beech and oak trees with fresh green tints, and attunes the lays of the feathered songsters to soft melody. But none of all its annual visitors sees all this, for the air is keen and can only be faced by the robust; even when the place is officially opened in the height of summer, there sometimes breaks out a "sauve qui peut" among the earliest guests, which only the boldest can withstand.

The neighboring Langen-Schwalbach, or familiarly Schwalbach, has a similar reputation as a health resort. It was known as early as 300, and was a fashionable watering-place in the seventeenth and eighteenth centuries. Its steel springs, and the air which is impregnated by them, attract all those whose complaints require such a tonic.

The company at Schwalbach are indeed at times reminded of the saying of the French writer, who thought that if a servant were engaged to go through all that a nervous lady voluntarily went through in a single winter season, he would sink under the attempt. The place itself lies in a pastoral valley, and makes its appearance in history in 1352 as the village of Swalhorn. Amongst the historical notabilities who have taken the waters here is Tilly, who stayed in the place in 1628. In later times the ex-Empress Eugénie arrived here and took up her abode in the boarding-house now called the "Villa Eugénie."

The most interesting points in the neighborhood are the Castles of Schwalbach, with their watchtower Adolfseck, which was reduced to ruins during the Thirty Years' War. These were once the dwelling-places of the favorite of the Emperor Adolf. The castles of Hohenstein and Hohlenfels should also be mentioned, the one situated on a lofty rock and the other on a chalk cliff.

CHAPTER XX.

AN EXCURSION TO THE TAUNUS.

As there is no other way to Castel, we must re-trace our steps and go back past Mosbach. The engine-sheds immediately on the banks of the Rhine have an inhospitable appearance, and the loopholes of the fortifications frown sullenly down upon us as we drive to the railway station along the outworks by the houses and hotels. But at length the fortifications lie behind us, and stretching out to our view stands the vine-clad hill of Hochheim. The church may be seen from a distance in all directions, as also its factory for the manufacture of sparkling wine, whilst its vineyards extend beyond the railway and slope down to the bank of the Main.

It is a noble fruit which grows up there on that yellow, sandy-looking hill, especially that on the piece beneath the church, the Hochheim Deanery. It glows through many a man's veins, and those who have quarrelled with it have done so only to become still more firmly attached to it again before long. A monument might indeed be raised here to England, for "sparkling hock," the Hochheim champagne, which is specially prepared for British palates, is sent across the Channel in enormous quantities.

The majestic proportions of the Taunus become more and more clearly defined before us as we approach. On the left yonder lies the modest Kurhaus of Weilbach, also called Lange-Weilbach, on account of the poetic repose which is met with there, even in the height of the season. It is well known for its sulphur springs, and for a newly-discovered mineral spring.

Shortly before we reach Frankfurt, at the Höchst station, the guard invites passengers for Soden to alight, while a swarm of children surround the carriages, crying "Bubeschenkel! Bubeschenkel!" a local kind of pastry, supposed to be in the shape of a leg, in which an active imagination may possibly trace a resemblance to the intended form. A little group of passengers respond to the cry of the guard by alighting. These being individuals either with pale faces, on which are written a longing for the healing waters of Sodon, or else persons in robust health, with an enterprising, travelling air, carrying thick plaids in strong hand-straps, wearing stout nailed shoes, and holding solid alpenstocks.

The remainder of the passengers, warding off the "Bubeschenkel," indulge in speculations as to whether they will go up to the interesting Church of St. Justinus, erected in 1090. They decide, however, that they have not the time.

In an hour we reach Soden, and with it the southern spur of the Taunus. Many invalids are annually attracted here by the mild climate, the tasteful gardens, and the springs containing salt, carbonic acid, and iron, a healing fountain for various ailments. They gaze with longing eyes after the mountain tourists who start from this place on foot, on horseback, and on donkeys. The usual tour is over Cronthal, Cronberg, Falkenstein, and Pfaffenstein to Königstein, where the first night is spent; then over the Fuchstanz, from which place two hours more brings them to the great Feldberg. They then go down over the Altkönig, in Oberursel, and reach the table-land of Homburg.

The Taunus has been adopted by the Taunus Club of Frankfurt, who regularly celebrate their festival at the most interesting points. It is covered by thick woods, and stretches between the Rhine, the Main, and the Lahn, for about a hundred miles, declining on the southwest, as the Rheingau chain forms the boundary between North and South Germany. Feldberg is its highest point, and is nearly three thousand feet above the sea-level; from it may be seen a splendid panorama extending over hundreds of miles in all directions.

The metallic wealth of these mountains once induced speculators to attempt the working of the mines, as the so-called "Goldgrube" at Homburg still testifies. They were, however, not productive enough to repay the trouble and outlay, for only peat and clay were found to be plentiful. It is not until the Lahn district is reached that the soil yields iron and manganese. The mountain district, which received its name from the Romans, who called it *mons taunus*, is, as is well known, very rich in mineral springs.

The Celtic race appear as the first inhabitants of the Taunus; they were succeeded by the Helvetii, especially between the Rhine and the Main; then came the Chatti; and lastly, the Alemanni and the Franks, who freed these mountains from the Romans in the fifth century after Christ. At the present day we may judge of the warlike nature of the Roman period from the Ring or Heathen Walls of the plateau, the entrances and exits of which formed the so-called " Rennwege," or courses, whilst the boundaries of the Roman domain are still to be recognized in the ditches fortified with stakes.

In the Middle Ages, which swept away the Old German districts, the land was divided among the noble families of Eppstein, Nüringen, Falkenstein, Münzenberg, and the Archbishop of Mayence, till in the course of time the Taunus (with the exception of Homburg and the Wetterau) passed into the hands of Nassau, and lastly, in 1866, into those of Prussia.

The road takes us uphill over Cronthal—a charming little bathing-place among green pastures—to Cronberg, whose bold inhabitants, supported by the banner of a knight of the Palatinate, once victoriously gave battle to the men of Frankfurt.

We then continue our way to the Castle of the Knight of Cronberg, built in the thirteenth century. Part of the Castle is still occupied, and the old chapel contains tombstones that were there before the castle was erected.

Lower down on the hill stands the stronghold of Falkenstein on a wooded rock. Kuno, of Sayn, whose castle on the Rhine now lies in ruins, fell in love with Irmingarde, the daughter of the surly Lord of Falkenstein. His love was returned, and he presented himself before her father, asking his consent to the marriage. The old Lord of Falkenstein smiled grimly, and told the impetuous lover that he would consider his proposal—on one condition. Kuno, delighted at what he considered so ready an assent, promised to do *anything*. Imagine his despair when Falkenstein told him that he could wed his daughter if he would build a road from the castle to the valley below, and ride up it on his war-horse before sunrise the next morning!

Kuno, of Sayn, went sadly away, for the castle of Falkenstein was perched high on a rock, and only a tortuous path led down to the valley, and he knew that it would take many men many months of hard labor to blast and cut out a road, and he had but one night in which to accomplish the impossible.

Suddenly he was roused from his gloomy thoughts by hearing a little voice call his name. He looked down and saw the King of the Gnomes, who told him not to despair, but to go to his inn, and have his war-horse ready for the morning, and he and his subjects would accomplish the work.

Kuno was incredulous, but knowing that he could effect nothing unaided, he obeyed the gnome, went to his inn, and waited, with what patience he could for the dawn. Meanwhile the gnome had waved his hand, and a mist rose and shrouded valley and hill in its dense vapor. Out of it came thousands of dwarf-like creatures, who began to use axes, picks, and spades with right good will.

All night long Kuno, of Sayn, lay awake and heard the crashing of forest trees, the breaking of stones, and occasionally a long rumbling sound like thunder. At dawn he emerged from the inn, and was met by the innkeeper, who told him that a terrible storm must have raged over the valley in the night. Kuno stayed not to listen to the man's tale, but called for his horse, and rode to the foot of the eminence upon which rose the castle of Falkenstein. There he was met by the King of the Gnomes, who showed him a broad highway leading from the shore to the very door of the castle. Kuno thanked him, and galloped bravely up, greeted on all sides by the smiling gnomes. As he rode over the bridge they were just finishing, he looked up and saw Irmingarde standing on the ramparts and waving him a greeting.

The Lord of Falkenstein could no longer withhold

his consent to their marriage ; and as the triumphant lover clasped Irmingarde to his heart, the sun rose over the horizon and flooded them with its golden rays.

Heinrich von Ofterdingen, the troubadour, it is said, plays here every night upon his harp, and wanders down the bank of the Liederbach to the Rhine ; whilst on the great cone of rock yonder, the Altkönig, tradition asserts that a gray mountain manikin sits and watches some treasure that lies hidden, winding at the same time his ever-growing beard on a reel.

On the heights of Altkönig are still visible the Giant Rings, or the Devil's Walls, which consist of two massive walls formed of rough stones loosely piled together, the exterior of which is two thousand paces in circumference. Three entrances lead into this stony circle, which is apparently of German work, for here formerly stood the Royal Seat of the "Gau-gericht," or district tribunal. According to tradition, Ariovistus and Rando, the sons of the Alemanni, were once enthroned here.

Feldberg is the King of the Taunus ; it commands the country round for a vast distance, reaching to Thuringia, to Inselsberg, to Hunsrück, and to the Wasgau. It was from this mountain that Queen Brunhilda, waking at daybreak, used to survey her beautiful empire, and on this account the precipitous northern side is called by the people of the locality "Brunhilda's bed."

Tradition asserts that it was to the summit of the Feldberg that Hermann der Cherusker summoned the German heroes, in order to form a League against the Roman yoke. Feldberg House, which was completed in 1860, annually entertains the athletic societies of the Main and Rhine districts, who meet here in July.

The fortress of Königstein rears itself proudly on its rocky height. At the foot of its throne lies the town of the same name, the gathering-place of all travellers to the Taunus, and especially of Frankfurt society. The Lords of Nüringen first governed here, then the Münzenbergs, and lastly the Falkensteiners and Stolzbergers, from whom it was wrested by Mayence.

History mentions Königstein as early as 1225. Since then many calamities have visited it, and among them that in 1793, when its gloomy walls were made to serve as a prison for the clubbists of Mayence. The interest in maintaining this splendid place is enhanced by the fact that Königstein has become, on account of its fine air, a much-frequented health resort.

The Duchess Adelaide of Nassau materially assisted in the embellishment of the town by building a large country residence in the immediate neighborhood. It must be somewhat melancholy for the ducal family to look down upon the beautiful land which they have lost; but still the bonds of home-love loosen but slowly, and they consequently appear at their old home every year in the early summer.

Every one who is afraid to attempt the Feldberg ascends Rossert, of which there is nothing to be said except that it is a great imposing group of rocks, to which the name of the " Teufelschloss," or Devil's Castle, has been given, on account of its weird appearance.

From here we have a splendid view of Königstein, Falkenstein, and the ruins which recall to us that mighty race renowned in history, the Eppsteiners. These airy strongholds are fortified by deep abysses and massive walls to withstand all attacks, save that of the unwearying enemy Time. Ruins now stand on the rock overhanging the town, which are clasped round by ivy, plantain, sloe-bushes, and brambles. Shattered towers and a broken chapel are all that remains of the once-proud citadel, which for four centuries kept the whole neighborhood under its sway, and maintained a bitter feud with the Counts of Nassau. At last, the race of its lowly rulers dying out, it passed to the dominion of the Counts of Stolberg, from whom it was handed over to the electoral city of Mayence.

Many ghastly remembrances are associated by the people with the name of the Eppsteiners. Within the arch of the gateway once hung a colossal skeleton in chains, supposed, in those days, to be that of a giant. It is now exhibited in the Museum at Wiesbaden as that of an antediluvian animal. There is another legend about a giant, namely, that of the Great and the Little Mannstein, two rocks which some people fancy, when seen from a distance, resemble two human forms. One of them is supposed to be a knight of Falkenstein, who is fighting with a giant for the possession of his stolen bride.

CHAPTER XXI.

FRANKFURT AND HOMBURG.

FRANKFORT-ON-THE-MAIN owes its name to Charlemagne, who one day wandered far into the Teutonic forests to wage war against the Saxons. In the battle that followed he was defeated, and forced to beat a hasty retreat with his beloved Franks. The country was unknown to Charlemagne—the enemy was in close pursuit—and, to make matters worse, a thick fog shut down, so that they could not see where they were going.

At last they reached the banks of the Main, and knowing that his small force would be destroyed by the enemy if they lingered where they were, yet not daring to cross the unknown river, Charlemagne in his perplexity had recourse to prayer. Immediately the fog lifted, and the Emperor saw a doe, followed by her young, crossing the river. Charlemagne bade his men keep close behind him, took the same way, and brought his little army safely over. As they reached the opposite bank the fog closed in behind them, concealing them from the pursuing Saxons, who declared, not seeing them, that the Franks must have perished in the Main. Charlemagne called the place *Franconofurd* (ford of the Franks), in commemoration of his deliverance.

We now step out of that legendary time into the battle-field of the Holy Roman Empire of the German nation. It was at Frankfurt that most of the German Emperors were chosen, from the time of Barbarossa. It was here that, by reason of the privileges of the Hohenstaufens, and on the authority of the golden bull of Charles IV., those powerful rulers were crowned whose portraits hang in the banquet-room of the Town Hall, which is called the " Römer." These same anointed heads also showed themselves to the shouting and excited people on the balcony, surrounded by the electoral princes.

Time has since passed both joyfully and sorrowfully over the town. It lost and regained its privileges several times over, until at length, after the Vienna Congress of 1816, it was chosen as the seat of the German Diet, and the powdered diplomatists of great and little States strutted through the streets.

The Revolution of 1848 brought the dawn of a new era over Frankfurt—a stormy, ominous era which preceded evil. The National Assembly sat in the Church of St. Paul, and this body, in a most melancholy manner, lost two of its most illustrious members, namely, Prince Felix von Lichnowsky and H. von Auerswald.

In 1863 the Emperor of Austria fruitlessly summoned his Congress of Princes hither. In 1866, the great and final change took place; General Vogel von Falkenstein occupied Frankfurt with his army of the Main, and thus it was incorporated with Prussia.

The political importance of the former Free Town, as regards its historical prerogatives as well as its geographical situation, was lost with the centralization of the German imperial interests in the North German capital, and those who at first advocated the preservation of the old traditional privileges were obliged to adapt themselves to moderating circumstances.

Another sun rose over Frankfurt in the year 1749, with the birth of Goethe; and Ludwig Börné claimed this as his native city. Poetry and the *belles-lettres* were also represented in Frankfurt by Clement Brentano, Bettina von Arnim, Fr. M. von Klinger, and others; science by A. von Feuerbach, Savigny, J. G. Schlosser, and a host of kindred spirits.

The particularly favorable situation of the city caused material interests to be even more in request, and the desire for them more deeply rooted than intellectual claims. The city became the great emporium of trade for South-west Germany. Its Exchange became a power even at that time, when the news of its transactions was carried northwards from Frankfurt and Paris by pigeon post, and the greedy stock-jobbers in Berlin strove to ascertain from the foam on the steaming horse left standing by the courier before one of the great banking-houses, whether the rate of exchange was likely to be high or low in Frankfurt.

The name of the town is inseparably connected with those of Rothschild, Bethmann, and others; and even at the present day there are not wanting signs that Frankfurt will not be long before she restores herself to her ancient rights in the monetary market of the world.

The most ancient memorial in Frankfurt is the "Römer," the town hall of the former free imperial city. It was erected in the early part of the fifteenth century, but has been altered many times since then. The "Römerberg," on which tournaments used to be held, is an open square in front of the Römer. Down to the end of the last century no Jew was allowed to enter it.

The old bridge over the Main is a most picturesque structure of red sandstone. It was built in 1342. On the middle of the bridge stands a statue of Charlemagne holding the imperial orb; though this, indeed, belongs to a later period. It was this monument which gave the honest Sachsenhäusers the idea that Charlemagne was the man who "invented Aeppelwei," a drink specially in favor in Frankfurt.

The gilded vane, which consists of a cock on an iron rod, has a legendary signification. The devil, it is said, did not approve of the building of the bridge, and claimed of the builder the first living being that should pass over it. This had to be granted, and as it is always a satisfaction in local tradition to outwit the devil, a poor, half-starved cock was driven over the bridge directly it was completed. In mockery of his Satanic Majesty, the poor creature was afterwards immortalized in the form of a gilded weathercock.

Pepin, the father of Charlemagne, is said to have been the founder of the Cathedral at Frankfurt. The building was not completed until 1512. Part of the tower and of the church itself was destroyed by a great fire in 1867, but has since been restored. At the time of the restoration the cloisters were completed from old plans, and the tower, which had been unfinished since 1512, was finished from the designs of the architect, Hans von Ingelnheim, which had been lying among the municipal archives for five hundred years.

Next it, in antiquity, are the churches of St. Leonard, of the Holy Virgin, and of St. Nicholas. St. Leonard's, begun in 1219, contains a Last Supper by Holbein the Elder, and on the north tower is seen the imperial eagle, bestowed on the abbey by Lewis the Bavarian for services rendered to him when he was under the papal ban. The celebrated church of St. Paul was not built until 1782.

The first objects that attract the eye of a stranger in walking through the town are the monuments of Gutenberg, Goethe, and Schiller. He will also visit

Goethe's house, with its marble tablet; Luther's house, from which the Reformer addressed the people on his journey to Worms; the Bethmann Museum, with Dannecker's incomparable Ariadne; the Städel'sche Art Institute; Rothschild's original house, at the entrance of the Jews' Street; the grave of " Frau Rath," Goethe's mother, in the old churchyard; the Eschenheim Tower, six hundred years old, the last relic of the ancient fortifications; the theatre; the Exchange; the Zoological Garden; and lastly, the splendid Palm Garden, with its wealth of leaf and blossom.

Sachsenhausen, said to have been founded by Charlemagne, and connected with Frankfurt by five bridges, forms a populous world of itself; the only particular point of interest it possesses is the house of the German Order which stands there. The same may also be said of Bornheim Heath, on which Lichnowsky was murdered. As in most large towns, modern times have added a new quarter, which gives the place quite a different appearance.

Frankfurt has one hundred and eighty thousand inhabitants, and the people are of a merry, active disposition. Strangers are constantly passing through their town, especially in summer. The river Main, with its clear stream, offers to the Frankfurt societies a fine opportunity for water sports, such as regattas, boating, etc. The woods, in which the annual spring festival is held, the Taunus, the Bergstrasse, and the neighboring towns with their various kinds of baths, are all visited by swarms of excursionists. This is especially the case with Homburg, which lies on a table-land within half an hour's ride, and is the favorite resort of the Frankfurt people.

Two dynasties have fallen in the course of a few years in this much-frequented town, the one favored by Heaven, the other by the powers below; the one expiring with the last Landgrave of Hesse-Homburg, who acted, as it were, the prelude of the Prussian war policy by dying in March, 1866, and giving up the government to Darmstadt, only to be readjusted later in the year; the other ruling according to the caprice of four kings, and in vain protesting, while packing up its rakes and cards, against the Parliament's decree of banishment.

The latter was the dynasty of Blanc the Gambler, who was really the Landgrave here, and who bore on his arms, according to a tradition of thirty years ago, the device: "Ici ne gagne ni rouge ni noir, mais toujours *Blanc.*"

The Landgrave Ferdinand Henry Frederick wished his capital to be described as " vor der Höhe;" the Bohemian population of the town called it " sur l'abyme." It did not matter which name it bore; but the former has been preserved.

In Goethe's time the Court of Homburg was a centre of intellectual life. Goethe's " Lila " was the Fraulein von Ziegler, a lady belonging to the Court.

Among the scholars who assembled there were Von Sinclair, Jung-Stilling, and Lavater, all of whom certainly visited the Court of Homburg. The unfortunate poet Hölderlin also lived here after his separation from his beloved Diotima.

The French Revolution drove a large number of the Waldenses to Homburg, and their descendants still live in the neighborhood. The town was indebted for many undesirable fugitives and guests to the closing of the Parisian gaming hells, and the cleansing of the Palais-Royal, in 1837.

The proprietors of the gaming-tables at this period, with Benazet at their head, crossed the frontier. Many of the West German Princes lent a willing ear to their offers, and thus *roulette* and *trente et quarante* were established in Germany. Benazet, and after him his nephew Dupressoir, ruled in Baden-Baden, and Blanc in Homburg. Both knew how to entice so-called society to their tables. They also loaded the French journalists with benefits, placing money and carriages at their disposal, well knowing that the former would in all probability return the same evening to their coffers. Things went on more respectably at Wiesbaden and Ems, whose united undertaking was at least under one control.

The surroundings of the Kurhaus are brilliantly arranged, and were formerly visited at every season of the year by a very cosmopolitan society, for the gambling went on all the year round. At the present time the season is very short on account of the climate, and the place is empty for the greater part of the twelve months.

The effect from the terrace of the Kurhaus with its glass roof is very magnificent, and there is a truly lovely view of the pleasure-gardens lying at its foot; these are bounded on both sides by villas and boarding-houses, and crowned by the verdure of the woods in the background. The orange-trees which adorn the banks under the terrace are of rare beauty.

The theatre is an elegant building; the Darmstadt company give performances there occasionally during the season. The castle, which used to be the residence of the Landgrave's family, and is now reserved for the occasional visit of the Prussian royal family, lies on a hill, surrounded by a green park. Many families of rank reside in the numerous villas and houses round about.

The environs of Homburg are particularly attractive, with fine promenades and places for recreation running out in various directions. The air is pure and invigorating, and is always fresh and clear owing to the proximity of the mountains and forests. The mineral springs, as well as the advantages of climate which Homburg possesses, has attracted an aristocratic society to the place now that the gaming-tables have been removed.

It was, it is true, difficult before the year 1872, which proved fatal to the gambling, to judge of the society by the luxury of their equipages, and the amount of show and wealth that was paraded. Adventure and immorality hid themselves here more than in the other watering-places, where society, indeed, often exhibited itself under false colors, beneath a luxury which covered its inner corruption and hid its social insignificance. That eventful year brought another stamp of visitors; the parvenus of the Exchange, the gilded mushrooms of a night's growth, who naturally could not show themselves without lackeys and carriages, disappeared—they vanished at the first touch of misfortune, to be seen no more. The thunderstorm cleared the air of Homburg society.

The town itself is of inconsiderable extent, with about nine thousand inhabitants, whose industry and occupations are principally carried on for the advantage of the visitors. Passing over the bridge from the railway station we enter the principal artery of the town, the Louisenstrasse. Here we see one hotel after another, while the buildings which are private houses are erected in the villa style and are beautifully adorned with gardens. These offer a retreat to strangers who have settled here, or who have come to use the waters.

It is curious to be here at the opening of the season, after the long winter sleep, when the earliest visitors arrive. The first cab which rolls over the Louisenstrasse laden with luggage makes quite a sensation. Heads are counted as yet individually; the musicians who throughout the winter have played to a small select society, sit ready in the music tent, and gain new spirit as they see foreign faces appearing which are unknown to them either as residents or as occasional visitors. Everything breathes once more; the hotels fill, slowly perhaps at first, till the height of the season approaches and the Spa bursts into full blossom.

Of the numerous interesting places in the neighborhood, we will here select the little town of Oberursel, with its Gothic church, built in the fifteenth century. This place had also, at one time, an intellectual prominence, for printing was carried on here as early as 1462. Nicodemus Frischlin's printing-press, which was raised here in 1590, was an important object in the history of literature.

In the neighborhood of Homburg also we come upon important Roman remains—indeed, upon one of the most important relics on the Rhine and Main, the so-called Saalburg. As early as 1830, some fine discoveries were made at Heddernheim, among others the foundation-walls of a Mithras temple, the finely-preserved relief of which is in the Museum at Wiesbaden. Many other mutilated relics were brought to light at that time, and prove the residence of the Roman legions here.

A Roman military road, which is clearly recognizable, leads almost directly to the ruins of the Roman citadel, the Saalburg, where a little Pompeii might long ago have been laid bare, if only the public had taken sufficient interest in the matter to provide the necessary funds. Imperfect as the excavations have necessarily been under the circumstances, having only been made by degrees by a private association formed for the purpose, this stronghold has been uncovered for an extent of more than twenty acres; the surrounding fortifications of walls and trenches have, for the most part, been brought to light; four gates with square towers, and behind them the buildings surrounding the citadel, which are tolerably well preserved, have also been disclosed. Among the former are the *porta prætoria* and the *porta decumana*.

We also find a prætorium 153 feet long and 132 feet broad, wells, bath-rooms, mosaic and other flooring, cellarage, all half ruined, and bearing here and there indications of the mortar which was on the walls. Urns and pitchers have been found at the place where the bodies used to be burnt. Weapons and coins have also been dug up plentifully, and on one occasion an urn containing 550 silver pieces was discovered.

Of especial interest is the grave-house which was erected on one of the old foundations, at a recent period, to cover the graves which were laid open; whilst two years ago the foundation-stone of a real columbarium was laid. The staked ditches which lie a few hundred paces off are also extremely interesting. It is supposed that this fortress was built by N. C. Drusus in the year 10 B.C., and that after being destroyed from the Germanic side in the year 15, it was rebuilt by his son Germanicus. Further excavations would no doubt supply a more definite solution of the history, but up to the present time they clearly testify to the residence in this place of the eighth and twenty-second legions.

CHAPTER XXII.

THE RHEINGAU.

The Rhine ! the Rhine ! Thereon our vines are growing—
 For ever bless the Rhine !
Along its shores the sunny grapes are glowing,
 That weep this racy wine.

WE now enter the splendid expanse of the river, which here lies before us like a polished lake, its surface dotted with islands. The green heights of the Bingerwald and Niederwald tower above it and enclose it in the background. Its waves dance upon the shore of the most favored and beautiful of the German districts. The sun's rays sparkle in the waters; their reflections kiss, as it were, the cheeks of the maidens who stand on the balconies and in the shady arbors, merrily greeting with waving handkerchiefs the steamer which is passing the bend in the river, leaving behind it a foamy track. Yonder, in softly ascending lines, are the golden-veined vine-gardens on that hill so blessed by heaven, and from which the rich produce goes forth yearly in such abundance.

On the right bank one little town stretches itself out almost to the next, the whole looking like a string

Cargo Boat on the Rhine.

of pearls, penetrated by the fragrance of the vines
and interspersed with gardens and villas, with churches
and chapels. In the background the vine-watchers'
houses seem to frown down on the scene, whilst the
grave-looking, weather-stained crucifixes smile benefi-
cently upon the gardens, like St. Januarius on the
coast of the Bay of Naples.

The little townlets of the Rheingau, with smiling
aspect, bathe their feet in the bright stream, and
cheerful human beings stroll along the banks. In
the snug summer-houses overhung with trailing vines
the glass filled with the golden wine sparkles, while
the humming of the bees announces how the grapes
are ripening once more to replenish the store of that
good wine, which for thousands of years has been a
joy and a blessing to those who know how to enjoy
its use without abusing it.

A gay and varied company are assembled on
board the steamer which carries us. On every face
we read the poet's words, "Wem Gott will rechte
Gunst erweisen, den schickt er in die weite Welt."
It would be difficult, indeed, to find a spot more truly
lovely than this; we never tire of its beauty. Every
visitor to these parts, besides admiring the beauties
of nature, should watch the vine-dresser at his heavy,
ceaseless work, which the autumn does not, however,
always repay. He should also see these slopes when
the fair bloom lies on the first half-open leaves; he
should mount through the vineyards when the grapes

are swelling, and when autumn tints the landscape. He would then, perhaps, better comprehend the enthusiasm of this honest, cheerful people; whose blood, it is true, is sometimes rather too hot and their actions rather too wild, as it has been since the old days of the Rheingau "Gebücks," when the club and the javelin had too great a license here.

Shadows, however, are not wanting in this sunny valley, and sometimes the vine-dresser has a heavy and careworn look, when, in spite of all his care, the bitter northeast wind has penetrated to his hill, and the frost of a single spring night has destroyed all the bloom which foretold for him so luxuriant a harvest. The fruit in this case, which should have been a source of pleasure to countless numbers, being nipped in the bud, hangs black and shrivelled on the stems that have been so carefully tended.

It is evening. The sun declines slowly towards the west and casts its rays obliquely over the Rhine, the shore, the villas, the vine-dressers' huts, the castles and the fortresses—lighting up the most delicate soft tints in the green wooded mountains and on the gray earth of the gardens, until it vanishes in the haze of the distant hills.

Yonder, on the left, a train is just steaming past the village of Budenheim, behind the Rhein-Au or Rettsbergs-Au. On the right lies Schierstein, the outer threshold of the Rheingau, surrounded by fruitful vineyards and orchards. The buildings which crown the hill on the land side are those of the Nürnberger Hof, on whose slopes the vine of the same name grows. Near it is a place frequented by Goethe in 1814, and at its feet is the Hof Armada. The left bank is uninteresting and bare, whilst, on the contrary, the right bank unfolds before us a panorama in which every minute shows a fresh picture.

Lower Walluf lies on the Waldava, a stream which once formed the boundary of the "Gebücks," a line of demarcation, protected by ditches, which at one time reached as far as Lorch, and by means of which the Rheingau fortresses, towns and villages sought to protect themselves against attack from without. The men of the Rheingau, as is well known, held fast to their own independence and acknowledged allegiance to no one, so that even the great lords were careful to keep on good terms with them.

The little town of Lower Walluf stretches itself invitingly under its vine-clad hills right along to the shore, facing which are the hospitable and much-frequented shady gardens of the burgomaster and Prince Wittgenstein. The town retains a mediæval look. In 1840 it is mentioned as a small village, presented by the Emperor Ludwig to Adalbert, who added considerably to his estate. Later it was held by the abbey of Fulda. Though the space is small the little dockyard is always full of life; and so is the boatman's inn, with its barrack-like appearance.

On summer afternoons the shore is always crowded with visitors eager to sail about on the river, or to make a journey up the Rhine. A large number also hang about the steamers as they land their passengers, either in small boats or at the pier, while in the shady arbors of the garden the burgomaster himself may be seen.

Up yonder, in the background above Walluf, where the mountains seem to beckon us, and the spires of the churches peep out at us from among the trees, lies Rauenthal—so called because it stands upon the mountain. Its vineyards stretch down towards the Rhine, receiving the full glow of the sun that ripens for us those priceless grapes which yield the wine that was crowned Queen of the Rhine at the Paris Exhibition.

This distinction is, however, not acknowledged by those proud lords, the princely Abbot of Johannisberg, the Master of Rüdesheim, the Knight of Stein, and the Dean of Hochheim. Since 1867 many a one has made a pilgrimage to Rauenthal in order to solve for himself the critical question. In doing this he has to mount to the splendid plateau of the "Schönen Aussicht," and look over that wonderful district—over that country on the other side of the Rhine, and over that which lies near him stretching far away to the Wasgau.

He enters the village and sits in the comfortable garden of the Nassau Hof, where he orders a bottle of the "best," and for which, even at the fountain-head, he has to pay two thalers at least. However low he may have doffed his hat to the newly-anointed queen, on his return to the Rhine, the chances are that he again drinks eternal brotherhood with the Lord of Rüdesheim, and that he is equally fickle when the princely Abbot of Johannisberg tries to convert him as to his claim to rule alone among the priceless products of the grape.

We pass on, along the foaming river; the vine-hills become higher and closer together as we proceed, for since passing Walluf we are in the "Gau" proper. Before us, on the left, lies the Eltville-Au, once the capital of the Rheingau. Before the town, on the right, extends the most beautiful park, with the usual little castles and pavilions, the estate of Julienheim, and the Castle of Rheinberg, which was once called also Christoffelsberg, from a figure of the saint on its tower. Until a few years ago this was the property of the Counts Grünne, but is now a public garden.

The name of the place has been said to be derived from the Roman *alta villa*, which time has corrupted into "Eltville;" but traces of the Romans have been sought for in vain. It is more probable that Bodmann is right when he traces the name from *alter Weiler*. The origin of the town must, at any rate, be sought for in the Frankish period.

During the residence of Charlemagne, Eltville

boasted a magistrate's court, whose jurisdiction extended over a wide circuit.

From a small beginning it became the principal place in the Mayence part of the Rheingau, and was a favorite resort and refuge to the archbishops when Mayence became too hot for them. In consequence of this the terrible Baldwin of Luxemburg erected the citadel in 1330, and Louis IV., on account of its fortifications, granted to the place the privileges of a town.

The castle and a portion of the walls are still preserved, as well as the watch-tower, although the Swedes and the French have greatly destroyed the fortress. One chronicle relates that Günther von Schwarzburg was poisoned here, but it is more correct to say that he had the fatal poison in his body when, seeing his end approach, he signed a peace with his opponent, Charles IV.

Eltville became a favorite resort for pilgrims when, in 1402, the miraculous Host was brought here from Gladbach. This raised the town to a state of great prosperity, for much more was ventured at that time in the way of pilgrimages and penances than now. The church of Eltville, which is built in the style of the fourteenth century, contains the tomb of Agnes of Hoppenstein, the wife of Frederick von Stockheim.

The place is indebted for one bright spot in its history to Gutenberg's pupil, Henry Bechtermünz

(also called Bechtelmünze), who, with the assistance
of his brother Nicholas and of Wigand Spiesz of
Ortenburg, set up a printing-press here in the middle
of the fifteenth century. A few specimens of its
work have been preserved. Simrock, indeed, ex-
presses an opinion that Gutenberg, towards the end
of his life, settled here with his relatives, but nothing certain is known on the subject except that the
neglected grave of one of his relatives, Jacob von
Sorgenloch, may be seen in the churchyard.

Eltville at the present day is a favorite resort of
the wealthy on account of its villas and parks. The
gardens of the houses join one another and form a
beautiful border to the shore, and although no wine
of Eltville figures in the list of the favorites of the
Rheingau, it has its factory of sparkling wine which
competes closely with champagne both at home and
abroad.

As we continue on our way, on the right the island
of Rheinau rises before us like a dark shady spot out
of the glittering surface of the river. On the shore
lies Erbach, which, as early as 954, formed a part of
the parish of Eltville; here we see the pointed
towers of the Gothic church peeping out of the chain
of villas, surrounded by the parsonage, the schools
and a little garden. These were all built in 1866,
and given to the people by the benefactress and
patroness of the place, the Princess Marianne of the
Netherlands, who resided here in her Castle of Rein-

hardshausen. Her castle contains an interesting collection of paintings and coins, and is open to the public on certain days.

Marcobrunnen, which belongs to the same province, is hardly distinguishable among the other vineyards, for we seek in vain for a monumental sign to indicate to us the wine-famed spot of the Strahlenberg. Only a well of red sandstone, called the "Marktbrunnen," or market-well, by the country people, stands by the highway; though it is probable that this rather represents a boundary-mark, for the vineyards here were, and still are, divided between ecclesiastical foundations and private persons.

The celebrated Steinberger also grows here, with similar modesty, on a slight declivity surrounded by a wall. The traveller in vain seeks the "Rose Garden." He shall not, however, be denied one glass of the fiery "golden beaker," but Heaven preserve him from some that bears the noble name of Steinberger. It is impossible that all so-called can be grown on this field of hardly eight acres in extent. The same may be said of the Gräfenberger yonder, which is a noble wine, but cannot be compared with the Steinberger.

The village of Kiedrich, and further inland the ruins of Scharfenstein with its round towers, have just come in sight, and with them the Eichberg lunatic asylum, established in 1843. A great number of historic associations are crowded together here, and from yonder Lower Ingelheim peers at us, while above us already towers the Johannisberg.

We must next mention Kiedrich and Scharfenstein, and the long-decayed family of Löwentrotz, the most powerful noble house of the Rheingau, rich in strongholds, with their different family branches, all of which have perished. Kiedrich appears as early as the tenth century, under the name of Cherdercho, while Scharfenstein, on the right bank of the Rhine, may be named as the oldest of the castles.

It was decidedly the largest if, as tradition tells us, it sheltered the whole of the tribe, whose common interests demanded their cohesion. The family of the Scharfenstein must have been one of the most wealthy, and consequently one of the most powerful, since it possessed the greatest number of castles and fiefs.

It seems that either the Scharfensteins began with the decline of the lords of Kiedrich, or that the latter merged into the Counts of Scharfenstein when this stronghold was given in fee to them by the Archbishop of Mayence, whose most trusty servants they became. The chronicle names as different branches of this family, the Greens, the Browns, the Blacks, the Gennens, the Eselwecks, the Steins, and the Crazzes von Scharfenstein. Their principal stronghold seems to have been specially destined to be a refuge for the archbishops, and under their protection there were often great doings within the walls of Scharfenstein, till Albert of Austria appeared before it in 1301, in order to besiege it. He retreated, after storming it in vain for thirty days.

The "Lion of Luxemburg," also, the bold Archbishop Baldwin of Treves—who was better acquainted with the sword than with the Cross—in vain laid siege to Scharfenstein. Albert of Brandenburg succeeded no better, and it was not until the Swedes came that the stubborn walls fell before an enemy on whom they had not reckoned, namely, Gunpowder. Mélac's French incendiaries laid waste what was left by the Swedes, and now nothing is to be found of the mighty Scharfenstein but a ruin.

Every one who has ever read a wine-card knows Hattenheimer. The place derives its name from Hatto II., who built it. The district itself is only an unimportant link in the chain which stretches, ring after ring, along the bank of the river.

More important to us is the Cistercian Abbey of Eberbach, lying inland in its idyllic green valley half enclosed by wooded hills, and the golden wine, the Steinberger Cabinet, which is hidden in its cellars. It once had a great and a splendid history, but it has experienced many changes, until at length it became an asylum for the insane, who were afterwards removed to the Eichberg. Last of all it was used as a prison.

Above it lies the Hallgart rampart, with the little village of Hallgarten, on the slopes of which the wine of the same name flourishes. A German,

Grape Arbor in the Anlagen, Coblentz.

Grape Arbor in the Anlagen, Coblentz.

named Adam von Itzstein, lies buried here: "a brave heart," says his gravestone, "weary of the youthful struggle for German freedom;" and here on his property, surrounded by his friends, he planned out and prophesied the existence of the German parliament.

It is said that when the pious Bernard of Clairvaux came here under the protection of Adalbert of Mayence, to seek a spot for a house in which to establish his order, a boar came out of the thicket, and rooting up the earth with his tusks, marked out the area which the saint destined for his monastery. Further than this, the boar also rolled hither the great stones for the foundation, and angels brought the smaller stones for the walls. In this way the building for the pious foundation was completed in the year 1116, under circumstances which, at the present day, we should consider somewhat exceptional and favorable, but which do not appear to have been so very remarkable in those periods.

When finished, the Archbishop Adalbert summoned the Augustine monks into the monastery, but the order of monks often changed; for the walls seem at first to have been somewhat deserted, indicating not a little ingratitude to the angels. The monks, however, soon took to wine-growing. It was they who had the finest Marcobrunner and who tended the Steinberger, so that the great cask in the cellar of the monastery of Eberbach had a world-wide reputation. It was capable of containing 12,000 gallons, and the entire harvest of the Steinberg was poured into it if there was room.

But in the Peasant War of 1525, the Rheingau insurrectionists drank to the very bottom of the great cask and sacked the interior of the monastery. The industrious monks, as soon as peace was restored, set to work again and repaired the damage that had been done, and worked on undisturbed until Albert of Brandenburg fell upon the abbey with equally insatiable thirst.

In the year 1803 the abbey was disestablished, and the property given to the domains whose noblest wines the monastery has since that time hidden in its cellars. The former refectory, now the press-house, dates from the twelfth century, and still reminds us, with its pillars and capitals, of the shrewd, industrious monks to whom vine-culture is so greatly indebted—wise men of business, who knew well how to obtain from emperors and princes free passage for their casks along the Rhine, till the stress of war destroyed all their blessings.

The ruins are still worth a visit: the church, dated 1186, with its monuments; the Cabinet cellar, with its true Rhine gold, and the magic names of Steinberg, Marcobrunner, Rüdesheim, Grafenberg, and Hallenheim! Even at the present day, the annual sale by auction of the wine which has been rejected as being unworthy of the "Cabinet" is an important

event in the life of the Rheingau. Whoever comes
to it, be he buyer or tourist, is invited to a "wine
meal," and at the end there is handed to him a sam-
ple of the finest wine, which does honor to Eberbach's cellar and to its hospitality.

Only speak to a native of the Rheingau of "wine-
testing," and his heart will rejoice. He may not,
indeed, be able to take part in the proceedings at
Eberbach, Hochheim, or any of the finest sources;
but he will do so probably at a peasant's, at a vine-
grower's, at the steward's of the castle, or at a rich
wine-grower's, who sets before us thirty different
sorts of his produce.

Wine-testing is, to the man of the Rhine, an act
of love—we might almost say of faith or religion—
which he performs with all his attention and devotion; and in one way or another a good deal is tested
on the Rhine, not only at the auctions, but, indeed,
whenever it is necessary or agreeable to look into
the goblet's golden depths.

Johannisberg! the pride, the King of the Rheingau! The castle stands on its vine-garlanded
heights, having the Mummische Schloss for its pedestal. At its feet lie stretched Oestrich, Winkel,
and Mittelheim, belonging, as it were, to one another.
To the right, above the last-named place, is the Castle of Vollrath; and yonder, on the left bank, on the
other side of the Au, basking in the sunshine, lies
Lower Ingelheim, which a thousand years ago was

the soul of the holy Roman Empire—Charlemagne's beautiful palace.

It was here, in these halls adorned with the art-treasures of the world, that the mighty emperor summoned the princes of his empire to assemble in order to determine the fate of nations, if not of Europe. It was also here that his own paternal heart had to bear the heaviest of all trials.

The glory is faded which once streamed from the mighty imperial crown of Ingelheim, where, perhaps, also the cradle of the noblest of men once rocked. The pillars are broken and decayed which supported the most magnificent, the most imposing of palaces. All the splendor has mouldered and perished to the last trace, and only a voice from the Thirty Years' War tells us, on a fragment of crumbling sandstone, that the hundred pillars which once adorned the "Saal" (so this place is still called, on which the palace stood) were conveyed hither from Ravenna by the Emperor Charlemagne.

It would be well if other stony records could tell us of those mighty bygone days; but all such witnesses have been destroyed by the rough events which have passed over these spots during the course of centuries. Ingelheim was, next to that of Aix-la-Chapelle, the most splendid of the imperial palaces, from which the great monarch looked over the loveliest of German river valleys to the Paradise on the farther bank.

At Ingelheim he promoted the planting and culture of the vine, which the Romans had already brought hither with the chestnut-tree. He also did a great deal for the cultivation of fruit in general.

A chronicler of the reign of Ludwig the Pious describes the castle as built of square blocks of hewn stone. It was of immense size, and in the form of a quadrangle enclosing a court-yard. Numerous apartments were contained within its walls.

He speaks especially of the principal hall. It must have been here that he assembled the diet of 788, at which Duke Thassilo of Bavaria was deposed from his dignity. The Danish king Harold fled hither in 826, with his wife and faithful followers, and was baptized by St. Alban. It was here that Charlemagne received ambassadors, whose arrival was celebrated with the most brilliant pageants.

It was at Ingelheim that Ernest of Swabia was condemned to excommunication and outlawry; and here also Henry V. summoned the diet in order to declare the deposition of his father Henry IV.—who was under the excommunication of the Pope—and to order him to be imprisoned at Bingen.

The palace, however, was allowed to fall to pieces; but Frederick I. restored it, and made it his favorite residence. Being again destroyed, it was rebuilt in 1354 by Charles IV., but only to be mortgaged to the Elector-Palatine. The people of Mayence set fire to it during the war between Frederick the Victorious and the Archbishop Adolf of Mayence. The Spaniards and the Swedes finished the work of destruction, and in 1689 the French cooled their courage on the empty ruins, so that now nothing remains of the former magnificent edifice but the fragments of a few pillars scattered about the spot.

Not even a breath of the spirit of its great past hovers now over the gardens to which we owe the dark juice of Ingelheim's grapes, and the traveller in vain seeks for a trace of it. From the Oestrich-Winkel shore, however, he will look up with a sensation of pleasure at the majestic hill, the foremost elevation of the " Rabenköpfe," where the renowned vineyards, the darlings of the sun, slope down with soft undulations. They look, indeed, like a carpet surrounding the cloister-castle of Johannisberg and its surrounding buildings.

The Archbishop, Hrabanus Maurus lived from 850 to 856 in the gray house in Winkel, which lies just below. With all his learning he must have found time to re-establish the old Roman wine-store. Goethe stayed at this place in the house of his friends, the Brentano family, which still shows some remembrances of him. It was here that Bettina wrote her letters to him, and it was from the river-bank at this place in 1806 that the unhappy poetess, Caroline von Günderode, sought death in the waters of the Rhine because of an unrequited attachment for the philologist Creuzer.

In a retired little house, almost hidden among vines and orchards, Robert von Hornstein, the composer, spent his summers. Many of his popular songs have been heard for the first time from that garden-terrace overlooking the Rhine. No traveller scans the heights of Johannisberg without being tempted to ascend them, although the place is not so rich in historical associations as Ingelheim. It presents to us in the main, as compared with its pious neighbor Eberbach, only the allegory of the idle and the industrious monks.

The extent of the prospect from here, over to Mayence and Donnersberg, to the peaks of the Eifel, and especially over the great river-bed and its luxuriant green pastures, is almost overpowering. It is a well-known fact that wherever the neighborhood is most beautiful, there stands a convent or an inn, or indeed usually both. The beauty of Johannisberg can only be compared with that of Camaldoli at Naples.

Perhaps, next to Charlemagne, we owe the culture of the divine grape of Johannisberg to the Bishop Hrabanus, for the hill was at first called the " Bishop's Mountain." After the well-known persecution of the Jews the Archbishop Ruthard built a monastery on the mountain, and placed it under the Abbot of St. Alban. He dedicated it to St. John the Baptist, perhaps as an atonement for the massacre of the children of Israel.

The Archbishop Adalbert gave over Eberbach also to Johannisberg, on account of the recklessness and extravagance of the monks in that establishment; and it is curious that in the course of time they should so completely have turned over a new leaf that Eberbach became a model of industry. Johannisberg then became independent of St. Alban, and was a free Benedictine abbey, in which the monks very soon had little else to do than to eat and drink and grow fat, whilst in Eberbach moderation and industry were more characteristic features

The crimes of the Abbey of Johannisberg increased; even the finding of a number of relics, which were exhibited, did not suffice to fill the empty coffers, and the scandal became so loud that Archbishop Dietrich commanded an examination of the monastery to be made, which resulted in the monks, who had not promised penance, being driven out, and others sent in from St. Jacobsberg to take their place. The revolted peasants plundered Johannisberg, and the casks of the monks were emptied and their monastery laid waste. What little prosperity was regained in later years soon again departed, and they were then obliged to sell some of their land.

Thirty years more had not passed over the country before Albert von Brandenburg and his wild host laid Johannisberg under contribution—that was in 1552. The monks were insulted, ill-treated and driven away, their wine drunk, their church plundered and the monastery set on fire. The spearmen then retired, but the monastery was a ruin.

The Abbot Valentine Horn was too indolent a man to set to work to repair the misfortune, but for the sake of his creature comforts he sold more land and mortgaged the slender rents, until the Archbishop Daniel of Mayence, in order to rescue the monastery again for the Benedictines, expelled both the monks and their abbot. Daniel himself undertook the management, but he also absorbed the revenues.

The Swedes then came and left the monastery behind them in ruins. At this period the distress was greater than ever, until Hubert von Bleymann came forward and took the property and the revenues on a mortgage of thirty thousand florins. The building rose from its ruins, and the cultivation of the vine was increased. When von Bleymann died the Abbot of Fulda paid off the mortgage, and, in 1716, took possession of the Johannisberg. But even then, there were merry days after the old fashion in the monastery. Alexander Kaufmann tells us, in his well-known poem, how the bold Abbot of Fulda came to Johannisberg, not to see if the faith prospered, but to ascertain, personally and experimentally, whether the vines were flourishing.

The princely Abbot Adalbert in the meantime erected a castle on the ruins, near the church which still stands. In 1803 the abbey passed into the hands of William of Orange. Napoleon presented it in 1807 to Marshal Kellermann in a moment of good-humor, the latter having cried out, on seeing it, "Oh! how beautiful it is!" "Would you like it?" asked Napoleon; "well, take it."

In the year 1815 it came into the possession of Austria, while Frederick William III. would gladly have had the beautiful castle for General Blucher. When the question arose among the Allies as to whom it should be given, the Emperor Alexander proposed that it should be presented to the brave Stein. The latter, however, is said to have remarked, "No, I thank your Majesty; the receiver is always as bad as the thief!" It was accordingly given in fee to Metternich, who gained by the transaction about sixty acres of the most incomparable vine land, and about a thousand acres of forest and arable land.

In the place where the monks neglected their duties, and themselves drank the best of the wine in copious draughts, and led so disorderly a life that no blessing or prosperity could enter their dwelling, careful accounts are now kept of the produce of the harvest, which was formerly recklessly sold, or pledged to the honor of Bacchus. The prince's managers supply strangers with samples for ready money at from three to fourteen florins the bottle. The stranger may, indeed, well depart satisfied with his draught and with a glance over the splendid panorama before him.

The interior of the castle presents nothing specially interesting, and in the chapel the only thing that deserves mention is the tomb of the Rhenish historian, Nicholas Vogt, who died in 1836. It was raised by his " friend and grateful pupil," Prince Metternich. His heart rests, according to his own wish, in the quartz rock in the Rhine at Bingen, in a silver case; a small iron cross marks the spot. A statue of St. John the Baptist stands in the open space before the church.

The whole of this fine property at present belongs to Richard von Metternich, who was formerly the Austrian ambassador in Paris, and he and his wife reside here in the summer. It may seem out of place to speak here—and to him whom we have just supposed to have drained a cup of the glowing " sixty-eight " at the castle—of the cold-water establishment in the village below; it may as well be mentioned, however, particularly as many may have need of such an institution.